The False Faces

Vance, Louis Joseph

Contents

THE FALSE FACES

BY

Vance, Louis Joseph

I
OUT OF NO MAN'S LAND

On the muddy verge of a shallow little pool the man lay prone and still, as still as those poor dead whose broken bodies rested all about him, where they had fallen, months or days, hours or weeks ago, in those grim contests which the quick were wont insensately to wage for a few charnel yards of that debatable ground.

Alone of all that awful company this man lived and, though he ached with the misery of hunger and cold and rain-drenched garments, was unharmed.

Ever since nightfall and a brisk skirmish had made practicable an undetected escape through the German lines, he had been in the open, alternately creeping toward the British trenches under cover of darkness and resting in deathlike immobility, as he now rested, while pistol-lights and star-shells flamed overhead, flooding the night with ghastly glare and disclosing in pitiless detail that two-hundred-yard ribbon of earth, littered with indescribable abominations, which set apart the combatants. When this happened, the living had no other choice than to ape the dead, lest the least movement, detected by eyes that peered without rest through loopholes in the sandbag parapets, invite a bullet's blow.

Now it was midnight, and lights were flaring less frequently, even as rifle-fire had grown more intermittent ... as if many waters might quench out hate in the heart of man!

For it was raining hard--a dogged, dreary downpour drilling through a heavy atmosphere whose enervation was like the oppression of some malign and inexorable incubus; its incessant crepitation resembling the mutter of a weary, sullen drum, dwarfing to insignificance the stuttering of machine-guns remote in the northward, dominating even a dull thunder of cannonading somewhere down the far horizon; lowering a vast and shimmering curtain of slender lances, steel-bright, close-ranked, between the trenches and over all that weary land. Thus had it rained since noon, and thus--for want of any hint of slackening--it might rain for another twelve hours, or eighteen, or twenty-four....

The star-rocket, whose rays had transfixed him beside the pool, paled and winked out in mid-air, and for several minutes unbroken darkness obtained while, on hands and knees, the man crept on toward that gap in the British barbed-wire entanglements which he had marked down ere daylight waned, shaping a tolerably straight course despite frequent detours to avoid the unspeakable. Only once was his progress interrupted--when straining senses apprised him that a British patrol was taking advantage of the false truce to reconnoitre toward the enemy lines, its approach betrayed by a nearing *squash* of furtive feet in the boggy earth, the rasp of constrained respiration, a muttered curse when someone slipped and narrowly escaped a fall, the edged hiss of an officer's whisper reprimanding the offender. In-continently he who crawled dropped flat to the greasy mud and lay moveless.

Almost at the same instant, warned by a trail of sparks rising in a long arc from the German trenches, the soldiers imitated his action, and, as long as those triple stars shone in the murk, made themselves one with him and the heedless dead. Two lay so close beside him that the man could have touched either by moving a hand a mere six inches; he was at pains to do nothing of the sort; he was sedulous to clench his teeth against their chattering, even to hold his breath, and regretted that he might not mute the thumping of his heart. Nor dared he stir until, the lights fading out, the patrol rose and skulked onward.

Thereafter his movements were less stealthy; with a detachment of their own abroad in No Man's Land, the British would refrain from shooting at shadows. One had now to fear only German bullets in event the patrol were discovered.

Rising, the man slipped and stumbled on in semi-crouching posture, ready to flatten to earth as soon as any one of his many overshoulder glances detected an-other sky-spearing flight of sparks. But this necessity he was spared; no more lights were discharged before he groped through the wires to the parapet, with almost uncanny good luck, finding the very spot where the British had come over the top, indicated by protruding uprights of a rough wooden scaling ladder.

As he turned, felt with a foot for the uppermost rung, and began to descend, he was saluted by a voice hoarse with exposure, from the black bowels of the trench:

"Blimy! but ye're back in a 'urry! Wot's up? Forget to put perfume on yer pocket-'andkerchief--or wot?"

The man's response, if he made any, was lost in a heavy splash as his feet slipped on the slimy rungs, delivering him precipitately into a knee-deep stream of foul water which moved sluggishly through the trench like the current of a half-choked sewer--a circumstance which neither suprised him nor added to his physical discomfort, who could be no more wet or defiled than he had been.

Floundering to a foothold, he cast about vainly for a clue to the other's whereabouts; for if the night was thick in the open, here in the trench its density was as that of the pit; the man could distinguish positively nothing more than a pallid rift where the walls opened overhead.

"Well, sullen, w'ere's yer manners? Carn't yer answer a civil question?"

Turning toward the speaker, the man replied in good if rather carefully enunciated English:

"I am not of your comrades. I am come from the enemy trenches."

"The 'ell yer are! 'Ands up!"

The muzzle of a rifle prodded the man's stomach. Obediently he lifted both hands above his head. A thought later, he was half blinded by the sudden spot-light of an electric flash-lamp.

"Deserter, eh? You kamerad--wot?"

"Kamerad!" the man echoed with an accent of contempt. "I am no German--I am French. I have come through the Boche lines to-night with important information which I desire to communicate forthwith to your commanding officer."

"Strike me!" his catechist breathed, skeptical.

There was a new sound of splashing in the trench. A third voice chimed in: "'Ello? Wot's all the row abaht?"

"Step up and tike a look for yerself. 'Ere's a blighter wot sez 'e's com from the Germ trenches with important information for the O.C."

"Bloody liar," the newcomer commented dispassionately. "Mind yer eye. Likely it's just another pl'yful little trick of the giddy Boche. 'Ere you!" The splashing drew nearer. "Wot's yer gime? Speak up if yer don't want a bullet through yer in'ards."

"I play no game," the man said patiently. "I am unarmed--your prisoner, if you like."

"I like, all right. Mike yer mind easy abaht that. But wot's all this 'important information'?"

"I shall divulge that only to the proper authorities. Be good enough to conduct me to your commanding officer without more delay."

"Wot do yer mike of 'im, corp'ril?" the first soldier enquired. "'Ow abaht an inch or two o' the bay'net to loosen 'is tongue?"

After a moment's hesitation in perplexed silence, the corporal took the flash-lamp from the private and with its beam raked the prisoner from head to foot, gaining little enlightenment from this review of a tall, spare figure clothed in the familiar gray overcoat of the German private--its face a mere mask of mud through which shone eyes of singular brilliance and steadiness, the eyes of a man of intelligence, determination, and courage.

"Keep yer 'ands 'igh," the corporal advised curtly. "Ginger, you search 'im."

Propping his rifle against the wall of the trench, its butt on the firing-step just out of water, the private proceeded painstakingly to examine the person of the prisoner; in course of which process he unbuttoned and threw open the gray overcoat, exposing a shapeless tunic and trousers of shoddy drab stuff.

"'E 'asn't got no arms--'e 'asn't got nothink, not so much as 'is blinkin' latch-key."

"Very good. Get back on yer post. I'll tike chaige o' this one."

Grounding his own rifle, the corporal fixed its bayonet, then employed it in a gesture of unpleasant significance.

"'Bout fice," he ordered. "March. Yer can drop yer 'ands--but don't go forgettin' I'm right 'ere be'ind yer."

In silence the prisoner obeyed, wading down the flooded trench, the spot-light playing on his back, striking sullen gleams from the inky water that swirled about his knees, and disclosing glimpses of coated figures stationed at regular intervals along the firing-step, faces steadfast to loopholes in the parapet.

Now and again they passed narrow rifts in the walls of the trench, entrances to dugouts betrayed by glimmers of candle-light through the cracks of makeshift doors or the coarse mesh of gunnysack curtains.

From one of these, at the corporal's summons, a sleepy subaltern stumbled to attend ungraciously to his subordinate's report, and promptly ordered the prisoner taken on to the regimental headquarters behind the lines.

A little farther on captive and captor turned off into a narrow and tortuous communication trench. Thereafter for upward of ten minutes they threaded a labyrinth of deep, constricted, reeking ditches, with so little to differentiate one from another that the prisoner wondered at the sure sense of direction which enabled the corporal to find his way without mis-step, with the added handicap of the abysmal darkness. Then, of a sudden, the sides of the trench shelved sharply downward, and the two debouched into a broad, open field. Here many men lay sleeping, with only waterproof sheets for protection from that bitter deluge which whipped the earth into an ankle-deep lake of slimy ooze and lent keener accent to the abiding stench of filth and decomposing flesh. A slight hillock stood between this field and the firing-line--where now lively fusillades were being exchanged--its profile crowned with a spectral rank of shell-shattered poplars sharply silhouetted against a sky in which star-shells and Verey lights flowered like blooms of hell.

Here the corporal abruptly commanded his prisoner to halt and himself paused and stood stiffly at attention, saluting a group of three officers who were approaching with the evident intention of entering the trench. One of these loosed upon the pair the flash of a pocket lamp. At sight of the gray overcoat all three stopped short.

A voice with the intonation of habitual command enquired: "What have we here?"

The corporal replied: "A prisoner, sir--sez 'e's French--come across the open to-night with important information--so 'e sez."

The spot-light picked out the prisoner's face. The officer addressed him directly.

"What is your name, my man?"

"That," said the prisoner, "is something which--like my intelligence--I should prefer to communicate privately."

With a startled gesture the officer took a step forward and peered intently into that mud-smeared countenance.

"I seem to know your voice," he said in a speculative tone.

"You should," the prisoner returned.

"Gentlemen," said the officer to his companions, "you may continue your rounds. Corporal, follow me with your prisoner."

He swung round and slopped off heavily through the mud of the open field.

Behind them the sound of firing in the forward trenches swelled to an uproar augmented by the shrewish chattering of machine-guns. Then a battery hidden somewhere in the blackness in front of them came into action, barking viciously. Shells whined hungrily overhead. The prisoner glanced back: the maimed poplars stood out stark against a sky washed with wave after wave of infernal light....

Some time later he was conscious of a cobbled way beneath his sodden foot-gear. They were entering the outskirts of a ruined village. On either hand fragments of walls reared up with sashless windows and gaping doors like death masks of mad folk stricken in paroxysm.

Within one doorway a dim light burned; through it the officer made his way, prisoner and corporal at his heels, passing a sentry, then descending a flight of crazy wooden steps to a dank and gloomy cellar, stone-walled and vaulted. In the middle of the cellar stood a broad table at which an orderly sat writing by the light of two candles stuck in the necks of empty bottles. At another table, in a corner, a sergeant and an operator of the Signal Corps were busy with field telephone and telegraph instruments. On a meagre bed of damp and mouldy straw, against the farther wall, several men, orderlies and subalterns, rested in stertorous slumbers. Despite the cold the atmosphere was a reek of tobacco smoke, sweat, and steam from wet cloth-ing.

The man at the centre table rose and saluted, offering the commanding officer a sheaf of scribbled messages and reports. Taking the chair thus vacated, the officer ran an eye over the papers, issued several orders inspired by them, then turned attention to the prisoner.

"You may return to your post, corporal."

The corporal executed a smart about-face and clumped up the steps. In answer to the officer's steadfast gaze the prisoner stepped forward and confronted him across the table.

"Who are you?"

"My name," said the prisoner, after looking around to make sure that none of the other tenants of the cellar was within earshot, "is Lanyard--Michael Lanyard."

"The Lone Wolf!"

Involuntarily the officer jumped up, almost overturning his chair.

"That same," the prisoner affirmed, adding with a grimace of besmirched and emaciated features that was meant for a smile--"General Wertheimer."

"Wertheimer is not my name."

"I am aware of that. I uttered it merely to confirm my identity to you; it is the only name I ever knew you by in the old days, when you were in the British Secret Service and I a famous thief with a price upon my head, when you and I played hide and seek across half Europe and back again--in the days of Troyon's and 'the Pack,' the days of De Morbihan and Popinot and...."

"Ekstrom," the officer supplied as the prisoner hesitated oddly.

"And Ekstrom," the other agreed.

There was a little silence between the two; then the officer mused aloud: "All dead!"

"All ... but one."

The officer looked up sharply. "Which--?"

"The last-named."

"Ekstrom? But we saw him die! You yourself fired the shot that--"

"It was not Ekstrom. Trust that one not to imperil his precious carcase when he could find an underling to run the risk for him! I tell you I have seen Ekstrom within this last month, alive and serving the Fatherland as the genius of that system of espionage which keeps the enemy advised of your every move, down to the least considerable--that system which makes it possible for the Boche to greet every regiment by name when it moves up to serve its time in your advanced trenches."

"You amaze me!"

"I shall convince you; I bring intelligence which will enable you to tear apart this web of treason within your own lines and...."

Lanyard's voice broke. The officer remarked that he was trembling--trembling so violently that to support himself he must grip the edge of the table with both hands.

"You are wounded?"

"No--but cold to my very marrow, and faint with hunger. Even the German soldiers are on starvation rations, now; the civilians are worse off; and I--I have been over there for years, a spy, a hunted thing, subsisting as casually as a sparrow!"

"Sit down. Orderly!"

And there was no more talk between these two for a time. Not only did the officer refuse to hear another word before Lanyard had gorged his fill of food and drink, but an exigent communication from the front, transmitted through the trench telephone system, diverted his attention temporarily.

Gnawing ravenously at bread and meat, Lanyard watched curiously the scenes in the cellar, following, as best he might, the tides of combat; gathering that German resentment of a British bombing enterprise (doubtless the work of that same squad which had stolen past him in the gloom of No Man's Land) had developed into a violent attempt to storm the forward trenches. In these a desperate struggle was taking place. Reinforcements were imperatively wanted.

Activities at the signallers' table became feverish; the commanding officer stood over it, reading incoming messages as they were jotted down and taking such action thereupon as his judgment dictated. Orderlies, dragged half asleep from their nests of straw, were shaken awake and despatched to rouse and rush to the front the troops Lanyard had seen sleeping in the open field. Other orderlies limped or reeled down the cellar steps, delivered their despatches, and, staggered out through a breach in the wall to have their injuries attended to in the field dressing-station in the adjoining cellar, or else threw themselves down on the straw to fall instantly asleep despite the deafening din.

The Boche artillery, seeking blindly to silence the field batteries whose fire was galling their offensive, had begun to bombard the village. Shells fled shrieking overhead, to break in thunderous bellows. Walls toppled with appalling crashes, now near at hand, now far. The ebb and flow of rifle-fire at the front contributed a background of sound not unlike the roaring of an angry surf. Machine-guns gibbered like maniacs. Heavier artillery was brought into play behind the British lines, apparently at no great distance from the village; the very flag-stones of the cellar floor quaked to the concussions of big-calibre guns.

Through the breach in the wall echoed the screams and groans of wounded. The foul air became saturated with a sickening stench of iodoform. Gusts of wet wind eddied hither and yon. Candles flickered and flared, guttered out, were renewed. Monstrous shadows stole out from black corners, crept along mouldy walls, crouched, sprang and vanished, or, inscrutably baffled, retreated sullenly to their lairs....

For the better part of an hour the struggle continued; then its vigour began to wane. The heaviest British metal went out of action; some time later the field batteries discontinued their activities. The volume of firing in the advance trenches dwindled, was fiercely renewed some half a dozen times, died away to normal. Once more the Boche had been beaten back.

Returning to his chair, the commanding officer rested his elbows upon the table and bowed his head between his hands in an attitude of profound fatigue. He seemed to remind himself of Lanyard's presence only at 'cost of a racking effort, lifting heavy-lidded eyes to stare almost incredulously at his face.

"I presumed you were in America," he said in dulled accents.

"I was ... for a time."

"You came back to serve France?"

Lanyard shook his head. "I returned to Europe after a year, the spring before the war."

"Why?"

"I was hunted out of New York. The Boche would not let me be."

The officer looked startled. "The Boche?"

"More precisely, Herr Ekstrom--to name him as we knew him. But this I did not suspect for a long time, that it was he who was responsible for my persecution. I knew only that the police of America, informed of my identity with the Lone Wolf, sought to deport me, that every avenue to an honourable livelihood was closed. So I had to leave, to try to lose myself."

"Your wife ... I mean to say, you married, didn't you?"

Lanyard nodded. "Lucy stuck by me till ... the end.... She had a little money of her own. It financed our flight from the States. We made a round-about journey of it, to elude surveillance--and, I think, succeeded."

"You returned to Paris?"

"No: France, like England, was barred to the Lone Wolf.... We settled down in Belgium, Lucy and I and our boy. He was three months old. We found a quiet little home in Louvain--"

The officer interrupted with a low cry of apprehension, Lanyard checked him with a sombre gesture. "Let me tell you...

"We might have been happy. None knew us. We were sufficient unto ourselves. But I was without occupation; it occurred to me that my memoirs might
make good reading--for Paris; my friends the French are as fond of their criminals
as you English of your actors. On the second of August I journeyed to Paris to negotiate with a publisher. While I was away the Boche invaded Belgium. Before I could
get back Louvain had been occupied, sacked...."

He sat for a time in brooding silence; the officer made no attempt to rouse him,
but the gaze he bent upon the man's lowered head was grave and pitiful. Abruptly,
in a level and toneless voice, Lanyard resumed:

"In order to regain my home I had to go round by way of England and Holland.
I crossed the Dutch frontier disguised as a Belgian peasant. When I reentered Lou-
vain it was to find ... But all the world knows what the blond beast did in Louvain.
My wife and little son had vanished utterly. I searched three months before I found
trace of either. Then ... Lucy died in my arms in a wretched hovel near Aerschot.
She had seen our child butchered before her eyes. She herself...."

Lanyard's hand, that rested on the table, clenched and whitened beneath its
begrimed skin. His eyes fathomed distances immeasurably removed beyond the
confines of that grim cellar. But he presently continued:

"Ekstrom had accompanied the army of invasion, had seen and recognized Lucy
in passing through Louvain. Therefore she and my son were among the first to be
sacrificed.... When I stood over her grave I dedicated my life to the extermination
of Ekstrom and all his breed. I have since done things I do not like to think about.
But the Prussian spy system is the weaker for my work....

"But Ekstrom I could never find. It was as if he knew I hunted him. He was seldom twenty-four hours ahead of me, yet I never caught up with him but once; and
then he was too closely guarded.... I pursued him to Berlin, to Potsdam, three times
to the western front, to Serbia, once to Constantinople, twice to Petrograd."

The officer uttered an exclamation of astonishment. Lanyard looked his way
with a depreciatory air.

"Nothing strange about that. To one of my early training that was easy--every-
thing was easy but the end I sought.... En passant I collected information concerning the workings of the Prussian spy system. From time to time I found means to

communicate somewhat of this to the Surete in Paris. I believe France and England have already profited a little through my efforts. They shall profit more, and quickly, when I have told all that I have to tell....

"Of a sudden Ekstrom vanished. Overnight he disappeared from Germany. A false lead brought me back to this front. Two days ago I learned he had been sent to America on a secret mission. Knowing that the States have severed diplomatic relations with Berlin and tremble on the verge of a declaration of war, we can surmise something of the nature of his mission. I mean to see that he fails.... To follow him to America, making my way out through Belgium and Holland, pursuing such furtive ways as I must in territory dominated by the Boche, meant much time lost. So I came through the lines to-night. Fortune was kind in throwing me into your hands: I count upon your assistance. As an ex-agent of the Secret Service you are in a position to make smooth my path; as an Englishman, you will advance the interests of a prospective ally of England if you help me to the limit of your ability; for what I mean to do in America will serve that country, by exposing the conspiracies of the Boche across the water, as much as it will serve my private ends."

The officer's hand fell across the table and closed upon the knotted fist of the Lone Wolf.

"As an Englishman," he said simply--"of course. But no less as your friend."

II
FROM A BRITISH PORT

And one man in his time plays many parts": few more than this same Lanyard. In no way to be identified with the hunted creature who crept into the British lines out of No Man's Land was the Monsieur Duchemin who, ten days after that wintry midnight, took passage for New York from "a British port," aboard the steamship ***Assyrian***.

Andre Duchemin was the name inscribed in the credentials furnished him in recognition of signal assistance rendered the British Secret Service in its task of scotching the Prussian spy system. And the personality he chose to assume suited well the name. A man of modest and amiable deportment, viewing the world with eyes intelligent and curious, his temper reacting from its ways in terms of grave humour, Monsieur Duchemin passed peaceably on his lawful occasions, took life as he found it, made the best of irksome circumstances.

This last idiosyncrasy stood him in good stead. For the ***Assyrian*** failed to clear upon her proposed sailing date and for a livelong week thereafter chafed alongside her landing stage, steam up, cargo laden and stowed, nothing lacking but the Admiralty's permission to begin her westbound voyage--a permission inscrutably withheld, giving rise to a common discontent which the passengers dissembled to the various best of their abilities, that is to say, in most cases thinly or not at all.

Yet they were none of them unreasonable beings. They had come aboard one and all keyed up to a high nervous pitch, pardonable in such as must commit their lives to the dread adventure of the barred zone, wanting nothing so much as to get it over with, whatever its upshot. And everlasting procrastination required them day after day to steel their hearts anew against that Terror which followed its furtive ways beneath the leaden waters of the Channel!

Alone among them this Monsieur Duchemin paraded successfully a false face of resignation, protesting no predilection whatsoever for a watery grave, no infatuate haste to challenge the Hun upon his chosen hunting-ground. In the fullness of time it would be permitted to him to go down to the sea in this ship. Meanwhile he found it apparently pleasant and restful to explore the winding cobbled ways of that antiquated waterside community, made over by the hand of War into a bustling seaport, or to tramp the sunken lanes that seamed those green old Cornish hills which embosomed the wide harbour waters, or to lounge about the broad white decks of the *Assyrian* watching the diurnal traffic of the haven--a restless, warlike pageant.

Daily, in earliest dusk of dawn, the wakeful might watch the faring forth of a weirdly assorted fleet of small craft, the day patrol, to relieve a night patrol as weirdly heterogeneous. Daily, at all hours, mine-sweepers came and went, by twos and twos, in flocks, in schools; and daily bellowing offshore detonations advertised their success in garnering those horned black seeds of death which the Hun and his kin were sedulous to sow in the fairways. While daily battleships both great and small rolled in wearily to refit and dress their wounds, or took swift departure on grim and secret errands.

There was, moreover, the not-infrequent spectacle of some minor ship of war--a truculent, gray destroyer as like as not--shepherding in a sleek submarine, like a felon whale armoured and strangely caparisoned in gray-brown steel, to be moored in chains with a considerable company of its fellows on the far side of the roadstead, while its crew was taken ashore and consigned to some dark limbo of oblivion.

And once, with a light cruiser snapping at her heels, a drab Norwegian tramp plodded sullenly into port, a mine-layer caught red-handed, plying its assassin's trade beneath a neutral flag.

Not long after its crew had been landed, volleys of musketry crashed in the town gaol-yard.

One of a group of three idling on the promenade deck of the *Assyrian*, Lanyard turned sharply and stared through narrowed eyelids into the quarter whence the sounds reverberated.

The man at his side, a loose-jointed American of the commercial caste, paused momentarily in his task of masticating a fat dark cigar.

"This way out," he commented thoughtfully.

Lanyard nodded; but the third, a plumply ingratiative native of Geneva, known to the ship as Emil Dressier, frowned in puzzlement.

"Pardon, Monsieur Crane, but what is that you say--'this way out'?"

"Simply," Crane explained, "I take the firing to mean the execution of our nootral friends from Norway."

The Swiss shuddered. "It is most terrible!"

"Well, I don't know about that. They done their damnedest to fix it for us to drown somewhere out there in the nice, cold English Channel. I'm just as satisfied it's them, instead, with their backs to a stone wall in the warm sunlight, getting their needin's. That's only justice. Eh, Monsieur Duchemin?"

"It is war," said Lanyard with a shrug.

"And war is ... No: Sherman was all wrong. Hell's got perfectly good grounds for a libel suit against William Tecumseh for what he up and said about it and war, all in the same breath."

Lanyard smiled faintly, but Dressler pondered this obscure reference with patent distress. Crane champed his cigar reflectively.

"What's more to our purpose," he said presently: "I shouldn't be surprised if this meant the wind-up of our rest-cure here. That's the third mine-layer they've collected this week--two subs, and now this benevolent nootral. Am I right, Monsieur Duchemin?"

"Who knows?" Lanyard replied with a smile. "Even now the mine-sweeping flotilla is coming home, as you see; which means, the neighbouring waters have been cleared. It is altogether a possibility that we may be permitted to depart this night."

Even so the event: as that day's sun declined amid a portentous welter of crimson and purple and gold, the moorings were cast off and the *Assyrian* warped out into mid-channel and anchored there for the night.

Inasmuch as she was to sail as the tide served, some time before sunrise, the passengers were advised to seek their berths at an early hour. Thirty minutes before the steamship entered the danger zone (as she would soon after leaving the harbour) they would be roused and were expected promptly to assemble on deck, with life-preservers, and station themselves near the boats to which they were individually assigned.

For their further comforting they were treated, in the ebb of the chill blue twi-light, to boat-drill and final instructions in the right adjustment of life-belts.

A preoccupied company assembled in the dining saloon for what might be its last meal. In the shadow of the general apprehension, conversation languished; ex-pressions of relief on the part of those who had been loudest in complaining at the delays were notably unheard; even Crane, Lanyard's nearest neighbour at table, was abnormally subdued. Reviewing that array of sobered and anxious faces, Lanyard remarked--not for the first time, but with renewed gratitude--that in all the roster of passengers none were children and but two were women: the American widow of an English officer and her very English daughter, an angular and superior spin-ster.

Avoiding the customary post-prandial symposium in the smoking room, Lan-yard slipped away with his cigar for a lonely turn on deck.

Beneath a sky heavily canopied, the night was stark black and loud with clash-ing waters. A fitful wind played in gusts now grim, now groping, like a lost thing blundering blindly about in that deep darkness. Ashore a few wan lights, widely spaced, winked uncertainly, withdrawn in vast remoteness; those near at hand, of the anchored shipping, skipped and swayed and flickered in mad mazes of goblin dance. To him who paced those vacant, darkened decks, the sense of dissociation from all the common, kindly phenomena of civilization was something intimate and inescapable. Melancholy as well rode upon that black-winged wind.

At pause beneath the bridge, the adventurer rested elbows upon the teakwood rail and with importunate eyes searched the masked face of his destiny. There was great fear in his heart, not of death, but lest death overtake him before that scarlet hour when he should encounter the man whom he must always think of as "Ek-strom."

After that, nothing would matter: let Death come then as swiftly as it willed....

He was not even middle-aged, on the hither side of thirty; yet his attitude was that of one who had already crossed the great divide of the average mortal span: he looked backward upon a life, never forward to one. To him his history seemed a thing written, lacking the one word Finis: he had lived and loved and lost--had arrayed himself insolently against God and Man, had been lifted toward the light a little way by a woman's love, had been thrust relentlessly back into the black pit of his damnation. He made no pretense that it was otherwise with him: remained now merely the thing he had been in the beginning, minus that divine spark which love had once kindled into consuming aspiration toward the right; the Lone Wolf prowled again to-day and would henceforth forevermore, the beast of prey callous to every human emotion, animated by one deadly purpose, existing but to destroy and be in turn destroyed....

Two decks below, about amidships, a cargo port was thrust open to the night. A thick, broad beam of light leaped out, buffeting the murk, striking evanescent glimmers from the rocking facets of the waters. Deckhands busied themselves rigging out an accommodation ladder. A tender of little tonnage panted nervously up out of nowhere and was made fast alongside. The light raked its upper deck, picking out in passing a group of men in uniforms. Fugitively something resembling a petticoat snapped in the wind. Then several persons moved toward the accommodation ladder, climbed it, disappeared through the cargo port. The wearer of the petticoat did not accompany them.

Lanyard noted these matters subconsciously, for the time altogether preoccupied, casting forward his thoughts along those dim trails his feet must tread who followed his dark star....

Ten minutes later a deck-steward found him, and paused, touching his cap.

"Beg pardon, sir, but all passingers is requested to report immediately in the music room."

Indifferently Lanyard thanked the man and went below, to find the music room tenanted by a full muster of his fellow passengers, all more or less indignantly waiting to be cross-examined by the party of port officials from the tender--the ship's purser standing by together with the second and third officers and a number of stewards.

Resentment was not unwarranted: already, before being suffered to take up quarters on board the *Assyrian*, each passenger had submitted to a most comprehensive survey of his credentials, his mental, moral, and social status, his past record, present affairs, and future purposes. A formality to be expected by all such as travel in war time, it had been rigid but mild in contrast with this eleventh-hour inquisition--a proceeding so drastic and exhaustive that the only plausible infer-ence was official determination to find excuse for ordering somebody ashore in irons. Nothing was overlooked: once passports and other proofs of identity had been scrutinized, each passenger was conducted to his stateroom and his person and luggage subjected to painstaking search. None escaped; on the other hand, not one was found guilty of flagitious peculiarity. In the upshot the inquisitors, baffled and betraying every symptom of disappointment, were fain to give over and return to their tender.

By this time Lanyard, one of the last to be grilled and passed, found himself as little inclined for sleep as the most timorous soul on board. Selecting an American novel from the ship's library, he repaired to the smoking room, where, established in a corner apart, he became an involuntary and, at first, a largely inattentive, eaves-dropper upon an animated debate involving some eight or ten gentlemen at a table in the middle of the saloon--its subject, the recent visitation.

Measures so extraordinary were generally held to indicate an incentive more extraordinary still.

"You can't get away from it," he heard Crane declare: "there's some sort of funny business going on, or liable to go on, aboard this ship. She wasn't held up for a solid week out of pure cussedness. Neither did they come aboard to-night to give us another once-over through sheer voluptuousness. There's a reason."

"And what," a satiric English voice enquired, "do you assume that reason to be?"

"Search me. 'Sfar's I'm concerned the processes of the British Intelligence Of-fice are a long sight past finding out."

"It is simple enough," one of Crane's compatriots suggested: "the *Assyrian* is suspected of entertaining a devil unawares."

"Monsieur means--?" the Swiss enquired.

"I mean, the authorities may have been led to believe some one of us a ques-tionable character."

"German spy?"

"Possibly."

"Or an English traitor?"

"Impossible," asserted another Briton heavily. "There is to-day no such thing in

England. Two years ago the supposition might have been plausible. But that breed has long since been stamped out--in England."

"Another guess," Crane cut in: "they've taken considerable trouble to clear the track for us. Maybe it occurred to somebody at the last moment to make sure none of us was likely to pull off an inside job."

"'Inside job?'" Dressler pleaded.

"Planting bombs in the coal bunkers--things like that--anything to crab our getting through the barred zone in spite of mines and U-boats."

"Any such attempt would mean almost certain death!"

"What of it? It's been tried before--and got away with. You've got to hand it to Fritz, he'll risk hell-for-breakfast cheerful any time he gets it in his bean he's serving Gott und Vaterland."

"Granted," said the Englishman. "But I fancy such an one would find it far from easy to secure passage upon this or any other vessel."

"How so? You may have haltered all your traitors, but there's still a-plenty German spies living in England. Even you admit that. And if they can get by your Secret Service, to say nothing of Scotland Yard, what's to prevent their fixing to leave the country?"

"Nothing, certainly. But I still contend it is hardly likely."

"Of course it's hardly likely. Look at these guys to-night--dead set on making an awful example of anybody that couldn't come clean. I didn't notice them missing any bets. They combed me to the Queen's taste; for a while I was sure scared they'd extract my pivot tooth to see if there wasn't something incriminating and degrading secreted inside it. And nobody got off any easier. *I* say the good ship ***Assyrian*** has a pretty clean bill of health to go sailing with."

"On the other hand"--yet another American voice was speaking--"no spy or criminal worth his salt would try to ship without preparations thorough enough to insure success, barring accidents."

"Criminal?" drawled the Briton incredulously.

"The enterprisin' burglar keeps a-burglin', even in war time. There have been notable burglaries in London of late, according to your newspapers."

"And you think the thief would attempt to smuggle his loot out of the country aboard such a ship as this?"

"Why not?"

"Scotland Yard to the contrary notwithstanding?"

"If Scotland Yard is as efficient as you think, sir, certainly any sane thief would make every effort to leave a country it was making too hot for him."

"Considerable criminal!" Crane jeered.

"Undeceive yourself, senor." This was a Brazilian, a quiet little dark body who commonly contented himself with a listening role in the smoking-room discussions. "There are truly criminals of intelligence. And war conditions are driving them out of Europe."

Of a sudden Lanyard--stretched out at length upon the leather cushions, in full view of these gossips--became aware that he was being closely scrutinised. By whom, with what reason or purpose, he could not surmise; and it were unwise to look up from that printed page. But that sixth sense of his--intuition, what you will--that exquisitely sensitive sentinel admonished that at least one person in the room was watching him narrowly.

Though he made no move other than to turn a page, his glance followed blindly blurring lines of text, and his quickened wits overlooked no shade of meaning or intonation as that talk continued.

"A criminal of intelligence," some one observed, "is a giddy paradox whose fatuous existence is quite fittingly confined to the realm of fable."

"You took the identical words right out of my mouth," Crane complained bitterly.

"Your pardon, senores: history confutes your incredulity."

"But we are talking about to-day."

"Even to-day--can you deny it?--men attain high places by means which the law would construe as criminal, were they not intelligent enough to outwit it."

"Big game," Crane objected; "something else again. What we contend is no man of ordinary common sense could get his own consent to crack a safe, or pick a pocket, or do second-story work, or pull any rough stuff like that."

"Again you overlook living facts," persisted the Brazilian.

"Name one--just one."

"The Lone Wolf, then."

"Unnatural history is out of my line," Crane objected. "Why is a lone wolf, anyway?"

The Brazilian's voice took on an accent of exasperation. "Senores, I do not jest. I am a student of psychology, more especially of criminal psychology. I lived long in Paris before this war, and took deep interest in the case of the Lone Wolf."

"Well, you've got me all excited. Go on with your story."

"With much pleasure.... This gentleman, then, this Michael Lanyard, as he called himself, was a distinguished Parisian figure, a man of extraordinary attainment, esteemed the foremost connoisseur d'art in all Europe. Suddenly, at the zenith of his career, he disappeared. Subsequently it became known that he had been identical with that great Parisian criminal, the Lone Wolf, a superman of thieves who had plundered all Europe with unvarying success for almost a decade."

"Then what made the silly ass quit?"

"According to my information, he won the love of a young woman--"

"And reformed for her sake, of course?"

"To the contrary, senor; Lanyard renounced his double life because of a theory on which he had founded his astonishing success. According to this theory, any man of intelligence may defy society as long as he will, always providing he has no friend, lover, or confederate in whom to confide. A man self-contained can never be betrayed; the stupid police seldom apprehend even the most stupid criminal, save through the treachery of some intimate. This Lanyard proved his theory by confounding not only the utmost efforts of the police but even the jealous enmity of that association of Continental criminals known as the Bande Noire--until he became a lover. Then he proved his intelligence: in one stroke he flouted the police, delivered into their hands the inner circle of the Bande Noire, and vanished with the woman he loved."

"And then--?"

"The rest," said the Brazilian, "is silence."

"It is for to-night, anyway," Crane observed, yawning. "It's bedtime. Here comes the busy steward to put the lights and us out."

There was a general stir; men drained glasses, knocked out pipes, got up, murmured good-nights. Lanyard closed the American novel upon a forefinger, looked up abstractedly, rose, moved toward the door. The utmost effort of exceptional powers of covert observation assured him that, at the moment, none of the company favoured him with especial attention; the author of that interest whose intensity had so weighed upon his consciousness had been swift to dissemble.

On his way forward he exchanged bows and smiles with Crane and one or two others, his gesture completely casual. Yet when he entered the starboard alleyway he carried with him a complete catalogue of those who had contributed to the conversation. With all, thanks to seven days' association, he stood on terms of shipboard acquaintance. Not one, in his esteem, was more potentially mischievous than any other--not even the Brazilian Velasco, though he had been the first to name the Lone Wolf.

It was, furthermore, quite possible that the mention of his erstwhile sobriquet had been utterly fortuitous.

And yet, one might not forget that sensation of being under intent surveillance....

In his stateroom Lanyard stood for several minutes gravely peering into the mirror above the washstand.

The face he scanned was lean and worn in feature, darkly weathered, framed in hair whose jet already boasted an accent of silver at either temple--the face of a man inured to hardship, seasoned in suffering, strong in self-knowledge. The incandescence of an intelligence coldly dispassionate, quick and shrewd, lighted those dark eyes. Distinctively a face of Gallic cast, three years of long-drawn torment had served in part to erase from it wellnigh all resemblance to both the brilliant social freebooter of ante-bellum Paris and that undesirable alien whom the authorities had sought to deport from the States. Amazing facility in impersonation had done the rest; unrecognisable as what he had been, he was to-day flawlessly the incarnation of what he elected to seem--Monsieur Duchemin, gentleman, of Paris.

Impossible to believe his disguise had been so soon penetrated....

And yet, again, that gossip of the smoking room....

Police work? Or had Ekstrom's creatures picked up his trail once more?

Beneath that urbane mask of his, a hunted, wild thing poised in question, mistrustful of the very wind, prick-eared, fangs agleam, eyes grimly apprehensive....

A little sound, the least of metallic clicks, breaking the hush of his solitude, froze the adventurer to attention. Only his glance swerved swiftly to a fastened door in the forward partition--his stateroom being the aftermost of three that might be thrown together to form a suite. The nickeled knob was being tried with infinite precaution. On the half turn it checked with a faint repetition of the click. Then the door itself quivered almost imperceptibly to pressure, though it yielded not a fraction of an inch.

Lanyard's eyes hardened. He did not stir from where he stood, but one hand whipped an automatic from his pocket while the other darted out to the switch-box by the head of his berth and extinguished the light.

Instantly a glimmer of light in the forward stateroom showed through a narrow strip of iron grill-work set in the top of the partition for ventilating purposes.

Simultaneously the door-knob was gently released, and with another louder click the light in the adjoining cubicle was blotted out.

Mystified, Lanyard undressed and turned in, but not to sleep--not for a little, at least.

Who might this neighbour be who tried his door so stealthily? Before to-night that room had had no tenant. Apparently one of the passengers had seen fit to shift his quarters. To what end? To keep a jealous eye on the Lone Wolf, perhaps? So much the better, then: Lanyard need only make enquiry in the morning to identify his enemy.

Deliberately closing his eyes, he dismissed the enigma. He possessed in marked degree that attribute of genius, ability to command slumber at will. Swiftly the troubled deeps of thought grew calm; on their placid surface inconsequent visions were mirrored darkly, fugitive scenes from the store of subconscious memory: Crane's lantern-jawed physiognomy, keen eyes semi-veiled by humorously drooping lids, the extreme corner of his mouth bulging round his everlasting cigar ... grimy lions in Trafalgar Square of a rainy afternoon ... the octagonal room of L'Abbaye Theleme at three in the morning, a swirl of Bacchanalian shapes ... Wertheimer's soldierly figure beside the telegraphers' table in that noisome cave at the Front ... the deck of a tender in darkness swept by a shaft of yellow light which momentarily revealed a group of folk with upturned faces, a petticoat fluttering in its midst....

III
IN THE BARRED ZONE

Day broke with rather more than half a gale blowing beneath a louring sky. Once clear of the bottleneck mouth of the harbour, the *Assyrian* ran into brutal quartering seas. An old hand at such work, for upward of a decade a steady-paced Dobbin of the transatlantic lanes, she buckled down to it doggedly and, remembering her duty by her passengers, rolled no more than she had to, buried her nose in the foaming green only when she must. For all her care, the main deck forward was alternately raked by stinging volleys of spray and scoured by frantic cascades. More than once the crew of the bow gun narrowly escaped being carried overboard to a man. Blue with cold, soaked to the buff despite oilskins, they stuck stubbornly to their posts. Perched beyond reach of shattering wavecrests, the passengers on the boat-deck huddled unhappily in the lee of the superstructure--and snarled in response to the cheering information that better conditions for baffling the ubiquitous U-boat could hardly have been brewed by an indulgent Providence. Sheeting spindrift contributed to lower visibility: two destroyers standing on parallel courses about a mile distant to port and to starboard were more often than not barely discernible, spectral vessels reeling and dipping in the haze. The ceaseless whistle of wind in the rigging was punctuated by long-drawn howls which must have filled any conscientious banshee with corrosive envy.

Toward mid-morning rain fell in torrents, driving even the most fearful passengers to shelter within the superstructure. A majority crowded the landing at the head of the main companionway close by the leeward door. Bolder spirits marched off to the smoking room--Crane starting this movement with the declaration that, for his part, he would as lief drown like a rat in a trap as battling to keep up in the frigid inferno of those raging seas. A handful of miserables, too seasick to care whether the ship swam or sank, mutinously took to their berths.

Stateroom 27--adjoining Lanyard's--sported obstinately a shut door. Lanyard, sedulous not to discover his interest by questioning the stewards, caught never a glimpse of its occupant. For his own satisfaction he took a covert census of passengers on deck as the vessel entered the danger zone, and made the tally seventy-one all told--the number on the passenger list when the *Assyrian* had left her landing stage the previous evening.

It seemed probable, therefore, that the person in 27 had come aboard from the tender, either with or following the official party. Lanyard was unable to say that more had not left the tender than appeared to sit in inquisition in the music room.

By noon the wind was beginning to moderate, and the sea was being beaten down by that relentlessly lashing rain. Visibility, however, was more low than ever. A fairly representative number descended to the dining saloon for luncheon--a meal which none finished. Midway in its course a thunderous explosion to starboard drove all in panic once more to the decks.

Within two hundred yards of the *Assyrian* a floating mine had destroyed a patrol boat. No more was left of it than an oil-filmed welter of splintered wreckage: of its crew, never a trace.

Imperturbably the *Assyrian* proceeded. Not so her passengers: now the smoking room was deserted even by the insouciant Crane, and the seasick to a woman brought their troubles back to the boat-deck.

Alone the tenant of 27 stopped below. And the riddle of this ostensible indifference to terrors that clawed at the vitals of every other soul on board grew to intrigue Lanyard to the point of obsession. Was the reason brute apathy or sheer foolhardihood? He refused either explanation, feeling sure some darker and more momentous motive dictated this obstinate avoidance of the public eye. Exasperation aroused by failure to fathom the mystery took precedence in his thoughts even to the personal solicitude excited by last night's gossip of the smoking room....

With no other disturbing incident the afternoon wore away, the wind steadily flagging, the waves as steadily subsiding. When twilight closed in there was nothing more disturbing to one's equilibrium than a sea of long and sullen rolls scored by the pelting downpour.

Perhaps as many as ten venturesome souls dined in the saloon, their fellows sticking desperately to the decks and contenting themselves with coffee and sandwiches.

Daylight waned, terrors waxed: passengers instinctively gravitated into little knots and clusters, conversing guardedly as if fearful lest their normal accents bring down upon them those Apaches of the underseas for signs of whom their frightened glances incessantly ranged over-rail and searched the heaving wastes.

The understanding was tacit that all would spend the night on deck.

Dusk at length blotted out the shadows of their guardian destroyers, and a great and desolating loneliness settled down upon the ship. One by one the passengers grew dumb; still they clung together, but seemingly their tongues would no more function.

With nightfall, the rain ceased, the breeze freshened a trifle, the pall of cloud lifted and broke, giving glimpses of remote, impersonal stars. Later a gibbous moon leered through the flying wrack, checkering the sea with a restless pattern of black and silver. In this ghastly setting the **Assyrian**, showing no lights, a shape of flying darkness pursuing a course secret to all save her navigators, strained ever onward, panting, groaning, quivering from stem to stern ... like an enchanted thing doomed to perpetual labours, striving vainly to break bonds invisible that transfixed her to one spot forever-more, in the midst of that bleak purgatory of shadow and moonshine and dread....

Sensitive to the eerie influence of the hour, Lanyard interrupted the tour of the decks which he had steadily pursued for the better part of the evening, and rested at the forward rail, looking down over the main deck, its bleached planking dotted with dark shapes of fixed machinery. In the bows the formless, uncouth bulk of the gun squatted in its tarpaulin. Its crew tramped heavily to and fro, shivering in heavy jackets, hands in pockets, shoulders hunched up to ears. Farther aft an iron door clanged heavily behind a sailor emerging from an alleyway; he approached the ship's bell, with practised hand sounded two double strokes, then turned and sang out in the weird minor traditional in his calling:

"Four bells--and a-a-all's well!"

Even as the wind made free with the melancholy echoes of that assurance, the spell upon the ship was exorcised.

Overhead, from the foremast crow's-nest, a voice screamed, hoarsely urgent:
"*Torpedo! 'Ware submarine to port!*"

Many things happened simultaneously, or in a span of seconds strangely scant.
The gunners sprang to station, whipping away the tarpaulin, while their lieutenant focussed binoculars upon the confused distances of the night. Obedient to his
instructions, the long, gleaming tube of steel pivoted smoothly to port.

From the bridge a signal rocket soared, hissing. The whistle loosed stentori-
an squalls of indignation and distress--one long and four short. Commands were
shouted; the engine-room telegraph wrangled madly. The momentum of the *Assyrian* was checked startlingly; her bows sheered smartly off to port.

A rumour of frightened voices and pounding feet came from the leeward boat-
deck, where the main body of the passengers was congregated, hidden from Lanyard
by the shoulder of the foreward deck-house. A number of men ran forward, paused
by the rail, stared, and scurried back, yelling in alarm. At this the din swelled to
uproar.

Scanning closely the surface of the sea, Lanyard himself descried a silvery ar-
row of spray lancing the swells, making with deadly speed toward the port bow of
the *Assyrian*. But now both screws were churning full speed astern; the vessel lost
headway altogether. Then her engines stopped. For a breathless instant she rested
inert, like something paralyzed with fright, bows-on to the torpedo, the telegraph
ringing frantically. Then the starboard screw began to turn full ahead, the port
remaining idle. The bows swung off still more sharply to port. The torpedo shot in
under them, vanished for a breathless moment, reappeared a boat's-length to starboard, plunged harmlessly on its unhindered way down the side of the vessel, and
disappeared astern.

Amidships terrified passengers milled like sheep, hampering the work of the
boat-crews at the davits. Ship's officers raged among them, endeavouring to restore
order. Half a mile or so dead ahead a tiny tongue of flame spat viciously in the murk.
A projectile shrieked overhead, and dropped into the sea astern. Another followed
and fell short.

The U-boat was shelling the *Assyrian*.

The forward gun barked violent expostulation, if without visible effect; the
submarine lobbing two more shells at the steamship with an indifference to its own

peril astonishing in one of its craven breed, trained to strike and run before counterstroke may be delivered. Its extraordinary temerity, indeed, argued ignorance of the convoying destroyers.

Coincident with the second shot, however, these unleashed searchlights slashed the dark through and through with their great, white, fanlike blades, till first one then the other picked up and steadied relentlessly upon a toy-boat shape that swam the swells about midway between the *Assyrian* and the destroyer off the port bows.

Simultaneously the quickfirers of the latter went into action, jetting orange flame. In the searchlights' glare, spurts of white water danced all round the submarine. A mutter of gunfire rolled over to the *Assyrian*, abruptly silenced by an imperative deep voice of heavier metal--which spoke but once.

With the lurid unreality of clap-trap theatrical illusion the U-boat vomited a great, spreading sheet of flame....

Someone at the rail, near Lanyard's shoulder, uttered a hushed cry of horror.

He paid no heed, his interest wholly focussed upon that distant patch of shining water. As his dazzled vision cleared he saw that the submarine had disappeared.

Unconsciously, in French, he commented: "So that is finished!"

Likewise in French, but in a woman's voice of uncommon quality, deep and bell-sweet, came the protest from the passenger at his side: "But, monsieur, what are we doing? We turn away from them--those poor things drowning there!"

That was quite true: under forced draught the *Assyrian* was heading away on a new course.

"They drown out there in that black water--and we leave them to that!"

Lanyard turned. "The destroyers will take care of them," he said--"if any survived that explosion with strength enough to swim."

He spoke from the surface of his thoughts and with a calm that veiled profound surprise. The woman by his side was neither the American widow nor her English daughter, but wholly a stranger to the ship's company he knew.

The training of the Lone Wolf had been wasted if one swift glance had failed to comprehend every essential detail: that tall, straight, slender figure cloaked in the folds of a garment whose hood framed a face of singular pallor and sweetness in the moonlight, its shadowed eyes wide with emotion, its lips a little parted....

With a shiver she lifted her hands to her eyes as if to darken the visions of her imagination.

"They die out there," she said, in murmurs barely audible…. "We turn our backs on them…. You think that right?"

"We play the game by the rules the enemy himself laid down," Lanyard returned. "They would have sunk us without one qualm of pity--would, in all probability, have shelled our boats had any succeeded in getting off. They have done as much before, and will again. It is out of reason to insist that the captain risk his ship in the hope of picking up one or two drowning assassins."

"Risk his ship? How? They are helpless--"

"As a rule, U-boats hunt in pairs; always, when specially charged to sink one certain vessel. It was so with the *Lusitania*, with the *Arabic* as well; I don't doubt it was so in this instance--that we should have heard from a second submarine had not the destroyers opened fire when they did."

The woman stared. "You think that--?"

"That the Boche had specific instructions to waylay and sink the *Assyrian*? I begin to think that--yes."

This declaration affected the woman curiously; she shrank away a little, as from a blow, her eyes winced, her pale lips quivered. When she spoke, it was, strangely enough, in English so naturally enunciated that Lanyard could not doubt that this was her mother tongue.

"Then you think it is because…."

Of a sudden she wilted, clinging to the rail and trembling wildly.

Lanyard shot a glance aft. The disorder among the passengers was measurably less, though excitement still ran so high that he felt sure they were as yet unnoticed. On impulse he stepped nearer.

"Pardon, mademoiselle," he said quietly; "you are excusably unstrung. But all danger is past; and there is still time to regain your stateroom unobserved. If you will permit me to escort you…."

He watched her narrowly, but she showed no surprise at this suggestion of intimacy with her affairs. After a brief moment she pulled herself together and dropped a hand upon the arm he offered. In another minute he was helping her over the raised watersill of the door.

Like all the ship the landing and main companionway were dark; but below, on the promenade deck, the second doorway aft on the starboard side stood ajar, affording a glimpse of a dimly lighted stateroom.

With neither hesitation nor surprise--for he was already satisfied in this matter--Lanyard conducted the woman to this door and stopped.

Her hand fell from his arm. She faltered on the threshold of Stateroom 27, eyeing him dubiously.

"Thank you, monsieur...?"

There was just enough accent of enquiry to warrant his giving her the name: "Duchemin, mademoiselle."

"Monsieur Duchemin.... Please to tell me how you knew this was my stateroom?"

"I occupy Stateroom 29. There was no one in 27 till after the tender came out last night. Furthermore, your face was strange, and I have come to know all others on board during our week's delay in port."

The light was at her back; he could distinguish little of her shadowed features, but fancied her a bit discountenanced.

In a subdued voice she said, "Thank you," once more, a hand resting significantly on the door-knob. But still he lingered.

"If mademoiselle would be so good as to tell me something in return--?"

"If I can...."

"Then why, mademoiselle, did you try my door last night?"

"It was neither locked nor bolted on my side. I wished to make sure--"

"So one fancied. Thank you. Good-night, mademoiselle...?"

She was impervious to his hint. "Good-night, Monsieur Duchemin," she said, and closed the door.

Now Lanyard's quarters opened not on this alleyway fore-and-aft but on a short and narrow athwartship passage. And as he turned away he saw out of the corner of an eye a white-jacketed figure emerge from this passageway and move hurriedly aft. Something furtive in the round of the fellow's shoulders challenged his curiosity. He called quietly:

"Steward!"

There was no answer. By now the white jacket was no more than a blur moving in that deep gloom. He cried again, more loudly:

"I say, steward!"

He could hardly see, but fancied that the man quickened his steps: in another instant he vanished altogether.

Smothering an impulse to give chase, the adventurer swung alertly into the narrow passage and opened the door to Stateroom 29. The room was dark, but as he fumbled for the switch, the door in the forward partition was thrust open and the girl's slight figure showed, tensely poised against the light behind her.

"Monsieur Duchemin!" she cried, in a voice sharp with doubt.

Lanyard turned the switch. "Mademoiselle," he said, and coolly crossed to the port, drawing the light-proof curtains.

"This door was locked all day--locked when the firing alarmed me and I went out to the deck."

"And on my side, mademoiselle, it was locked and bolted when last I was here, shortly before dinner." "Whoever unfastened it entered my room during my absence and tampered with my luggage."

"You have missed something?"

Gaze intent to his she nodded. He shrugged and cast shrewdly round his quarters for some clue to the enigma. His glance fastened on a leather bellows-bag beneath the berth. Dropping to his knees he pulled this out, and looked up with a quizzical grimace, his forefinger indicating the lock, which was uncaught.

"I left this latched but not locked," he said. "Perhaps I, too, have lost something."

Opening the bag out flat, he sat back on his heels, with practised eye inspecting its neat arrangement of intimate things.

"Nothing has been taken, mademoiselle," he announced gravely. "But something--I think--has been generously added. I seem to have an anonymous admirer on board."

Bending forward, he rummaged beneath a sheaf of shirts and brought forth a small jewel-box of grained leather, with a monogram stamped on the lid--"C.B."

"The lock is broken," he observed, and handed it up to the woman. "As to its contents, mademoiselle herself knows best...."

The woman opened the box.

"Nothing is missing," she said in a thoughtful voice.

"I am relieved." Lanyard closed the bag, thrust it back beneath the berth, and got upon his feet. "But you are quite sure--?"

"My jewels are all in order," she affirmed, without meeting his gaze.

"And you miss nothing else?"

"Nothing."

Was there an accent of hesitation in this response?

"Then, I take it, the thief was disappointed."

Now she glanced quickly at his eyes. "Why do you say that?"

"If the thief had found what he sought, he would never have presented it to me, mademoiselle would never again have seen her jewels. Failing in his object, after breaking that lock, and interrupted by your unexpected return, he planted the case with me, hoping to have me suspected. I am fortunately able to prove the best of alibis.... So then," said Lanyard, smiling, "it would appear that, though we met ten minutes ago for the first time--and I have yet to know mademoiselle by name--we are allies in a common cause."

"My name is Brooke--Cecelia Brooke," she said quietly--"if it matters. But why 'allies'?"

"It appears we own a common enemy. Each of us possesses something which that one desires--you a secret, I a good name. (Duchemin, indeed, I have always held to be an excellent name.) I shall not hesitate to call on you if my treasure is again violated. May I venture to hope mademoiselle will prove as ready to command my services?"

"Thank you. I fancy, however, there will be no need."

She moved irresolutely toward the communicating door, paused in its frame, eyeing him speculatively from under level brows. He detected, or imagined, a tremor of impulse toward him, as though she faltered on the verge of some grave confidence. If so, she curbed her tongue in time. Her gaze dropped, fixed itself abstractedly on the door.... "This must be fastened," she said, in a tone of complete disinterest.

"I will speak to the chief steward immediately."

"Don't trouble." She roused. "It doesn't matter, really, for to-night. I shall leave what valuables I have in the purser's care and stop on deck till daybreak."

He gave a gesture of bewilderment. "You abandon your seclusion--leave your secret unguarded?"

"Why not?" She shrugged slightly with a little *moue* of discontent. "If, as you assume, I had a secret, it was that for certain reasons I did not wish my presence on board to become known. But it seems it has become known: my secret is no more. So I need no longer risk being cut off from the boats in the event of any accident."

Momentarily her gravity was dissipated by a smile at once delightful and provocative.

"Once more, monsieur--good-night!"

After some moments Lanyard, with a start, found himself staring blankly at a blankly incommunicative communicating door.

IV
IN DEEP WATERS

Following this abrupt introduction to his interesting neighbour, Lanyard went back to his deck-chair and, bundling himself up against the cold, settled down to ponder the affair and await developments in a spirit of chastened resignation. That a denouement would duly unfold he was quite satisfied; that he himself must willy-nilly play some part therein he was too well persuaded.

Not that he wished to meddle. If this Miss Cecelia Brooke (as she named herself) fostered any sort of intrigue, he wanted nothing so fervently as to be left altogether out of it. But already he had been dragged in, without wish or consent of his; whoever coveted her secret--whatever that was, more precious to her than jewels--harboured designs upon his own as well. It was his duty henceforth to go warily, overlooking no circumstance, however trifling and inconsiderable it might appear. The slenderest thread may lead to the heart of the most intricate maze--and the heart of this was become Lanyard's immediate goal, for there his enemy lay perdu.

It was never this man's fault to underrate an enemy, least of all an unknown; and he entertained wholesome respect for Secret Service operators--picked men, as a rule, the meanest no mean antagonist. And this business, he fancied, had all the flavour of Secret Service work--one of those blind duels, desperate and grim affairs of masked combatants feinting, thrusting, guarding in the dark, each with the other's sword ever feeling for his throat, fighting for life itself and making his own rules as the contest swayed.

But what was this Brooke girl doing in that galley? What conceivable motive induced her to dabble those slender hands in the muck and blood of Secret Service work?

Lanyard was fain to let that question rest. After all, it was no concern of his. There she was, up to her pretty eyebrows in some dark, bad business; and it was not for him to play the gratuitous ass, rush in unasked, and seek to extricate her....

Through endless hours he sat brooding, vision blindly focussed upon the misty, shimmering mystery of that night.

Ekstrom!... Slowly in his understanding intuition shaped the conviction that it was Ekstrom whom he was fighting now, Ekstrom in the guise of one of his creatures, some agent of the Prussian spy system who had contrived to smuggle himself aboard this British steamship.

Out of those nine in the smoking room the previous night, then, he must beware of one primarily, perhaps of more.

Four he was disposed, with reservations, to reckon negligible: Baron von Harden, head of a Netherlands banking house, a silent body whose acute mental processes went on behind a pallid screen of flabby features; Julius Becker, a theatrical manager of New York, whose right name ended in ski; Bartlett Putnam, late charge d'affaires of the American embassy in Madrid; Edmund O'Reilly, naturalized citizen of the United States, interested in the manufacture of motor tractors somewhere in Michigan.

Of the other five, two were English: Lieutenant Thackeray, a civilly reticent gentleman whose right arm rested in a black silk sling, making a flying trip to visit a married sister in New York; Archer Bartholomew, Esq., solicitor, a red-cheeked, bright-eyed, white-haired, brisk little Cockney, beyond the military age.

There remained Dressier, the stout, self-satisfied Swiss, whose fawning manner was possibly accounted for by his statement that he journeyed to New York to engage in the trade of restaurateur in partnership with his brother; Crane, long and awkward and homely, of saturnine cast, slow of gesture and negligent as to dress, his humorous sense clouding a power of shrewd intelligence; and Senor Arturo Velasco, of Buenos Aires, middle-aged, apparently extremely well-to-do, a thoughtful type, more self-contained than most of his countrymen.

One of these probably ... But which?...

Nor must he permit himself to forget that the *Assyrian* carried fifty-nine other male passengers, in addition to her complement of officers, crew, and stewards, that any one of these might prove to be Potsdam's cat's-paw.

Awesome pallor tinged the eastern horizon, gaining strength, spread in imperceptible yet rapid gradations toward the zenith. Stars faded, winked out, vanished. Silver and purple in the sea gave place to livid gray. Almost visibly the routed night rolled back over the western rim of the world. Shafts of supernal radiance lanced the formless void between sky and sea. Swollen and angry, the sun lifted up its enormous, ensanguined portent. And the discountenanced moon withdrew hastily into the immeasurable fastnessness of a cloudless firmament, yet failed therein to find complete concealment. Keen, sweet airs of dawn raked the decks, now to port, now to starboard, as the ***Assyrian*** twisted and writhed on her corkscrew way.

Passengers whose fears had become sufficiently numb to permit them to drowse, stirred in their chairs, roused blinking and blear-eyed, arose and stretched cramped, cold bodies. Others lay listless, enervated by the sleepless misery of that night. Crane found Lanyard awake and marched him off for coffee and cigarettes in the smoking room.

Later, starting out for a turn around the decks, they passed a deck-chair sheltered in a jog where the engine-room ventilating shaft joined the forward deckhouse, in which Miss Brooke lay cocooned in wraps and furs, her profile, turned aside from the sea, exquisitely etched against the rich blackness of a fox stole. She slept as quietly as the most carefree, a shadowy smile touching her lips.

Crane's stride faltered. He whistled low.

"In the name of all things wonderful! how did that get on board?"

Lanyard mentioned the girl's name. "She has the stateroom next to mine--came off that tender, night before last."

"And me sore on that darn' li'l boat because it brought aboard all the nosey Johnnies! Ain't it the truth, you never know your luck?"

The American ruminated in silence till another lap of their walk took them past the girl again.

"Funny," he mused, "if that's why they held us up...."

"Comment, monsieur?"

"Oh, I was just wondering if it was on that young lady's account they kept us kicking our heels back there so long."

"I am still stupid," Lanyard confessed.

"Why, she might be a special messenger, you know--something like that--the

British Government wanted to smuggle out of the country without anybody suspecting."

"Monsieur is a romantic."

"You can't trust me," Crane averred unblushingly.

When they passed the chair again it was empty.

At breakfast Lanyard saw the girl from a distance: their places were separated by the width of the saloon. She had no neighbours at her table, did not look up when Lanyard entered, finished her meal some time before he did, and retired immediately to her stateroom, in whose seclusion she remained for the rest of the day.

That second day was altogether innocent of untoward incident. At least superficially the life of the ship settled into the groove of "business as usual." Only the company of the *Assyrian's* faithful convoys was an ever-present reminder of peril.

And in the middle of the afternoon she passed close by a derelict, a torpedoed tramp, deep down by the stern, her bows helplessly high in air and crimson with rust, the melancholy haunt of a great multitude of gulls.

More than slightly to Lanyard's surprise he received no quiet invitation to the captain's quarters to be interrogated concerning the burglary in Stateroom 27. Apparently, the young woman had contented herself with reporting merely that the communicating door had carelessly been left unfastened.

For his own part, neither seeking nor avoiding individual members of the smoking-room group, Lanyard permitted himself to be drawn into their company, and sat among them amiably receptive. But this profited him scantily; there was no further talk of the Lone Wolf; he was not again aware of that covert surveillance.

But when--the evening chill driving him below to don a fur-lined topcoat--the Brooke girl, coming up the companionway, acknowledged his look of recognition with the most distant of nods, he accepted the apparent rebuff without resentment. He understood. She was playing the game. The enemy was watching, listening. After that he was studious to refrain from seeming either to avoid or to seek her neighbourhood; and if he did keep a sharp eye on her, it was so circumspectly as to mock detection. To the best of his observation she found no friends on board, contracted no new acquaintances, kept herself to herself within walls of inexorable reserve.

Dawn, ending the second night at sea, found the **Assyrian** pursuing a course still devious, and now alone; the destroyers had turned back during the night. The western boundary of the barred zone lay astern. Ahead, at the end of a brief interval of time, the ivory towers of New York loomed, a-shimmer with endless sunlight, glorious in golden promise. Accordingly, the spirits of the passengers were exalted. The very ship seemed to grin in self-complacence; she had won safely through.

Unremitting vigilance was none the less maintained. No hour of the twenty-four found either gun, forward or aft, wanting a full working crew on the keen qui vive. The life boats remained on outswung davits; boat drills for passengers as well as crew were features of the daily programme. Regulations concerning light and smoking on deck after dark were rigidly enforced. Fuel was never spared in the effort to widen the blue gulf between the steamship and those waters wherein she had so nearly met her end. By day a hunted thing, racing frantically toward a port of refuge in the West, all her stout fabric labouring with titanic pulsations, shying in panic from the faintest suspicion of smoke upon the horizon, the **Assyrian** slipped into the grateful obscurity of night like a snake into a thicket, made herself akin to its densest shadows, strained hopelessly not to be outdistanced by its fugitive mantle.

And the benison of unseasonably clement weather was hers; day after shining day, night after placid night, the Atlantic revealed a singularly gracious humour, mirrored the changeful panorama of the heavens in a surface little flawed. So that the most squeamish voyagers, as well as those most beset with fears, slept sweetly in the comfort of their berths.

Lanyard, however, never went to bed without first securing his door so that it might be opened by force alone; and never slept without a pistol beneath his pillow.

But the truth is, he slept little. For the first time in his history he learned what it meant to will sleep to come and have his will defied. He lay for hours staring wide-eyed into darkness, hearkening to the steady throbbing of the engines, unable to dismiss the thought that their every revolution brought him so much nearer to America, so much the nearer to his hour with Ekstrom. In vain he sought to fatigue his senses by over-indulgence in his weakness for gambling. Day-long sessions at poker and auction in the smoking room--where he found formidable antagonists, principally in the persons of Crane, Bartlett Putnam, Velasco, Bartholomew, Julius Becker and Baron von Harden--served only to forward his financial fortunes; his luck was phenomenal; he multiplied many times that slender store of English banknotes with which he had embarked upon this adventure. But he left each exhausting sitting only to toss upon a wakeful pillow or to roam uneasily the dark and desolate decks, a man haunted by ghosts of his own raising, hagridden by passions of his own nurturing....

About two o'clock on the third night (the first outside the danger zone, when every other passenger might reasonably be expected to be in his berth) Lanyard lay in a deck-chair deep in shadows, wondering if it was worthwhile to go below and woo sleep in his stateroom. By way of experiment he shut his eyes. When after a moment he opened them again he was no longer alone.

Some distance away, at the rail, the woman of Stateroom 27 was standing with her back to Lanyard, looking intently forward, unquestionably ignorant of his presence.

Without moving, he watched in listless incuriosity till he saw her straighten and stand away from the rail as if bracing herself against some crisis.

A man was coming aft from the entrance to the main companionway, impatience in his stride--a tall man, of good carriage, muffled almost to the heels in a heavy ulster, a steamer-cap well forward over his eyes. But the light was poor, the pale shine of the aged moon blending trickily with the swaying shadows; Lanyard was unable to place him among the passengers. There was a suggestion of Lieutenant Thackeray--but that one was handicapped by one shell-shattered arm, whereas this man had the use of both.

He demonstrated that promptly, taking the girl into them. She yielded herself gladly, with a hushed little cry, hiding her face in the bosom of his ulster, clinging to him.

This, then, was an assignation prearranged! Miss Cecelia Brooke had a lover aboard the *Assyrian*, a lover whom she denied by day but met in stealth by night!

And yet, after that first, swift embrace, their conduct became oddly unloverlike. The man released her of his own initiative, held her by the shoulders at arm's length. There was irritation in his manner. He seemed tempted to shake the young woman.

"Celia! what madness!"

So much, at least, Lanyard overheard; the rest was a mumble into the hand which the girl placed over the man's lips. She cried breathlessly: "Hush! not so loud!"

And then she remembered to guard her own voice. In an undertone she spoke passionately for a moment. The man interrupted in a tone of profound vexation. She drew away, as if hurt, caught him up as he hesitated for a word, returned, clung to the lapels of his coat, her accents rapid and pitiful, eloquent of explanation, entreaty, determination. The man lifted his hands to her wrists, broke her grasp, cut her brusquely short, put her forcibly from him. She sobbed softly....

Thus swiftly the scene suffered disillusioning transition. The pretty fiction of lovers meeting in secret was no more. Remained a man annoyed to the verge of anger, a woman desperately importunate.

The wind, sweeping aft, carried broken snatches of their communications:

"... *all I have ... could not let you go*...."

"*Insanity*!"

"*I was desperate*...."

"... *drive me mad with your nonsense*...."

Lanyard sat up, scraping his chair harshly on the deck. Stricken mute, the pair at the rail moved only to turn his way the pallid ovals of their faces.

Heedless of the prohibition, he struck a vesta, cupped its flame in his hands, bending his face close and deliberately lighting a cigarette. Appreciably longer than necessary he permitted the flare to reveal his features. Then he blew it out, rose, sauntered to the rail, cast the cigarette into the sea, went aft and so below, satisfied that the girl must have recognised him and so knew that her secret was safe.

But it was in an oddly disgruntled humour that he turned in--he who had been so ready to twit Crane with his fantastic speculations concerning the English girl, who had himself been the readiest to endue her with the romantic attributes becoming a heroine of her country's Secret Service! What if he must now esteem her in the merciless light of to-night's exposure, as the most pitiable of all human spectacles, a poor lovesick thing sans dignity, sans pride, sans heed for the world's respect, a woman pursuing a man weary of her?

He resented unreasonably the unreasonable resentment which the affair inspired in him.

What was it to him? He who had struck off all fettering bonds of common human interests, who had renounced all common human emotions, who had set his hand against all mankind that stood between him and that vengeful purpose to which he had dedicated his life! He, the Lone Wolf, the heartless, soulless, pitiless beast of prey!

God in Heaven! what was any woman to him?

V
ON THE BANKS

Unaccountably enough in his esteem, and more and more to Lanyard's exasperation, the evil flavour of that overnight incident lasted; it tinctured distastefully his first waking thoughts; and through all that fourth day at sea his mood was dark with irrational depression.

And the fifth day and the sixth were like unto the fourth.

Constantly he caught himself on watch for the young woman, wondering how she would comport herself toward him, unwilling witness though he had been to that shabby scene.

But, save distantly at meal times, he saw nothing of her.

And though he knew that she was much on deck after midnight, he was studious to keep out of her way. The tedium of stopping in a stuffy stateroom, when the spell of restlessness was on him, waiting for the sounds of his neighbour's return before he might venture forth, was nothing; anything were preferable to figuring as the innocent bystander at another encounter between the Brooke girl and her reluctant lover....

Then that happened which lent the business another complexion altogether. Its second phase, of close development, drew toward an end. Subtle underlying forces began to stir in their portentous latency.

The rapiers which thus far had merely touched, shivering lightly against each other, measuring each its opponent's strength, feeling out his skill, fell apart, then re-engaged in sharp and deadly play. Steel met steel and, clashing, struck off sparks whose fugitive glimmerings lightened measurably the murk....

On the sixth night out, at eleven o'clock as a matter of routine, the smoking room was closed for the night, terminating an uncommonly protracted and, in

Lanyard's esteem, irksome sitting at cards. Well tired, he went immediately to his quarters, undressed, stretched out in his berth, and switched off the light.

Incontinently he found himself bedevilled by thoughts that would not rest.

For upward of an hour he lay moveless, seeking oblivion in that very effort to preserve immobility, while the **Assyrian**, lunging heavily on her way, moaned and muttered tedious accompaniment to the chant of the working engines.

Despairing at length, and fretted by the closeness of his quarters, he got up, dressed sketchily, and was shrugging into his fur-lined coat when he heard the door to the adjoining stateroom open and close, stealth in the sound of it.

At that he hung up his overcoat, and threw himself down with a book on the lounge seat beneath the port. The novel was dull enough in all conscience; for that matter no tale within the compass of the cunningest weaver of words could have enthralled his temper at that time.

He read and read again page after page, but without intelligence.

Between his eyes and the type-blackened paper mirages of the past trembled and wavered; old faces, old scenes, old illusions took unsubstantial form, dissolved, blended, faded away: a saddening show of shadows.

His heavy eyelids drooped; slumber's drowsy vestments trailed lazily athwart the sea of consciousness....

A slight noise startled him, either the shutting of the door to Stateroom 27, or the sound of the book dropping from his relaxed grasp. He sat up and consulted his watch. The hour was half after twelve.

The ship's bell sounded remotely a single, doleful stroke.

He might have dozed five minutes or fifteen--long enough at least to leave its tantalising effect of sleep desperately desirable, mockingly elusive, almost grasped, whisked beyond grasping. And with this he was aware of something even less tangible, a sense of something amiss, of something vaguely wrong, as of an evil spirit stalking furtively through the darkened labyrinth of the ship ... as impalpable and ineluctable as miasmic exhalations of a morass....

Lanyard passed a hand across his forehead. Had he been dreaming, then? Was this merely the reaction from some bitter nightmare? He could not remember.

On sheer impulse he stood up, extinguished the light, opened the door. As he did this he noted that a light burned in Stateroom 27, visible through the ventilating grille. So the girl must have returned while he slept. Or had she neglected to turn the switch when she went out? He could not be certain.

On the threshold he paused a little, attentive to the familiar rumour of the ship by night: the prolonged sloughing of riven waters down the side, gnashing of swells hurled back by the bows, sibilance of draughts in alleyways, groaning of frames, a thin metallic rattle of indeterminate origin, the crunching grind of the steering gear, the everlasting deep-throated diapason of the engines, somewhere aft in that tier of staterooms a persistent human snore ... nothing unusual, no alarming discordance....

Yet the feeling that mischief was afoot would not be still.

Lanyard moved down to the junction of the thwartship passage with the fore-and-aft alleyway.

Here he commanded a view of the promenade-deck landing and the main companionway, all in darkness but for a feeble glimmer of reflected starlight through the open deck port on the far side of the vessel. Beyond this the rail was stencilled against the dull face of the sea with its far lifting and falling horizon; within, no more was visible than the dimmed whiteness of the forward partition, the dense, indefinite mass of balusters winding up to the boat-deck, and the flat plane of the tiled landing.

On this last, near the mouth of the port alleyway, half obscured by the intervening balusters, something moved, something huge, black, and formless swayed and writhed strangely, and in the strangest silence, like a dumb, tormented misshapen brute transfixed to one spot from which its most anguished efforts might not avail to budge it.

Lanyard ran forward, rounded the well of the companionway, and pulled up.

Now the nature of the thing was revealed. Blackly silhouetted against the square of the doorway two human figures were close-locked and struggling desperately, straining, resisting, thrusting, giving, recovering ... and all with never a sound more than the deadened thump of a shifting foot or the rasp of hard-won breathing.

For several seconds the spectator could not distinguish one contestant from the other. Then a change in the fortunes of war enabled him to make out that one was a woman, the other, and momentarily more successful, a man. Slender and youthful and strong, she fought with the indomitable fury of a pantheress. He on his part had won this much temporary advantage--had broken the woman's clutch upon his throat and was bending her back over his hip, one hand fumbling at her windpipe, the other imprisoning her two wrists.

Yet she was far from being vanquished. Even as Lanyard moved toward the pair, she drove a savage knee into the man's middle and, as he checked instantaneously with a grunt of pained surprise, regained her footing and planted both elbows against his chest, striving frantically to free her hands.

Simultaneously Lanyard took the fellow from behind, wound an arm around his neck, jerked his head sharply back, twisted his forearm till he released the woman's wrists, and threw him with a force that must have jarred his every bone.

The woman staggered back against the partition, panting and sobbing beneath her breath. The man rebounded from his fall with astonishing agility, and flew back at Lanyard. An object in his right hand gave off the dull gleam of polished steel.

Lanyard, his automatic in his stateroom, in the pocket of the overcoat where he had deposited it when meaning to go out on deck, lacked any means of defense other than his two hands; but his one-time fame as an amateur pugilist had been second only to his fame as a connaisseur d'art; and to one whose youth had been passed in association with the Apaches of Paris, some mastery of la savate was an inevitable accomplishment.

A lightning coup de pied planted a heel against one of the man's shins, and his onslaught faltered in a gust of curses. Then the point of his jaw received the full force of Lanyard's right fist with all the ill will imaginable behind it. The man reared back, reeled into the black mouth of the alleyway, fell heavily.

Even so, he demonstrated extraordinary vitality and appetite for punishment. He had no more gone down than the adventurer, peering into the gloom, saw him struggle up on his knees. Instantly Lanyard made toward him, intent on finishing this work so well begun, but in his second stride tripped over a heavy body hidden in the shadows, and pitched headlong. Falling, he was conscious of a flashing thing that sped past his cheek, immediately above his shoulder. There followed an echoing thud against the forward partition.

Picking himself up smartly, Lanyard crept several paces down the alleyway, flattening against the wall, straining his vision, listening intently, rewarded by neither sign nor sound of his antagonist.

That one must have been swift to advantage himself of Lanyard's tumble. If he had not vanished into thin air, or gone to earth in some untenanted stateroom thereabouts, he found in the close blackness of that narrow passage a cloak of positive invisibility to cover his escape.

And there is little wisdom in stalking an armed man whom one cannot see, with what little light there is at one's own back.

So Lanyard went back to the landing, stepping carefully over the obstacle which had both thrown him and saved his life--the supine body of a third man, motionless; whether dead or merely insensible, he did not stop to investigate. His immediate concern was for the woman.

As he came upon her now, she stood en profile to the partition, tugging strongly at something embedded in the woodwork close by her side, between her waist and armpit. At the sound of his approach she looked up with a tremor of apprehension quickly calmed.

"Monsieur Duchemin! If you please--"

Lanyard, in no way surprised to recognise the voice of Miss Cecelia Brooke, stepped closer. "What is it?" he enquired; and then, bending over to look, found that her cloak was pinned to the partition by the blade of a heavy knife buried a full half of its considerable length.

"He threw it as you fell," the girl explained. "I was in the direct line."

"Permit me, mademoiselle...."

He laid hold of the haft of the weapon and with some difficulty withdrew it.

"Who was it?" he asked, weighing the knife in his palm and examining it as closely as he could without the aid of light.

There was no reply. Directly her cloak was freed, the girl had moved hastily away to the body over which Lanyard had stumbled. He heard an imploring whisper--"Please!"--and looked up to see her on her knees.

"Who, then, is this?" he demanded, joining her.

"Lionel--Lieutenant Thackeray. Please--O please!--tell me he is not dead."

Her voice broke; he saw her slender body convulsed with racking emotions. Kneeling, Lanyard made a hasty and superficial examination, necessarily no more under the conditions.

"His heart beats," he announced--"he breathes. I do not think him seriously injured." He made as if to get up. "I will get a light--a flash-lamp from my stateroom--or, better still, the ship's surgeon--"

Her hand fell upon his arm. "Please, no! Not that--not now. Later, if necessary; but now--surely, you can help me carry him to his stateroom."

"You know the number?"

"It's close by--30."

"Find it, and light up. No--leave this to me; I can carry him without assistance."

The girl rose and disappeared. Lanyard passed his arms beneath the Englishman's body, gathered him into them, and struggled to his feet: no inconsiderable task.

Light gushed from an open doorway, the third aft from the landing. Staggering, the adventurer entered and deposited the body upon the berth. Immediately the girl closed and bolted the door, then passed between him and the berth to bend over the unconscious man. He lay in deep coma, limbs a-sprawl, unpleasant glints of white between his half-closed eyelids, his breathing stertorous through parted lips. Free of its sling, his wounded arm dangled over the edge of the berth. In putting him down, Lanyard had remarked that its sleeve had been slit to the shoulder, and that its bandages were undone. Now, in amazement, he saw the arm was firm and muscular, with an unbroken skin, never a sign of any injury in all its length.

Gently the girl lifted the lieutenant's head to the light, discovering a hideously bruised swelling at the base of the skull, blood darkly matting the close-clipped hair.

She requested without looking round: "Water, please--and a towel."

Obediently Lanyard ran hot and cold water into the hand-basin in equal proportions.

"Would it not be well now to call the ship's surgeon?" he suggested diffidently.

"Is that necessary? I am something of a nurse. This is simply a bad contusion--no worse, I believe. He was struck down from behind, a cowardly blow in the dark, as he started to go up on deck. I had been waiting for him. When he didn't come I suspected something was wrong. I came down, found him lying there, that brute kneeling over him."

She spoke coolly enough, in contrast with the high excitement that inflamed her eyes as she turned away from the berth.

"Monsieur Duchemin, are you armed?"

"I have this," he said, exhibiting the knife thrown by the would-be murderer--a simple trench dagger, without distinguishing marks of any sort.

"Then take this, please." Extracting an automatic pistol from a holster belted beneath Thackeray's coat, she proffered it. "You won't mind staying here a moment, standing guard, while I fetch a dressing from my room?"

Before he could utter a word of protest she had slipped out into the alleyway, shutting the door behind her.

When several minutes had passed the adventurer found himself beset by increasing concern. This long delay seemed not only inconsistent with her solicitude, but indicated a possibility that the girl had braved unwisely the chance of a resumption of hostilities on the part of her late and as yet anonymous assailant.

Darkening the room as a matter of common-sense precaution, Lanyard, pistol in hand, stepped out into the alleyway in time to see the girl in the act of rising from her knees on the landing, near the spot where Thackeray had fallen. The light of her flash-lamp was blotted out as she came hurriedly aft.

Perplexed, he turned back and switched on the light as she entered.

Her eyes challenged his almost defiantly.

"Was I long?" she asked, breathless. "I dropped something...."

Lanyard bowed without speaking. Instinctively he knew that she was lying; and divining this in his attitude, she coloured and, disconcerted, turned away. For a moment, while she busied herself arranging on a convenient chair an assortment of first-aid accessories, he fancied that her half-averted face wore a look of sullen chagrin, with its compressed lips, downcast eyes, and faintly gathered brows.

But directly she needed assistance, and requested it of him in a subdued and impersonal manner, showing a countenance devoid of any incongruous emotion.

Lanyard, lifting the lieutenant's head and heavy torso, helped turn him face downward on the berth, then stood aside, thoughtfully watching the girl's deft fingers sop absorbent cotton in an antiseptic wash and apply it to the injury.

After a little, he said: "If mademoiselle has no more immediate use for me--"

"Thank you, monsieur. You have already done so very much!"

"Then, if mademoiselle will supply the name of this assassin--"

"I know it no more than you, monsieur!" She glanced up at him, startled. "What do you mean to do?"

"Why, naturally, lodge an information with the captain concerning this outrage--"

"Oh, please, no!"

At a loss, Lanyard shrugged eloquently.

"Not yet, at all events," she hastened to amend. "Let Lionel judge what is best to be done when he comes to."

"But, mademoiselle, who can say when that will be?" He pointed out the ugly, ragged abrasion in the young Englishman's scalp exposed by the cleansing away of the clotted blood. "No ordinary blow," he commented; "something very like a slung-shot or a loaded cane did that work. If I may venture again to advise--unless mademoiselle is herself a surgeon--"

Her colour faded and she caught her breath sharply. "You think it as serious as all that?"

"I do not know. Such a blow might easily fracture the skull, possibly bring about a concussion of the brain. Regard, likewise, his laborious breathing. I most assuredly advise consulting competent authority."

She did not immediately answer, turning back undivided attention to her task; but he noticed that her hands were tremulous, however, dextrously they finished dressing and bandaging the hurt; and deep distress troubled the handsome eyes she turned to his when she rose.

"You are right," she murmured--"unquestionably right, monsieur. We must have the surgeon in...."

But when Lanyard advanced a hand toward the bell-push, to call the steward, she interposed in quick alarm:

"No--if you please, a moment; I must have time to think!" Her slender fingers writhed together in her agony of doubt and irresolution. "If only I knew what to do...."

Lanyard was dumb. There was, indeed, nothing helpful he could offer, who was without a solitary tangible or trustworthy clue to the nature of this strange business.

He owned himself sadly mystified. In the light--or, rather, the shadow--of this latest development, his revised suspicions seemed unwarranted to the point of impertinence; unless, of course, one assumed the unknown assailant to be a rejected lover or wronged husband. And somehow one did not, in the presence of this clear-eyed, straight-limbed, courageous young Englishwoman, so wanting in self-consciousness.

And yet ... what the deuce was she to this man whom, indisputably, she followed against his wish?

And what conceivable chain of circumstances linked their fortunes with his, and that double burglary of the first night out with this murderous assault of to-night?

Nor was to-night's work, considered by itself, lacking in questionable features.

Why had Thackeray carried that sound arm in a sling? How had its bandages come to be unwrapped? Not in struggles before being placed hors de combat, for he had never had a chance to resist. Had his assailant, then, unwrapped it subsequently? If so, with what end in view?

Why had this Miss Cecelia Brooke, surprising the thug at his work, joined battle with him so bravely and so madly without calling for help?

What hidden motive excused this singular hesitation to summon the surgeon, this reluctance to inform the officers of the ship?

What duplicity was that which the girl had paraded concerning her procrastination when Lanyard had surprised her on her knees out there on the landing?

If this were what Lanyard had first inclined to think it, Secret Service intrigue, surely it was weirdly intricate when an English girl hesitated to safeguard an Englishman by taking into her confidence the officers of a British ship, British manned!

Nevertheless, and however much he might wonder and doubt, Lanyard would never question her. Never of his own volition would he probe more deeply into this mystery, take one farther step into the intricacies of its maze.

So, in silence, he waited, passively courteous, at her further service if she had need of him, content if she had not, tolerant of her tacit prayer for time in which to think a way out of her difficulties.

After some few moments he grew uncomfortably aware that he had become the object of a speculative regard not at all unfavourable.

He indulged in a mental gesture of resignation.

Then what he had feared befell, not altogether as he had apprehended, but in the girl's own fashion, if without material difference in the upshot.

"I am afraid," said she in an even voice, so quietly pitched as to be inaudible to any eavesdropper. "This becomes a task greater than I had dreamed, more than my wits can cope with. Monsieur Duchemin...."

She hesitated. He bowed slightly. "If mademoiselle can make any use of my poor abilities, she has but to command me."

"We--I have much to thank you for already, monsieur, much more than I can ever hope to reward adequately--"

"Reward?" he echoed. "But, mademoiselle--!"

"Please don't misunderstand." She flushed a little, very prettily. "I am simply trying to express my sense of obligation, not only for what you have already done, but for what I mean to ask you to do."

Again he bowed, without comment, amiably receptive.

She resumed with perceptible effort: "I can trust you--"

"You must make sure of that before you do," he warned her, smiling.

"I am sure," she averred gravely.

"You know nothing concerning me, mademoiselle--pardon! For all you know I may be the greatest rogue in Christendom. And I must tell you in all candour, sometimes I think I am."

"What I may or may not know concerning you, Monsieur Duchemin, is immaterial as long as I know you are what you have proved yourself to me, a gentleman, considerate, generous, brave, and--not inquisitive."

He was frankly touched. If this were flattery, tone and manner robbed it of fulsomeness, rendered it subtle beyond the coarser perceptions of the man. He knew himself for what he was, knew himself unworthy; and that part of him which was unaffectedly French, whether by accident of birth or influence of environment, and so impulsive and emotional, reacted in spontaneous gratitude to this implicit acceptance of him for what he strove to seem to be.

"Mademoiselle is gracious beyond my deserts," he protested. "Only let me know how I may be of use...."

"In three ways: Continue to be lenient in your judgments, and ask me no more questions than you must because ... I may not answer...." Her hands worked together again. She added unhappily, in a faint voice: "I dare not."

That, too, moved him, since he had been far from lenient in his judgments. He responded the more readily: "All that is understood, mademoiselle."

"Please go at once back to your stateroom, and as quietly as possible. There is a bare chance you were not recognised, that nobody knows who came to my aid tonight. If you can slip away without attracting attention, so much the better for us, for all of us. You may not be suspected."

"Trust me to use my best discretion."

"Lastly ... take and keep this for me, till I ask you for it again. Hide it as secretly as you can. It may be sought for, is certain to be if you are believed to be in my confidence. It must not be found. And I may not want it again before we land in New York."

She extended a hand on whose palm rested a small and slender white cylinder, no longer and little thicker than the toy pencil that dangles from a dance-card: a tight roll of plain white paper enclosed in a wrapping of transparent oiled silk, gummed fast down its length and, at either end, sealed with miniature blobs of black wax.

"Will you do this for me, Monsieur Duchemin? I warn you, it may cost you your life."

He took it, his temper veering to the whimsical. "What is life?" he questioned. "A prelude--perhaps an overture to that great drama, Death. Who knows? Who cares?"

She heard him in a stare. "You place no value on life?"

"Mademoiselle," he said, "I have lived nearly thirty years in this world, three years in the theatre of war, seldom far from the trenches of one front or another. I tell you, I know death too well...."

He shrugged and put the roll of paper away in a pocket.

"You understand it must not be taken from you under any circumstance? As a last resort, it must be destroyed rather than yielded up."

"It shall be," he said quietly. "Is there anything more?"

She shook her head, thoughtfully knuckling her underlip.

"How can I communicate with you in event of necessity after we get to New York?" she asked.

"I shall stop for a week or two at the Hotel Knickerbocker."

"If anything should happen"--with a swift glance of anxiety toward the motionless figure in the berth--"if anything should prevent my calling for it within a week after our arrival, you will be good enough to deliver it to--" She caught herself up quickly, the unuttered words trembling on her lip. "I will write down the address of the person to whom you will deliver it, and slip it underneath the door between our rooms--first making certain you are there to receive it--if I do not ask you to return the--thing--before we land."

"That shall be as you will."

"When you have memorized the address you will destroy it?"

"Depend on that."

"I think that is all. Thank you, Monsieur Duchemin--and good-night."

She extended her hand. He saluted it punctiliously with fingertips and lips.

"If you will put out the light, mademoiselle, it may aid me to get away unseen."

She nodded and offered him Thackeray's pistol. "Take this. O, I have another with me."

Lanyard accepted the weapon and, when she had darkened the room, opened the door, slipped out, and closed it behind him so noiselessly that the girl could not believe he was gone.

Nothing hindered his return to Stateroom 29.

Fully two minutes after he had locked himself in he heard the distant clamour of the annunciator, calling a steward to Stateroom 30.

VI
UNDER SUSPICION

He sat for a long time on the edge of his berth, elbow on knee, chin in hand, unstirring, gaze fixed upon that little cylinder of white paper resting in the hollow of his palm, in profoundest concentration pondering the problems it presented: what it was, what possession of it meant to Michael Lanyard, what safe disposition to make of it pending welcome relief from this unsought and most unwelcome trust.

This last question alone bade fair to confound his utmost ingenuity.

As for what it was, Lanyard was well satisfied that he now held the true focus of this conspiracy, a secret of the first consequence, far too momentous to the designs of England to be entrusted, though couched in the most cryptic cipher ever mind of man devised, even to cables or mails which England herself controlled.

Solely to prevent this communication from reaching America, Lanyard believed, Germany had sown mines broadcast in all the waters which the *Assyrian* must cross, and had commissioned her U-boats, without fail and at whatever cost, to sink the vessel if by any accident she won safely through the mine-fields.

In the effort to steal this secret, German spies had sailed on the *Assyrian* knowing well the double risk they ran, of being shot like rats if found out, of being drowned like neutrals if the ship went down through the efforts of their compatriots.

It was the zeal of Potsdam's agents, seeking the bearer of this secret, which had caused the rifling of Miss Brooke's luggage when she fell under suspicion, thanks to her clandestine way of coming aboard; and through the same agency young Thackeray had been all but murdered when suspicion, for whatever reason, shifted to him.

To insure safe transmission of this communication, England had held the *As-syrian* idle in port, day after day, while her augmented patrols scoured the seas, hunting down ruthlessly every submarine whose periscope dared peer above the surface, and while her trawlers innumerable swept the channels clear of mines.

To prevent its theft, Lieutenant Thackeray had invented the subterfuge of the "wounded" arm, amid whose splints and bandages (Lanyard never doubted) the cylinder had been secreted.

Finally, it was as a special agent, deep in her country's confidence, that this English girl had smuggled herself aboard at the last moment, bringing, no doubt, this very cylinder to be transferred to the keeping of Lieutenant Thackeray or, per-haps, another confrere, should she find reason to think herself suspected, her trust endangered.

Nothing strange in that; women had served their countries in such capaci-ties before; the secret archives of European chancellories are replete with their re-cords. Lanyard himself remembered many such women, brilliant mondaines from many lands domiciled in that Paris of the so-dead yesterday to serve by stealth their respective governments; but never, it was true, a woman of the caste of Cecelia Brooke; unless, indeed, this were an actress of surpassing talent, gifted to hoodwink the most skeptical and least susceptible of men.

And yet....

Lanyard's train of thought faltered. New doubt of the girl began to shadow his meditations. Contradictory circumstances he had noted intruded, uninvited, to challenge overcredulous conclusions concerning her.

Would any secret agent worth her salt invite suspicion by making such a con-spicuously furtive embarkation, by such ostentatious avoidance of her fellow pas-sengers, by surrounding herself with an atmosphere of such palpable mystery? Would such an one confess she had a "secret" to an utter stranger, as she had to Lanyard that first night out? Would she, under any conceivable circumstances, en-trust to that same stranger that selfsame secret upon whose inviolate preservation so much depended?

And would she make love-trysts on the decks by night?

Would a brother-agent take her in his arms, then reprove her with every symp-tom of vexation for her "madness," her "insanity," her "nonsense" that was like to "drive me mad"?--Thackeray's own words!

Vainly Lanyard cudgelled his wits for some plausible reading of this riddle.

Was this Brooke girl possibly (of a sudden he sat bolt upright) a Prussian agent infatuated with this young Englishman and by him beloved in spite of all that forbade their passion?

Did not this explanation reconcile every apparent inconsistency in her conduct, even to the entrusting to a stranger of the stolen secret, the purloined paper she dared not keep about her lest it be found in her possession?

Lanyard's eyes narrowed. Visibly his features hardened. If this surmise of his were any way justified in the outcome, he promised Miss Cecelia Brooke an hour of most painful penitence.

Woman or not, she need not look for mercy from him, who must ever be merciless in his dealings with Ekstrom's crew.

To be made that one's tool!

The very thought was intolerable....

As for himself, possession of this paper meant that pitfalls were digged for his every step.

If ever the British found cause to suspect him, his certain portion would be to face a firing squad in dusk of early day.

If, on the other hand, these Prussian agents on board the *Assyrian* ever got wind of the fact that the cylinder was in his care, his fate was apt to be a knife between his ribs the first time he was caught alone and--with his back to the assassin.

Two courses, then, were open to him: the most sensible and obvious, to go straightway to the captain of the *Assyrian*, report all that he knew or surmised, and turn over the paper for safekeeping; one alternative, to hide the cylinder so absolutely that the most drastic search would overlook it, yet so handily that he could rid himself of it at an instant's notice.

But the first course involved denunciation of the Brooke girl. And what if she were innocent? What if, after all, these doubts of her were the specious spawn of facts misinterpreted, misconstrued? What if she proved to be all she seemed? Could he, even though what he had warned her he might be, the greatest rogue unhung, be false to a trust reposed in him by such a woman?

As to that, there was no question in his mind; he would never betray her, lacking irrefutable conviction that she was an employee of the Prussian spy system.

Then how to hide the paper?

Kneeling, Lanyard drew from beneath the berth his bellows-bag, selected from its contents a black japanned tin case containing a rather elaborate though compact trench medicine kit, the idle purchase of an empty afternoon in London. Extracting from its fittings a small leather-covered case, he replaced the kit, relocked and shoved the bag back beneath the berth.

Then, standing over the hand-basin, he opened the leather-covered case. Its velvet-lined compartments held a hypodermic syringe and needle, and a glass phial of twenty-four one-thirtieth grain morphia tablets.

Uncorking the phial, he shook out all the tablets, replaced three, then slid the paper cylinder into the tube; it fitted precisely, concealed by the label of the manufacturing chemist, leaving room for six more tablets. Lanyard inserted four on top of the cylinder, moistening the lowermost slightly to make it stick, recorked the phial, and returned it to its compartment.

Next he dissolved three morphia tablets in a little water in the bottom of a glass, filled the syringe with the strong solution, fitted on the needle, squirted most of the contents down the waste-pipe, and consigned the remaining tablets to the same innocuous fate.

Finally he replaced needle and syringe in the case, let the glass which had held the solution stand without rinsing, and put the open case upon the shelf above the basin.

A light tapping sounded on the panels of his door.

"Well? Who's there?"

"Your steward, sir. Captain Osborne's compliments, an' 'e'd like to see you in 'is room as soon as convenient, sir."

"You may say I will come at once."

"'Nk you, sir."

A summons to have been expected as a sequel to the surgeon's report after attending Lieutenant Thackeray; none the less, Lanyard had not expected it so soon.

Authority, he reflected, ran true to form afloat as well as ashore; it was prompt enough when required to apply a pound or so of cure. Surely the officers, at least the captain, must have been advised why this voyage was apt to prove exception-ally hazardous; and surely in the light of such information it had been wiser to set armed watches on every deck by night, rather than permit the lives of passengers to be imperilled through the possible activities of Prussian agents among them in-cogniti.

And now that he was reminded of it, was not this, perhaps, but a device of the enemy's to decoy him from the comparative safety of his stateroom?

It was with a hand in his jacket pocket, grasping Thackeray's automatic, that he presently left the room. The alleyway, however, was deserted except for his stew-ard; who, as he appeared, turned and led the way up to the boat-deck.

Rounding the foot of the companionway, Lanyard contrived a hasty glance down the port alleyway. The door to Stateroom 30 was on the hook; a light burned within. Outside a guard was stationed, a sailor with a cutlass: the first application of the pound of cure!

At the heels of his guide, he approached a door in the deck-house, devoted to officers' accommodations, beneath the bridge. Here the steward knocked discreet-ly. A heavy voice grumbling within was stilled for a moment, then barked a sharp invitation to enter. The steward turned the knob, announced dispassionately "Mon-seer Duchemin," and stood aside. Lanyard entered a well-lighted room, simply but comfortably furnished as the captain's office and sitting room; sleeping quarters adjoined, the head of a berth with a battered pillow showing through a door a foot or so ajar.

Four persons were present; the notion entered Lanyard's head that a fifth possi-bly lurked in the room beyond, spying, eavesdropping: not a bad scheme if Thacker-ay had an associate on board whose identity it was desirable to keep under cover.

The door closed gently behind him as he stood politely bowing, conscious that the four faces turned his way were distinguished by a singular variety of expres-sion.

Miss Cecelia Brooke was nearest him, beside a chair from which she had evi-dently just risen, her pretty young face rather pale and set, a scared look in her candid eyes.

Beyond her, the captain sat with his back to a desk: a broad-beamed, vigorous body, intensely masculine, choleric by habit, and just now in an extraordinarily grim temper, his iron-gray hair bristling from his pillow, and his stout person visibly suffering the discomfort of wearing night-clothes beneath his uniform coat and trousers. Bending upon Lanyard the steel-hard regard of small, steel-blue eyes, he drummed the arms of his chair with thick and stubby fingers.

To one side, standing, was the third officer, a Mr. Sherry, a youngish man with a pleasant cast of countenance which temporarily wore a look, rarely British, of ingrained sense of duty at odds with much embarrassment.

Lastly Mr. Crane's lanky person was draped, with its customary effect of carelessness, on one end of the lounge seat. He looked up, nodded shortly but cheerfully to Lanyard, then resumed a somewhat quizzical contemplation of the half-smoked cigar which etiquette obliged him to neglect in the presence of a lady.

"This is the gentleman?" Captain Osborne queried heavily of the girl. Receiving a murmured affirmative, he continued: "Good morning, Monsieur Duchemin.... Thanks, Miss Brooke; we won't keep you up any longer to-night."

He rose, bowed stiffly as Mr. Sherry opened the door for the girl, and when she was gone threw himself back into his chair with a force which made it enter a violent protest.

"Sit down, sir. Daresay you know what we want of you."

"It is not difficult to guess," Lanyard admitted. "A sad business, monsieur."

"Sad!" the captain iterated in a tone of harsh sarcasm. "That's a mild name to give murder."

Even had it not been blurted violently at him, that word was staggering. The adventurer echoed it blankly. "You can't mean Lieutenant Thackeray--?"

"Not yet, though doctor says it may come to that; the poor chap's in a bad way--concussion."

"So one feared. But monsieur said 'murder'...."

Captain Osborne sat forward, steely gaze mercilessly boring into Lanyard's eyes. "Monsieur Duchemin," he said slowly, "Lieutenant Thackeray was not the only passenger to suffer through to-night's villainy. The other died instantly."

"In God's name, monsieur--who?"

"Bartholomew."

"Mr. Bartholomew!" A memory of that brisk little body's ruddy, cheerful, British personality flashed athwart the screen of memory. Lanyard murmured: "Incredible!"

"Murdered," the captain proceeded, "in Stateroom 28. Lieutenant Thackeray and he were friends, shared the suite. Apparently Mr. Bartholomew heard some unusual noise in 30 and left his berth to investigate. He was struck down from behind as he approached the communicating door. The murderer had got in by way of the sitting room, 26."

Mr. Sherry added in an awed voice: "Frightful blow--skull crushed like an eggshell."

There was a pause. Crane thoughtfully relighted his cigar, and wrapped his right cheek round it. The captain glared glassily at Lanyard. Mr. Sherry looked, if possible, more uncomfortable than ever. Lanyard pondered, aghast.

Ekstrom's work, of a certainty! This was his way, the way he imposed upon his creatures. Ekstrom, ever a killer, obsessed by the fallacious notion that dead men tell no tales....

And Bartholomew had been in this mess with Thackeray, both of them operatives of the British Secret Service!

"Miss Brooke has given her version of the attack on Lieutenant Thackeray," the captain pursued. "Be good enough to let us have yours."

Succinctly Lanyard recounted the happenings between the moment when premonition of evil drew him from his stateroom and the moment when he returned thereto.

He was at pains, however, to omit all mention of the cylinder of paper; that, pending definite knowledge to the contrary, was a sacred trust, a matter of his honour, solely the affair of the Brooke girl.

The captain squared himself toward Lanyard, his face louring, his jaw pugnacious.

"How did you happen to be up and dressed at that late hour, so ready to respond to this--ah--premonition of yours?"

"I sleep not well, monsieur. It was my intention to go on deck and endeavour to walk off my insomnia."

Captain Osborne commented with a snort.

"Why did you leave Miss Brooke alone before she called the doctor?"

"At mademoiselle's request, naturally."

"You'd been deuced gallant up to that time. I presume it didn't occur to you that the young woman might need further protection?"

Lanyard shrugged. "It did not occur to me to refuse her request, monsieur."

"Didn't it strike you as odd she should wish to be left alone with Lieutenant Thackeray?"

"It was not my affair, monsieur. It was her wish."

"Excuse me, cap'n." Crane sat up. "I'd like to ask Mr. Lanyard a question."

But Lanyard had prepared himself against that, and acknowledged the touch with a quiet smile and the hint of a bow.

"Monsieur Crane...."

"U.S. Secret Service," Crane informed him with a grin. "Velasco spotted you--had seen you years ago in Paruss--tipped me off."

"So one inferred. And these gentlemen?" Lanyard indicated the captain and third officer.

"I wised them up--had to, when this happened."

"Naturally, monsieur. Proceed...."

"I only wanted to ask if you noticed anything to make you think perhaps there was an understanding between Miss Brooke and the lieutenant?"

"Why should I?"

"I ain't curious why you should. What I want to know is, did you?"

"No, monsieur," Lanyard lied blandly.

"The little lady didn't seem to take on more'n she naturally would if the lieutenant'd been a stranger, eh?" "How to judge, when one has never seen mademoiselle distressed on behalf of another?"

Crane abandoned his effort, resuming contemplation of his cigar.

"Now we come to the point. Monsieur Lanyard, or whatever your name is."

"I have found Duchemin very agreeable, monsieur le capitaine."

"I daresay," Captain Osborne sneered. He hesitated, glowering in the difficulty of thinking. "See here, Monsieur Duchemin--since you prefer that style--I'm not going to beat about the bush with you. I'm a plain man, plain-spoken. They tell me you reformed. I don't know anything about that. It's my conviction, once a thief, always a thief. I may be wrong."

"Right or wrong, monsieur might easily be less offensive."

The captain's dark countenance became still more darkly congested. Implacable prejudice glinted in his small eyes. Nor was his temper softened by the effrontery of this offender in giving back look for look with a calm poise that overshadowed his arrogance of an honest, law-abiding man.

He made a vague gesture of impatience.

"The point is," he said, "this crime was accompanied by robbery."

"Am I to understand I am accused?"

"Nobody is accused," Crane cut in hastily.

"You have found no clues--?"

"Nary clue."

"What I want to say to you, Monsieur Duchemin, is this: the stolen property has got to be recovered before this ship makes her dock in New York. It means the loss of my command if it isn't. It means more than that, according to my information; it means a disastrous calamity to the Allied cause. And you're a Frenchman, Monsieur--Duchemin."

"And a thief. Monsieur le capitaine must not forget his pet conviction."

"As to that, a man can't always be particular about the tools he employs. I believe the old saying, set a thief to catch a thief, holds good."

"Do I understand," Lanyard suggested sweetly, "you are about to honour me by utilizing my reputed talents, by commissioning a thief to catch this thief of to-night?"

"Precisely. You know more of this matter than any of us here. You were at hand-grips with the murderer--and let him get away."

"To my deep regret. But I have told you how that happened."

"Seems a bit strange you made no real effort to find out what the scoundrel looked like."

"It was dark in that alleyway, monsieur."

The captain made an inarticulate noise, apparently meant to convey an effect of ironic incredulity. More intelligible comment was interrupted by a ring of the telephone. He swung around, clapped receiver to ear, snapped an impatient "Well?" and listened with evident exasperation.

Lanyard's eyes narrowed. This business of telephoning was conceivably well-timed; not improbably the captain was receiving the report of somebody who had been sent to search Stateroom 29 in Lanyard's absence. He wondered and, wondering, glanced at Crane, to find that gentleman watching him with a whimsical glimmer which he was quick to extinguish when the captain said curtly, "Very good, Mr. Warde," and turned back from the telephone, his manner more than ever truculent.

"Mr. Lanyard," he said--"Monsieur Duchemin, that is--a valuable paper has been stolen, an exceedingly valuable document. I don't know which carried it, Lieutenant Thackeray or Mr. Bartholomew. But I do know such a paper was in their possession. And to the best of my knowledge, we three were the only ones on board that did know it. And it has disappeared. Now, sir, you may or may not be deeper in this affair than you have admitted. If you are, I'd advise you to own up."

"Monsieur le capitaine implies my complicity in this dastardly crime!"

Osborne shook his head doggedly. "I imply nothing. I only say this: if you know anything you haven't told us, my advice is to make a clean breast of it."

"I have nothing to tell you, monsieur, beyond the fact that I find you, your tone, your manner, and your choice of words, intolerably insolent."

"Then you know nothing--?"

"Monsieur!" Lanyard cried sharply.

"Very good," the captain persisted. "I'll take your word for it--and give you till we take on our pilot to find the real criminal and make him give up that paper."

"And if I fail?"

"Not a soul on board leaves the *Assyrian* till the murderer and thief are found--if they are not one."

"But that is a general threat; whereas monsieur has honoured me by making this a personal matter. What punishment have you prepared for me specifically, if I fail to accomplish this task which baffles your--shrewdness?"

"I'll at least inform the port authorities in New York, tell them who you are, and have you barred out of the country."

"I want to say, Lanyard," Crane interposed, "this isn't my notion of how to deal with you, or in any way by my advice."

"Thank you, monsieur," the adventurer replied icily, without removing his attention from the captain. "What else, Captain Osborne?"

"That is all I have to say to you to-night, sir. Good-night."

"But I have something more to say to you, monsieur le capitaine. First, I desire to give over to you this article which it will doubtless please you to consider stolen property." Lanyard placed the automatic pistol on the desk. "One of Lieutenant Thackeray's," he explained; "at Miss Brooke's suggestion, I borrowed it as a life-preserver, in event of another brush with this homicidal maniac."

"She told us about that," Osborne said heavily, fumbling with the weapon. "What else, sir?"

"Only this, monsieur le capitaine: I shall use my best endeavour to uncover the author of these crimes. If I succeed, be sure I shall denounce him. If I succeed only in securing this valuable paper you speak of, be equally sure you will never see it; for it shall leave my hands only to pass into those which I consider entirely trustworthy."

"The devil!" Captain Osborne leaped from his chair quaking with fury. "You dare accuse me of disloyalty--!"

"Now you mention it...." Lanyard cocked his head to one side with a maddening effect of deliberation. "No," he concluded--"no; I wouldn't accuse you of intentional treason, monsieur; for that would involve an imputation of intelligence...."

He opened the door and nodded pleasantly to Crane and the third officer.

"Good-night, gentlemen," he said silkily. "Oh, and you, too, Captain Osborne--good-night, I'm sure."

VII
IN STATEROOM 29

In spite of his own anger, something far from being either assumed or inconsiderable, Lanyard was fain to pause, a few paces from the deck-house, and laugh quietly at a vast and incoherent booming which was resounding in the room he had just quitted--Captain Osborne trying to do justice to the emotions inspired in his virtuous bosom by the cheek of this damned gaol-bird.

But suddenly, reminded of the grim reason for all this wretched brawling, Lanyard shrugged off his amusement. Beneath his very feet, almost a man lay dead, another perhaps dying, while the beast who had wrought that devilishness remained at large.

He comprehended in a wondering regard that wide, star-blazoned arch of skies, that broad, dark, restful mystery of waters, that still, sweet world of peace through which the *Assyrian* forged, muttering contentedly at her toil ... while Murder with foul hands and slavering chops skulked somewhere in the darkened fabric of her, somewhere beyond that black mouth of the deck-port yawning at Lanyard's elbow.

From that same portal a man came abruptly but quietly, saw Lanyard standing there, gave him a staring look and grudging nod, and strode forward to the captain's quarters: Mr. Warde, the first officer.

Lanyard recollected himself, and went below.

Still the sailor guarded the door in that port alleyway; but now it stood wide, and Cecelia Brooke was on its threshold, conversing guardedly with the surgeon. Even as Lanyard caught sight of them, the latter bowed and turned aft, while the girl retreated and refastened the door on its hook.

Thus reminded of Crane's shrewd questions, Lanyard was speculating rather foggily concerning the reason therefor as he turned down the passage to his own quarters. What had the American noticed, or been told, to make him surmise covert sympathy between the girl and the lieutenant?

He caught himself yawning. Drowsiness buzzed in his brain. He had an incoherent feeling that he would now sleep long and heavily. Entering his stateroom, he put a shoulder against the door, pushing it to as he fumbled for the switch. The circumstance that the lights were no longer burning as he had left them failed to impress him as noteworthy in view of his belief that, by the captain's orders, Mr. Warde had been ransacking his effects in his absence.

But when no more than a click responded to a turn of the switch, the room remaining quite dark, Lanyard uttered an imprecation, abruptly very wide awake indeed.

Before he could move he stiffened to positive immobility: the cool, hard nose of a pistol had come into contact with his skull, just behind the ear.

Simultaneously a softly-modulated voice advised him in purest German: "Be quite still, Herr Lanyard, and hold up your hands--so! Also, see that you utter no sound till I give you leave.... Karl, the handkerchief."

Lanyard stood motionless, hands well elevated, while a heavy silk blindfold was whipped over his eyes and knotted tight at the back of his head.

"Now your paws, Herr Lone Wolf--put them together behind your back, prudently making no attempt to reach a pocket."

Obediently Lanyard permitted his wrists to be caught together with a second silk handkerchief. He could feel a slight sensation of heat upon his hands, and guessed that this was caused by the light of a flash-lamp held close to the flesh. None the less he took the chance of clenching his fists and tensing the muscles of his wrists.

"Tightly, Karl."

The bonds were made painfully fast. Still it did not seem to occur to his captors to oblige their prisoner to open his hands and relax his wrists. Lanyard perceived a glimmer of hope in this oversight: the enemy was normally stupid.

"Now the lights again."

After a little wait, during which he could hear the bulbs being pressed back into their sockets, the switch clicked once more.

"And now, swine-dog!"--the pistol tapped his skull significantly--"if you value your life, speak, and speak quickly. Where is that document?"

"Document?" Lanyard repeated in a tone of wonder.

"Unless you are eager to explore the hereafter, tell us where we may find it without delay."

"Upon my word, I don't know what you're talking about."

"You lie!" the German snapped. "Face about!"

Somebody grasped his shoulders roughly and swung him round to the light, the nose of the pistol shifting to press against his abdomen.

"Search him, Karl."

Unseen hands investigated his pockets cunningly. As they finished, the man who answered to the name of Karl became articulate for the first time, following a grunt of disappointment:

"Nothing--he has it not upon him."

"Look more thoroughly. Did you think him idiot enough to carry it where you'd find it at the first dip? Imbecile!"

For the purpose of this second search Lanyard's garments were ripped open, and the enemy made sure that he carried nothing next his skin more incriminating than a money-belt, which was forcibly removed.

"His shoes--see to his shoes!" the first speaker insisted irritably. "Sit down, Lanyard!"

A petulant push sent the adventurer reeling across the cabin to fall upon the lounge seat beneath the port. With some effort he assumed a sitting position, while Karl, kneeling, hastily unlaced and tore off his shoes and socks.

"Nothing, captain," was the report.

"Damnation!... Continue to search his luggage. Leave nothing unexamined. In particular look into every hole and corner where none but a fool would attempt to hide anything. This fine gentleman imagines we value his intelligence too highly to believe he would leave the paper in plain sight."

To an accompaniment of sounds indicating that Karl was obeying his superior, this last resumed in a tone of lofty contempt:

"How is it you have abandoned the habit of going armed, Herr Lone Wolf? That is not like you. Is it that you grow unwary through drug-using? But that matters nothing. We have more important business to speak over, you and I. You will be very, very docile, and answer promptly, also in a low voice, if you would avoid getting hurt. Do you understand?"

"Perfectly," Lanyard replied, furtively working at the bonds on his wrists.

"Good. We speak together like good friends, yes?"

"Naturally," said Lanyard. "It is so conducive to chumminess to be caressed with an automatic pistol--you've no idea!"

"Oblige by speaking German. Our ears are sick with all this bastard English. Also, more quietly speak. Do not put me to the regrettable necessity of shooting you."

"How regrettable? You didn't stick at braining those others--"

"Hardly the same thing. You are not like those English swine. You are French; and Germany has no hatred for France, but only pity that it so fatuously opposes manifest destiny. In truth, you are not even French, but a great thief; and criminals have no patriotism, nor loyalty to any State but their own, the state of moral turpitude."

The speaker interrupted himself to relish his wit with a thick chuckle. And Lanyard's jaws ached with the strain of self-control. He continued to pluck at the folds of silk while concentrating in effort to memorise the voice, which he failed utterly to place. Undoubtedly this animal was a shipboard acquaintance, one who knew him well; but those detestable German gutturals disguised his accents quite beyond identification.

"For all that, you are not wise so to try my patience. I permit you five minutes by my watch in which to make up your mind to surrender that document."

"How often must I tell you," Lanyard enquired, "all this talk of documents is Greek to me?"

"Then you have five minutes to brush up your classical education, and translate into terms suited to your intelligence. I will have that document from you or--in four more minutes--shoot you dead."

To this Lanyard said nothing. But his patient attentions to the handkerchief round his wrists were beginning perceptibly to be rewarded.

"Moreover, Herr Lanyard, you will do yourself a very good turn by confessing--entirely aside from saving your life."

"How is that?"

"Providing you persuade me of your good faith, I am empowered to offer you employment in our service."

Lanyard's breath passed hardly through a throat swollen with rage, chagrin, and hatred, all hopelessly impotent. But he succeeded in preserving an unruffled countenance, as his captor's next words demonstrated.

"You are surprised, yes? You are thinking it over? Take your time--you have three minutes more. Or perhaps you are sulky, resenting that our cleverness has found you out? Be reasonable, my good man. Think: you cannot be insensible to the honour my offer does you."

"What do you want of me?"

"First, that paper--thereafter to use your surpassing talents to the glory of God and Fatherland. In addition, you will be greatly rewarded."

"Now you do begin to interest me," Lanyard said coolly.... Surely he could contrive some way to slay this beast with his naked hands! He must play for time.... "How rewarded?"

"As I say, with a place in the Prussian Secret Service, its protection, freedom to ply your trade unhindered in America, even countenanced, till that country becomes a German province under German laws."

"But do I hear you offer this to a Frenchman?"

"Undeceive yourself. Men of all nations to-day, recognising that the star of Germany is in the ascendant, that soon all nations will be German, are hastening to make their peace beforehand by rendering Germany good service."

"Something in that, perhaps," Lanyard admitted thoughtfully.

"Think well, my friend.... Yes, Karl?"

The voice of the other spy responded sullenly: "Nothing--absolutely nothing."

"Two minutes, Herr Lanyard."

Of a sudden Lanyard's face was violently distorted in a grimace of terror. He lurched his shoulders forward, openly struggling with his bonds.

"But--good God!" he protested in a voice of terror, "you can't possibly be so unreasonable! I tell you, I haven't got your damned paper!"

A loop of the handkerchief slipped over one hand.

"Be still! Cease your struggles. And not so loud, my friend!" The peremptory voice dropped into mockery as Lanyard, pale and exhausted, sat back trembling--and a second loop of silk dropped over the other hand. "So you begin to appreciate that we mean business, yes? One minute and thirty seconds!"

"Have mercy!" the adventurer whined desperately--and licked his lips as if he found them dry with fear. Now both hands were all but wholly free. True: he remained blindfolded and covered by a deadly weapon. "Give me a chance. I'll do anything you wish! But I can't give you what I haven't got."

"Be silent! Here, Karl."

There was a sound of unintelligible murmuring as the two spies conferred together. Lanyard writhed in apparent extremity of terror. His hands were free. He sought hopelessly for inspiration. What to do without arms?

"Be grateful to Karl. He urges that perhaps you know nothing of the document."

"Don't you think I'd tell if I did know?"

"Then you have one minute--no, forty seconds--in which to pledge yourself to the Prussian Secret Service."

"You want me to swear--?"

"Certainly."

"Then hear me," said Lanyard earnestly: "*You damned canaille*!" And in one movement he tore the bandage from his eyes and launched himself head foremost at the man who stood over him.

He caught part of an oath drowned out by the splitting report of a pistol that went off within an inch of his ear. Then his head took the man full in the belly, and both went sprawling to the deck, Lanyard fighting like a maniac.

Sheer luck had guided clawing fingers to the right wrist of his antagonist, round which they shut like jaws of a trap. At the same time he wrenched the other's arm high above his head.

Momentarily expecting the shock of a bullet from the pistol of the second spy, he found time to wonder that it was so long deferred, and even in the fury of his struggles, out of the corner of one eye caught a fugitive glimpse of a tallish man, masked, standing back to the forward partition in a pose of singular indecision, pistol poised in his grasp.

Then the efforts of his immediate adversary threw him into a position in which he was unable to see the other.

Of a sudden the stateroom was filled with the thunder of an automatic, its seven cartridges discharged in one brisk, rippling crash.

It was as if a white-hot iron had been laid across Lanyard's shoulder. Beneath him the man started convulsively, with such force as almost to throw him off bodily, then relaxed altogether and lay limp and still, pinning one of Lanyard's arms under him.

Its visor displaced, the face of Baron von Harden was revealed, features distorted, eyes glaring, a frozen mask of hate and terror.

His arm free, the adventurer rolled away from the corpse in time to see the open window-port blocked by the body of the other spy.

Gathering himself together, he snatched up the pistol that dropped from the inert grasp of the dead man, and levelled it at the port.

But now that space was empty.

He rose and paused for an instant, his glance instinctively seeking the ledge above the hand-basin.

The hypodermic outfit was there, but minus the phial.

In the alleyway rose a confusion of running feet and shouting tongues. A heavy banging rang on the door to Stateroom 29. Crane's nasal accents called upon Lanyard to open.

VIII
OFF NANTUCKET

Upon the authors of that commotion Lanyard wasted no consideration whatever. Let them knock and clamour; he had more urgent work in hand, and knew too well the penalty were he stupid enough to unbolt to them. Their bodies would dam the doorway hopelessly; insistent hands would hinder him; innumerable importunate enquiries would be dinned at him, all immaterial in contrast with this emergency, a catechism one would need an hour to satisfy. And all attempts would be futile to make them understand that, while they plagued him with futile questions, a murderer and spy and thief was making good his escape, being afforded ample opportunity to slough all traces of his recent work and resume unchallenged his place among them.

No; if by any freak of good fortune, any exertion of wit or daring, that one were to be apprehended, it must be within the next few minutes, it could only be through immediate pursuit.

Nor did the adventurer waste time debating the better course. With him, whose ways of life were ceaselessly beset by instant and mortal perils, each with its especial and imperative demand upon his readiness and ingenuity, action must ever press so hard upon the heels of thought as to make the two seem one.

For that matter, the whole transaction had been characterised by almost unbelievable rapidity. And that square opening of the window-port was hardly vacant when Lanyard sprang to his feet; the fugitive had barely time to find his own upon the outer deck before Lanyard leaped after him; the first thumps upon the panels of his door were still echoing when he thrust head and shoulders out of the port and began to pump the automatic at a shadow fleeing aft upon that narrow breadth of planking between rail and wall.

Then, at the third shot, the automatic jammed upon a discharged shell.

Exasperated, the adventurer cast the weapon from him, shrugged hastily out of his unfastened coat and waistcoat, hitched tight his belt, and clambered through the port.

Dropping to the deck, he turned in time to see the fugitive dart round the shoulder of the superstructure.

As Lanyard gained the after rail of the promenade deck a man standing on the boat-deck at the head of the companion-ladder greeted him with pistol fire. He dodged back, untouched, and instantaneously devised a stratagem to cope with this untoward development.

Overhead, at the side, a lifeboat hung on its davits, ready for emergency launching, the gap in the rail which it filled when normally swung inboard spanned only by a length of line. And the darkness in the shadow of the boat was dense, an excellent screen.

Climbing upon the rail, Lanyard grasped the edge of the deck overhead and drew himself up undetected by his quarry, whom he espied still holding the head of the companion ladder, hidden from the bridge by the after deck-house, standing ready to shoot Lanyard should he attempt to renew the pursuit by that approach.

At the same time, "Karl" seemed mysteriously occupied with some object or objects in whose manipulation he was hampered to a degree by the necessity under which he laboured of holding his pistol ready and dividing his attention.

A man of good stature, broad at the shoulders, slender at the hips, he poised himself with athletic grace--the lower part of his face masked by what Lanyard took to be a dark silk handkerchief.

Lanyard heard him swearing in German.

Then a brisk little spray of sparks jetted from the flint and steel of a patent cigar-lighter in the hands of the spy. And as Lanyard rose from his knees after ducking beneath the line, a stream of fatter sparks spat from the end of a fuse.

The man leaned over the rail and cast a small black object to which the sputtering fuse was attached, down to the main deck.

As it struck midway between superstructure and stern it burst into brilliant flame, releasing upon the night an electric-blue glare that must have been visible from any point within the compass of the horizon.

A yell of profane remonstrance saluted the light, and throughout the brief passage that followed Lanyard was conscious that pistols and rifles on the after deck below were making him and his antagonist their targets.

Before the German could face about, Lanyard, moving almost noiselessly in his bare feet, had covered more than half the intervening space. In another breath he might have had the fellow at a disadvantage. But the distance was too great. Twice the automatic blazed in his face as he closed in, the bullets clearing narrowly--or else he fancied that their deadly cold breath fanned his cheek.

Then the spy's weapon in turn went out of action. Half blinded, Lanyard clipped the man round the body and hugged him tight, exerting all his skill and strength to effect a throw.

That effort failed; his onslaught was met with address and ability that all but matched his own. The animal he embraced had muscles like tempered springs and the cunning and fury of a wild beast in a trap. For a moment Lanyard was able to accomplish no more than to smother resistance in a rib-crushing embrace; no sooner did he relax it than all attempts to shift his hold were anticipated and met half way, forcing him back upon the defensive.

Yet he was given little chance to prove himself the master. The first phase of the struggle was still in contest when the rear door of the smoking room opened and a man stepped out, paused, summed up the situation in a glance, seized Lanyard from behind.

The adventurer felt his arms grasped by hands whose strength seemed little short of superhuman, and wrenched back so violently that his very bones cracked. Fairly lifted from his feet, he was held as helpless as an infant kicking in the arms of its nurse.

Released, the other spy stepped back and swung his left fist viciously to Lanyard's jaw. Something in the brain of the adventurer seemed to let go; his head dropped weakly to one side. The man who had struck him said quietly, "Loose the fool, Ed," and followed as Lanyard reeled away, striking him repeatedly.

For a giddy moment Lanyard was darkly conscious--as one dreams an evil dream--of blows raining mercilessly about his head and body, blows that drove him back athwartships toward a fate dark and terrible, a great void of blackness. He felt unutterably weary, and was weakened by a sensation of nausea. Beneath him his knees buckled. There fell one final blow, ruthless as the wrath of God.

He was falling backward into nothingness, into an everlasting gulf of night that yawned for him....

As he shot under the guard rope and into space between the edge of the deck and the keel of the lifeboat, the spy rounded smartly on a heel and darted to the smoking-room door. His confederate was in the act of stepping across the raised threshold. He followed, closed the door.

The first officer, charging aft from the bridge, rounded the deck-house and pulled up with a grunt of surprise to find the deck completely deserted....

The shock of icy immersion reanimated Lanyard.

He felt himself plunging headlong down, down, and down to inky depths unguessable. The sheer habit of an accustomed swimmer alone bade him hold his breath.

Then came a pause: he was no more descending; for a time of indeterminate duration, an age of anguish, he seemed to float without motion, suspended in frigid purgatory. Against his ribs something hammered like a racing engine. In his ears sounded a vast roaring, the deafening voices of a thousand waterfalls. His head felt swollen and enormous, on the point of bursting wide.

Without warning expelled from those depths, he shot full half-length out of water, and fell back into the milky welter of the *Assyrian's* wake.

Instinctively he kept afloat with feeble strokes.

The cold was bitter, as sharp as the teeth of death; but his head was now clear, he was able to appreciate what had befallen him.

Already the *Assyrian*, forging onward unchecked, had left him well astern, her progress distinctly disclosed by that infernal bluish glare spouting from her after deck.

She seemed absurdly small. Incredulity infected Lanyard's mind. Nothing so tiny, so insignificant, so make-believe as that silhouette of a ship could conceivably be that great liner, the *Assyrian*....

Temporarily a burning pain in his left shoulder drove all other considerations out of mind. The salt water was beginning to smart in the raw, superficial wound made by that assassin's bullet ... back there in the stateroom ... long ago....

Then the cold began to bite into his marrow, and he struggled manfully to swim, taking long, slow strokes, at first comparatively powerful, by insensible degrees losing force.

Just why he took this trouble he did not know: for some dim reason it seemed desirable to live as long as possible. Withal he was aware he could not live. Whether careless or utterly ignorant of his fate, the **Assyrian** was trudging on and on, leaving him ever farther astern, lost beyond rescue in that weird, bleak waste. Even were an alarm to be given, were she to stop now and put out a boat, it would find him, if it found him at all, too late.

The cold was killing.

He felt very sleepy. Drowsily he apprehended the beginning of the end. His senses, growing numb with cold, presently must cease to function altogether. Then he would forget, and nothing would matter any more.

Yet the will to live persisted amazingly. Had Lanyard wished it he could not have ceased to swim, at least to keep afloat. Vaguely he wondered how people ever managed to commit suicide by drowning; it seemed to pass human power to resist that buoyancy which sustained one, to let go, let one's self go down. Impossible to conceive how that was ever done....

Why should he care to go on living?

No reading that riddle!...

On obscure impulse he gave up swimming, turned upon his back, floated face to the sky, derelict, resigning himself to the cradling arms of the sea. The gradual, slow rocking of the swells soothed his passion like a kindly opiate. The cold no more irked him, but seemed somehow strangely anodynous. Imperturbably he envisaged death, without fear, without welcome. What must be, must....

For all that, life clutched at him with jealous hands. More than ever sleepy, before he slept that last, long sleep he must somehow solve this enigma, learn the reason why life continued so to allure his failing senses.

Athwart the drab texture of consciousness wild fancies played like heat lightning in a still midsummer night.

Death's countenance was kind.

That wide field of stars, drooping low and lifting away with rhythmic motion, would sometime dip swiftly down to the very sea itself and, swinging back, take with it his soul to some remote bourne....

The deeps were yielding up their mysteries. Past him a huge pale monster swept at furious pace, hissing grimly as it passed, like some spectral Nemesis pursuing the *Assyrian*.

Indifferently he speculated concerning the reality of this phenomenon.

The heave of a swell enabled him to glance incuriously after the steamship. She seemed smaller, less genuine than ever, a shadow shape that boasted visibility solely through that unearthly light on her after deck. Even that now had waned to a mere glimmer, the flicker of a candle lost in the immensities of that night-bound world of empty sky and empty ocean. Even as he that had been named Michael Lanyard was a lost light, a tiny flame that guttered toward its swift extinction....

Why live, when one might die and, dying, find endless rest?

Like a blazing thunderbolt one word rent the slumbrous web of sentience: *Ekstrom*!

Galvanised by the flood of hatred unpent by the syllables of that name, Lanyard began again to swim, flailing the water with frantic arms as if to win somewhither by the very violence of his efforts.

This the one cogent reason why he must not, could not, die....

Unjust to require him to give up life while that one lived. Unfair.... It must not be!...

Across the sea rolled a dull, brutish detonation. The swimmer, swung high on the bosom of a great swell, saw a vast sheet of fire raving heavenward from the *Assyrian*.

It vanished instantly.

When his dazzled vision cleared, he could see no more of the ship. He imagined a faint, wild rumour of panic voices, conjured up scenes of horror indescribable as that great fabric sank almost instantaneously, as if some gigantic hand plucked her under.

What had happened? Had the accomplices of the dead Baron von Harden set off an infernal machine aboard the vessel? In the name of reason, why? They had got what they sought, that accursed document, whatever it was, that page torn from the Book of Doom. Then why...?

And to what end had they exploded that light bomb on the after deck?

To make the *Assyrian* a glaring target in the night--what else? A target for what?...

Of a sudden all rational mental processes were erased from Lanyard's consciousness. A wave of pure fear flooded him, body, mind, and soul. He began to struggle like a maniac, fighting the waters that hindered his flight from some hideous thing that was lifting up from the ocean's ooze to drag him down.

He heard a voice screaming thinly, and knew it was his own.

The impossible was happening to him, out there, alone and helpless on the face of the waters. A shape of horror was rising out of the deep to engorge him. He could feel distinctly the slow, irresistible heave of its bulk beneath him. His feet touched and slipped upon its horrible sleek flanks.

His most desperate efforts were all unavailing. He could not escape. The thing came up too rapidly. Following that first mad thrill of contact with it underfoot, he was lifted swiftly and irresistibly into the air. Almost instantly he was floundering in knee-deep waters that parted, cascading away on either hand. Then, elevated well above the sea, he slid and fell prone upon a slimy wet surface.

His clawing hands clutched something solid and substantial, an upright bar of metal.

Incredulously Lanyard pawed the body of the monster beneath him. His hands passed over a riveted joint of metal plates. Looking up, he made out the truncated cone of a conning tower with its antennae-like periscope tubes stencilled black upon the soft purple of the star-strewn sky.

Slowly the truth came home: a submarine had risen beneath him. He lay upon its after deck, grasping a stanchion that supported the small raised bridge round the conning tower.

He sobbed a little in sheer hysteric gratitude, that this miracle had been vouchsafed unto him, that he had thus been spared to live on against his hour with Ekstrom.

But when he sought to drag himself up to the bridge, he could not, he was too weak and faint. Ceasing to struggle, he rested in half stupour, panting.

With a harsh clang a hatch was thrown back. Rousing, Lanyard saw several figures emerge from the conning tower. Men uncouthly clothed in shapeless, shiny leather garments, straddled and stretched above him, filling their lungs with the sweet air. He tried to call to them, but evoked a mere rattle from his throat.

Two came to the edge of the bridge and stood immediately over him, fixing binoculars to their eyes, their voices quite audible.

A pang of despair shot through Lanyard when he heard them conferring together in the German tongue.

Death, then, was but a little delayed.

Thereafter he lay in dumb apathy, save that he shivered and his teeth chattered uncontrollably.

Through the torpor that rested like a black cloud upon his senses he caught broken phrases, snatches of sentences:

"... *sinking fast ... struck square amidships ... broke her back....*"

"... *trouble with her boats. There goes one over*!..."

"... *fools jumping overboard like cattle....*"

"*What's that rocket? Do the swine want us to shell their boats*?"

"*Why not? They're asking for it*!"

One of the officers lowered his glasses and barked a series of sharp commands. The crew on deck leaped to attention. One leaned over the conning-tower hatch and shouted to his mates below. A hatch forward of the tower opened, and a quick-firing gun on a disappearing carriage swung smoothly and silently up from its lair.

The other officer, looking down, started violently.

"*Verdammt*! What's this?"

The first rejoined him. "Impossible!"

"Impossible or not--a man or a cadaver!"

"Have him up and see...."

By order, two of the crew dragged Lanyard up to the bridge, supporting him by main strength while the officers examined him.

"At the last gasp, but alive," one announced.

"How the devil did he get out here?"

"From the *Assyrian*--"

"Impossible for any man to swim this far since our torpedo struck--"

"Then he must have gone overboard before it struck--or was thrown--"

A cry of alarm from the group about the gun, awaiting final orders to open fire upon the *Assyrian's* boats, interrupted the conference. The officers swung away in haste.

"Hell's fury! what's that searchlight?"

"A Yankee destroyer--in all probability the one we dodged yesterday afternoon."

"She'll find us yet if we don't submerge. Forward, there--house that gun! And get below--quickly!"

During a moment of apparent confusion, one of the men sustaining Lanyard caught the attention of an officer.

"What shall we do with this fellow, sir?" he enquired.

"Leave him here to sink or swim as we go down," snapped the officer--"and be damned to him!"

With a supreme effort the adventurer sank his fingers deep into the arms of the two men.

"Wait!" he gasped faintly in German. "On the Emperor's service--"

"What's that?" The officer turned back sharply.

"Imperial Secret Service," Lanyard faltered--"Personal Division--Wilhelm-strasse Number 27--"

A brilliant glare settled suddenly upon the deck of the submarine, and was welcomed by a panicky gust of oaths. One officer had already popped through the conning-tower hatch, followed by several of the crew. There remained only those supporting Lanyard, and the second officer.

"Take him below!" the latter ordered. "He may be telling the truth. If not...."

In the distance a gun boomed. A shell shrieked over the submarine and dropped into the sea not a hundred yards to starboard. The men rushed Lanyard toward the conning tower. He tried feebly to help them. In that effort consciousness was altogether blotted out....

IX
SUB SEA

When he opened his eyes again he was resting, after a fashion, naked between harsh, damp blankets in a narrow, low-ceiled bunk inches too short for one of his stature.

After an experimental squirm or two he lay very still; his back and all his limbs were stiff and sore, his bullet-seared shoulder burned intolerably beneath a rudely applied first-aid dressing, and he was breathing heavily long, labouring inhalations of an atmosphere sickeningly dank, close, and foul with unspeakable stenches, for which the fumes of sulphuric acid with a rank reek of petroleum and lubricating oils formed but a modest and retiring background.

Also his head felt very thick and dull. He found it extremely difficult to think, and for some time, indeed, was quite unable to think to any purpose.

His very eyes ached in their sockets.

In the ceiling glowed an electric bulb, dimly illuminating a cubicle barely big enough to accommodate the bunk, a dresser, and a small desk with a folding seat. The inner wall was a slightly concave surface of steel plates whose seams oozed moisture. In the opposite wall was a sliding door, open, beyond which ran a narrow alleyway floored with metal grating. Everything in sight was enamelled with white paint and clammy with the sweat of that foetid air.

Over all an unnatural hush brooded, now and again accentuated by a rumble of distant voices and gusts of vacant laughter, once or twice by a curious popping. For a long time he heard nothing else whatever. The effect was singularly disquieting and did its bit to quicken torpid senses to grasp his plight.

Sluggishly enough Lanyard pieced together fragments of lurid memories, reconstructing the sequence of last night's events scene by scene to the moment of his rescue by the U-boat.

So, it appeared, he was aboard a German submersible, virtually a prisoner, though posing as an agent of the Personal Intelligence Department of the German Secret Service.

To that inspiration of failing consciousness he owed his life, or such of its span as now remained to him, a term whose duration could only be defined by his ability to carry off the imposture pending problematic opportunity to escape. And, assuming that this last were ever offered him, there was no present possibility of guessing how long it might not be deferred.

Its butcher's mission successfully accomplished, the U-boat was not improbably even now en route for Heligoland, beginning a transatlantic cruise of weeks that might never end save in a nameless grave at the bottom of the Four Seas.

Only the matter of impersonation failed to embarrass in prospect. A natural linguist, Lanyard's three years within the German lines had put a rare finish upon his mastery of German. More than this, he was well versed in the workings of the Prussian spy system. As Dr. Paul Rodiek, Wilhelmstrasse Agent Number 27, he was safe as long as he found no acquaintance of that gentleman in the complement of the submarine; for, largely upon information furnished by Lanyard himself, Dr. Rodiek had been secretly apprehended and executed in the Tower the day before Lanyard left London to join the *Assyrian*.

But the question of the U-boat's present whereabouts and its movements in the immediate future disturbed the adventurer profoundly. He was elaborately incurious about Heligoland; and several weeks' association with the Boche in the close quarters of a submarine was a prospect that revolted. Wellnigh any fate were preferable....

Uncertain footsteps sounded in the alleyway, paused at the entrance to his cubicle. He turned his head wearily on the pillow. In the doorway stood a man whose slenderly elegant carriage of a Prussian officer was not disguised even by his shapeless wreck of a naval lieutenant's uniform, a man with a countenance of singularly unpleasant cast, leaving out of all consideration the grease and grime that discoloured it. His narrow forehead slanted back just a trace too sharply, his nose was thin and overlong, his mouth thin and cruel beneath its ambitious mustache a la Kaiser; his small black eyes, set much too close together, blazed with unholy exhilaration.

As soon as he spoke Lanyard understood that he was drunk, drunk with more than the champagne of which he presently boasted.

"Awake, eh?" he greeted Lanyard with a mirthless snarl. "You've slept like the dead man I took you for at first, my friend--a solid fourteen hours, my word for it! Feeling better now?"

Lanyard's essays to reply began and ended in a croak for water. The Prussian nodded, disappeared, returned with an aluminium cup of stale cold water mixed with a little brandy.

"Champagne if you like," he offered, as Lanyard, painfully propping himself up on an elbow, gulped like an animal from the vessel held to his lips. "We are holding a little celebration, you know."

Lanyard dropped back to the pillow, the question in his eyes.

"Celebrating our success," the Prussian responded. "We got her, and that means much honour and a long furlough to boot, when we get home, just as failure would have spelled--I don't like to think what. I shouldn't care to fill the shoes of those poor devils who let the *Assyrian* escape them off Ireland, I can tell you."

Something very much like true fear flickered in his small eyes as he pondered the punishment meted out to those who failed.

So the U-boat was homeward bound! Strange one noticed no motion of her progress, heard no noise of machinery.

"Where are we?" Lanyard whispered.

"Peacefully asleep on the bottom, about five miles south of Martha's Vineyard, waiting till it is dark enough to slip in to our base."

"Base?"

The Prussian hiccoughed and giggled. "On the south shore of the Vineyard," he confided with alcoholic glee: "snuggest little haven heart could wish, well to the north of all deep-sea traffic; and the coastwise trade runs still farther north, through Vineyard Sound, other side the island. Not a soul ever comes that way, not a soul suspects. How should they? The admirable charts of the Yankee Coast and Geodetic Survey"--he sneered--"show no break in the south beach of the island, between the ocean and the ponds. But there is one. The sea made the breach during a gale, our people helped with a little Trotyl, tides and storms did the rest. Now we can enter a secluded, landlocked harbour with just enough water at low tide, and lie hidden there till the word comes to move again--three miles of dense scrub forest, all privately owned as a game preserve, fenced and patrolled, between us and the nearest cultivated land--and friends in plenty on the island to keep all our needs supplied--petroleum, fresh vegetables, champagne, all that. Just the same we take no chances--never make our landfall by day, never enter or leave harbour except at night."

He paused, contemplating Lanyard owlishly. "Ought not to tell you all this, I presume," he continued, more soberly, though the wild light still flickered ominously in his eyes. "But it is safe enough; you will see for yourself in a few hours; and then ... either you are all right, or you will never live to tell of it. We radio'd for information about Wilhelmstrasse Number 27 just before dawn, after we had dodged that damned Yankee destroyer. Ought to get an answer to-night, when we come up."

Heavier footsteps rang in the alleyway. The Prussian made a grimace of dislike.

"Here comes the commander," he cautioned uneasily.

A great blond Viking of a German in the uniform of a captain shouldered heavily through the doorway and, acknowledging the salute of the rat-faced subaltern with a bare nod, stood looking down at Lanyard in taciturn silence, hostility in his blood-shot blue eyes.

"How long since he wakened?" he asked thickly, with the accent of a Bavarian.

"A minute or two ago."

"Why did you not inform me?"

The tone was offensively domineering, thanks like enough to drink, nerves, and hatred of his job and all things and persons pertaining to it.

The subaltern coloured. "He asked for water--I got it for him."

The commander stared churlishly, then addressed Lanyard: "How are you now?"

"Very faint," Lanyard said truthfully. But he would have lied had it been otherwise with him. It was his book to make time in which to collect his thoughts, concoct a bullet-proof story, plan against an adverse answer to that wireless enquiry.

"Can you eat, drink a little champagne?"

Lanyard nodded slightly, adding a feeble "Please."

The Bavarian glanced significantly at his subaltern, who hastened to leave them.

"Who are you? What is your name?"

"Dr. Paul Rodiek."

"Your employment?"

"Personal Intelligence Bureau--confidential agent."

"What were you doing on board the *Assyrian*?"

Lanyard mustered enough strength to look the man squarely in the eye.

"Pardon," he said coldly. "You must know your question is indiscreet."

"I must know more about you."

"It should be enough," Lanyard ventured boldly, "to know that I set off that flare as arranged, at risk of my life."

"How came you overboard?"

"In the scuffle caused by my lighting the flare."

"So you tell me. But we found you half clothed, lacking any sort of identification. Am I to accept your unsupported word?"

"My papers are naturally at the bottom of the sea, in the garments I discarded lest their weight drag me down. If you have doubts," Lanyard continued firmly, "it is your privilege to settle them by communicating via radio with Seventy-ninth Street."

He shut his eyes wearily and turned his head aside on the pillow, confident that this reference to the headquarters and secret wireless station of the Prussian spy system in New York would win him peace for a time at least.

After a moment the commander uttered a non-committal grunt. "We shall see," he prophesied darkly, and went away.

Later, one of the crew brought Lanyard a dish of greasy stew and potatoes, lukewarm, with bread and a half-bottle of excellent champagne.

He ate all he could stomach of the first, devoured the second ravenously, and drained the bottle of its ultimate life-giving drop.

Then, immeasurably refreshed and fortified in body and spirit, he turned face to the wall, composed himself as if to sleep, shut his eyes, adjusted the tempo of his respiration, and lay quite still, wide awake and thinking hard.

After a while somebody tramped into the cubicle, bent over Lanyard inquisitively and, satisfied that he slept, retired, taking away the empty bottle and dishes.

Otherwise his meditations were disturbed only by those echoes of revelry in honour of the late manifestation of the Hun's divine right to do wanton murder on the high seas.

The rumour waxed and waned, died into dull mutterings, broke out afresh in spurts of merriment that held an hysterical note. Once a quarrel sprang up and was silenced by the commander's deep, unpleasant tones. Corks popped spasmodically. Again there were sounds much like a man's sobbing; but these were promptly blared down by a phonograph with a typically American accent. When that palled, a sentimental disciple of frightfulness sang Tannenbaum in a melting tenor.

Everything tended to effect an impression that all, commander and meanest mechanic alike, were making forlorn efforts to forget.

Devoutly Lanyard prayed they might be successful, at least until the submarine made her secret base. If too much alcohol was bad, too much brooding was infinitely worse for the German temperament. He remembered one U-boat commander who, returning to the home port after a conspicuously successful cruise, had been taken ashore in a strait-jacket.

Lanyard himself did not care to dwell upon those scenes which must have been enacted on board the ***Assyrian*** after the torpedo struck....

Deliberately ignoring all else, he set himself the task of reviewing those events which had led up to his going overboard.

One by one he considered the incidents of that night, painstakingly dissected them, examined their every phase in minute analysis, weighing for ulterior meaning every word uttered in his presence, harking even farther back to reconstruct his acquaintance with each actor from the very moment of its inception, seeking that hint which he was convinced must be somewhere hidden in the history of the affair, waiting only recognition to lead straightway out of this gloomy maze of mystery into a sunlit open of understanding.

In vain: there was an ambiguity in that business to baffle the keenest and most pertinacious investigation.

The conduct of Cecelia Brooke alone bristled with inconsistencies inexplicable, the conduct of the German spies no less.

To get better perspective upon the problem, he reduced the premises to their barest summary:

A valuable dossier brought on board the *Assyrian* (no matter by whom) had come into the possession of British agents, with the knowledge of Captain Osborne. Thackeray had secreted it in that fraudulent bandage. German agents, apparently under the leadership of Baron von Harden, had waylaid him, knocked him senseless, unwrapped the bandage, but somehow (probably in the first instance through the interference of the Brooke girl) had overlooked the document. Subsequently the Brooke girl had found and entrusted it to Lanyard. (No matter why!) He on his part had exerted his utmost inventiveness in hiding it away. Nevertheless it had been discovered and abstracted within an hour.

By whom?

Not improbably by the Brooke girl herself. Repenting her impulsiveness, after leaving Lanyard with the captain, from whom she had doubtless learned the truth about "Monsieur Duchemin," she might well have gone directly to Lanyard's stateroom and hit upon the morphia phial as the likeliest hiding place without delay, thanks to prior acquaintance with the proportions of the paper cylinder.

But why should she have assumed that Lanyard had not disposed of the trust about his person?

Not impossibly the thing had been found by the first officer of the *Assyrian*, searching by order of the captain--as Lanyard assumed he had.

But, if Mr. Warde had found it, he had not reported his find when telephoning to Captain Osborne; or else the latter had gone to great lengths to mystify Lanyard.

There remained the chance that the paper had been stolen by one of the two German agents--by either without the knowledge of the other.

If Baron von Harden had found it--necessarily before Lanyard returned to the room--he had subsequently been at elaborate pains to conceal his success from both his victim and his confederate. Why? Did he distrust the latter? Again, why?

If "Karl" had been the thief, it must have been after Lanyard's return, and while the Baron was preoccupied with the task of keeping the prisoner quiet, to let the search proceed.

In that event "Karl" had lied deliberately to his superior. Why? Because the document was salable, and "Karl" intended to realize its value for his personal benefit?

Not an unlikely explanation. Nor could this be called the first instance in which the Prussian spy system, admirably organized though it was, had been betrayed by one of its own agents.

This hypothesis, too, accounted for that most perplexing circumstance of all, the murder of Baron von Harden. For Lanyard was fully persuaded that had been nothing less than premeditated murder, in no way an accident of faulty aim. Even the most nervous and unstrung man could hardly have missed six shots out of seven, point blank. A nervous man, indeed, could hardly have gained his own consent to take so hideous a chance of injuring or killing a collaborator.

It appeared, then, that one of four things had happened to the cylinder of paper:

Miss Brooke had taken it back into her own care. In which case Lanyard was no more concerned.

Captain Osborne had secured it through Mr. Warde. This, however, Lanyard did not seriously credit.

It had gone to the bottom when the *Assyrian* sank with the body--among others--of Baron von Harden.

Or "Karl" had stolen it.

Privately, indeed, Lanyard rather inclined to hope that the last might prove to be the true solution. He desired earnestly to meet "Karl" once more, on equal terms. And the more counts in the score, the greater his satisfaction in exacting a reckoning in full.

But he anticipated. That chapter might only too possibly have been closed forever by the hand of Death. As yet he knew nothing concerning the mortality of the *Assyrian* debacle. He had not enquired of the officers of the U-boat because they knew little if anything more than he. Their glasses had discovered to them trouble with the lifeboats; they had spoken of one boat capsizing, of "people going overboard like cattle." There must have been many drownings, even with a United States destroyer near by and speeding to the rescue.

A single question troubled Lanyard greatly. Officers and crew of the U-boat had betrayed profoundest consternation upon the advent of that destroyer, presumably a warship of a neutral nation. And that same ship had without hesitation fired upon the submarine.

Was it possible, then, that the United States had already declared war on Germany?

It seemed extremely probable; in such event these Germans would have been notified instantly by wireless from the New York bureau of their country's Secret Service; whereas, Captain Osborne, receiving the same advice by wireless, might reasonably have kept it quiet lest the news stir to more formidable activity those agents of the Wilhelmstrasse whose presence among the passengers he must at least have strongly suspected.

Presently the closeness of the atmosphere began to work upon Lanyard's perceptions. In spite of his long rest, a new drowsiness drugged his senses. He yielded without struggle, knowing he would soon need every ounce of strength and vitality that sleep could give him....

The din of an inferno startled him awake. Those narrow metal walls were echoing a clangour of machinery maniacal in character and overpowering in volume. Clankings, tappings, hissings, coughings, clatterings, stridulation of a wireless spark, drone of dynamos, shrewdish scolding of Diesel motors developing two thousand horsepower, individual efforts of some two thousand valves, combined-- or, declined to combine--in a cacophony like nothing under the sun but the chant of a submersible under way on the surface.

Lanyard, gratefully aware of a current of fresh air sweeping through the hold, rolled out of his bunk to find that, while he slept, clothing had been provided for him, rough but adequate; heavy woollen underwear and socks, a sweater, a dungaree coat, trousers of the same stuff, all vilely damp, and a friendless pair of oil-sodden shoes: the sweepings of a dozen lockers, but as welcome as disreputable.

Dressed, he turned aft through the alleyway, entering immediately the central operating room and storm center of that typhoon of noise, a wilderness of polished machinery in active being.

Of the score or more leather-clad machinists silent at their posts, none paid him more heed than a passing, incurious glance as he crossed to a narrow steel companion ladder and ascended to the conning tower. This he found deserted; but its deck-hatch was open. He climbed out to the bridge.

The night was calm and heavily overcast, with no sea more than long, slow swells. Through its windless quiet the U-boat racketed with the raving abandon of the Spirit of Discord on a spree in a boiler factory. To the riot of its internal strife was added the remonstrance of waters sliced by the stem and flung back by the sides, a prolonged and stertorous hiss like the rending of an endless sheet of canvas.

To eyes new from the electric illumination of the hold, the blackness was positive, with the palpable quality of an element, relieved alone by the dull glow of the binnacle housing the gyroscope telltale, from which the faintest of golden reflections struck back to pick out a pair of seemingly severed fists gripping the handles of the bridge steering wheel with a singular effect of desperation.

For some moments Lanyard could see nothing more.

The mirthless chuckle of the lieutenant sounded at his elbow.

"So the good Herr Doctor thought he had better come up for air, eh? My friend, the very dead might envy you the sincerity of your slumbers. We have been half an hour on the surface, with all this uproar--and you are only just wakened!"

"Half an hour?" Lanyard repeated thoughtfully. "Then we should be close in...."

"Give us ten minutes more ... if we don't go aground in this accursed blackness!"

A broad-shouldered body passed between Lanyard and the binnacle, momentarily eclipsing its light. Down below in the operating room a bell shrilled, and of a sudden the Diesels were silenced.

The dead quiet that followed the sharp extinction of that hubbub was as startling as the detonation of high explosive had been.

Through this sudden stillness the submarine slipped stealthily, the hissing beneath her bows dying down to gentle sibilance.

From forward the calls of an invisible leadsman were audible. In response the commander uttered throaty orders to the helmsman at his elbow, and those unattached hands shifted the wheel minutely.

Lanyard started to speak, but a growl from the captain, and a touch of the lieutenant's hand on his sleeve cautioned him to silence.

There was a small pause. The vessel seemed to have lost way altogether, to swim like a spirit ship that Stygian tide. The lieutenant moved forward, leaving

Lanyard alone. The voice of the leadsman was stilled. By the wheel the captain stood absolutely motionless, his body vaguely silhouetted against the glow of the binnacle. The hands that gripped the wheel so savagely were as steady as if carven out of stone. An atmosphere of suspense enveloped the boat like a cloud.

Lanyard grew conscious of something huge and formidable, a denser shadow in the darkness beyond the bows, the loom of land. Off to starboard a point of light appeared abruptly, precisely as if a golden pin had punctured the black blanket of the night. The captain growled gutturals of relief and command. The hands on the wheel shifted, steering exceeding small. A second light shone out to port, then shifted slowly into range with the first, till the two were as one. Again the bell sang in the operating room, and the vessel forged ahead quietly to the urge of electric motors alone. A third light and a fourth appeared, well apart to port and starboard, the range lights precisely equidistant between them. Between these the U-boat moved swiftly. They swam back on either hand and were abruptly extinguished as if the night, resenting their insolent trespass, had gobbled both at a gulp.

The temperature became sensibly warmer and the salt air of the sea was strongly tinctured with the sweet smell of pines and forest mould.

Up forward carbons sputtered and spat; a searchlight was unsheathed and carved the gloom as if it was butter, ranging swiftly over the tree-clad shore of a burnished black lagoon, picking out en passant several unpainted wooden structures, then steadying on a long and substantial landing stage, on which several men stood waiting.

X
AT BASE

As the U-boat, with motors dead and way lessening, glided up alongside the head of that T-shaped landing stage and was made fast, the wireless operator popped up from below, saluted the commander, and delivered a written message.

Lanyard, instinctively aware that this was the expected report from Seventy-ninth Street on Dr. Paul Rodiek, quietly pulled himself together and took quick observations.

At best his chances in the all-too-probable emergency were far from brilliant. Yet one might better perish trying, however hopelessly, than passively submit to being shot down.

The lieutenant, waspishly superintending the work of crew and base guards at the mooring lines, stood preoccupied within an arm's length; while the landing stage was a fair six feet away. From its T-head to the shore, the distance was nothing less than two hundred yards.

Desperate action and miraculous luck might take the Prussian by surprise and enable one to snatch the service automatic from its holster at his belt, leap to the stage, and shoot a way landward through the guards clustered there; after which everything would depend on swiftness of foot and the uncertain light permitting one to gain a refuge in the surrounding woodland without a bullet in one's back.

It was a sorry hope....

With catlike attention Lanyard watched the hands holding that paper to the binnacle light--large hands, heavy and muscular but tremulous with drink and nervous reaction from the long strain and cumulative horror of the cruise then ending. Their aim would not be good, except by accident. None the less, if the report were unfavourable, their first gesture would be toward the holster, signalling to Lanyard that the moment had come to initiate heroic measures.

The Bavarian was an unconscionable time absorbing the import of the message. Bending his face close to the paper, the better to make out the writing, he read with moving lips, slowly, a doltish frown of concentration clouding his congested countenance.

At length, however, he stood up, swaying a little as he folded and pocketed the paper.

Lanyard relaxed. The man was too far gone in drink to be crafty, too sure of his absolute power of life and death to imagine a need for craft. Since his hand had not immediately sought the holster, it would not.

Turbid accents uttered the name of Dr. Rodiek.

Lanyard stepped forward alertly. "Yes, Herr Captain?"

"New York says it had no knowledge of your intention to leave England on the *Assyrian*, but that you may well have done so. The Wilhelmstrasse will know, of course. It has already been telegraphed. Pending its reply, I am to detain you."

"How long?" Lanyard demurred.

"As you know, transatlantic communications must now go by land telegraph to the Border, by hand into Mexico, thence by radio via Venezuela to Berlin. All that takes time. Also, we may not signal New York but at stated times of night. You will be detained another twenty-four hours at least, possibly longer."

"My errand cannot wait."

"It must."

"You will obstruct the business of the Imperial Government at your peril."

"I would incur still greater peril did I let you go," the commander replied nervously. "With these swine-dogs at war with the Fatherland, our lives are not worth *that* should this base be betrayed."

"Do I understand America has declared war?"

"Two days since. Did you not know?"

"The *Assyrian's* wireless room was under guard: the captain published no bulletins whatever."

The Bavarian gave a gesture of impatience.

"You will remain on board for the night," he announced heavily.

"Pardon!" Lanyard insisted with every evidence of anxious excitement. "What you tell me makes it more than ever imperative that I reach New York without an hour's avoidable delay. I warn you, think well before you hinder the discharge of my duty."

"It is not necessary that I think," the commander replied. "My thinking has all been done for me. Me, I obey my orders; it is not my part to question their wisdom. Moreover, Herr Doctor, to my mind your insistence is to say the least suspicious. Even had I discretion in the matter, I should hold you. Therefore, you will keep a civil tongue in your head, or go below in irons immediately!"

He swung on his heel, showing an insolent back while he conferred with his subaltern.

And Lanyard shrugged appreciation of the futility of more contention against such mulishness. Not that the Bavarian was not right enough! As to that, one had really hoped for no better issue; but every shift is worth trial till proved worthless; and he was no worse off now than if he had submitted without complaint. Still one had Chance to look to for aid and comfort in this stress; and Chance, the jade, is not always unkind to her audacious suitors.

Even now she flashed upon Lanyard a provoking intimation of her smile. He began to divine possibilities in this overt ill-feeling between the officers; advantage might be made of the racial hostility of Prussian and Bavarian.

The commander's attitude and tone were consistently overbearing, if his words were inaudible to Lanyard. The lieutenant quite evidently submitted only in form; his salute was punctiliously correct and curt; and as the commander lumbered off down the landing stage, he grumbled indistinctly in Lanyard's hearing:

"Dog of a Bavarian!"

"The good Herr Captain," Lanyard suggested pleasantly, "is not in the most agreeable of tempers, yes?"

The high and well-born lieutenant spat comprehensively into the darkness overside. After a moment of hesitation he moved nearer and spoke in confidential accents. And the fragrant air of the night was tainted with the vinous effluvium of his breath.

"Always he prattles of his precious duty!" the Prussian muttered. "Damn his duty! Look you, Herr Doctor: months we have been on this cruise, yes, more than three months out of Heligoland, penned together in this ramshackle stinkpot, or isolated here in this God-forgotten hole, seeing nothing of life, hearing nothing of the world but what little the radio tells us--sick of the very sight of one another's faces! And now, when we have accomplished a glorious feat and have every right to look for prompt recall and the rewards of heroes, orders come to remain indefinitely and operate against the North Atlantic fleet of the contemptible Yankee navy! The life of a dog! And that noble commander of mine pretends to welcome it, talks of one's duty to the Fatherland--as if he liked the work any better than I!--solely to spite me!"

"But why?"

"Because he hates me," the lieutenant snarled passionately--"hates me even as I hate him--he knows how well!"

He interrupted himself to define his conception of the commander's character in the freest vernacular of the Berlin underworld.

Lanyard laughed amiably. "They are like that," he agreed--"those Bavarians!"

Which inspired the Prussian to deliver a phosphorescent diatribe on the racial traits of the Bavarian people as comprehended by the North German junker.

"To be cooped up God knows how long in this putrescent death-trap with such cattle," he concluded mutinously--"it passes all endurance!"

"I wonder you stand it," Lanyard sympathised--"a man of spirit and good birth, as one readily perceives. Though the life of a secret agent is not altogether heavenly either, if you ask me," he added gratuitously. "Regard me now, charged with a mission of most vital moment--more than ever so since the Yankees have shown their teeth--delayed here indefinitely because your excellent Herr Captain chooses to doubt my word."

"Patience. Maybe your release comes quickly. Then he will regret--or would had he wit enough. There is no cure for a fool." The sententiousness of this aphorism was unhappily marred by a hiccough. "Anybody with eyes in his head could see you are what you are...."

The last of the operating-room crew piled up the hatchway, saluted, and hurried ashore to join in noisy jubilations. There remained on the U-boat only the lieutenant with Lanyard, and two base guards detailed as anchor watch.

"I must go," the lieutenant volunteered. "And believe me, one welcomes a change of clothing and a dry bed after a week in this reeking sieve. As for you, my friend, if it lay with me, you should receive the treatment due a gentleman." A wave of maudlin camaraderie affected him. He passed an affectionate arm through Lanyard's and was suffered, though the gorge of the adventurer revolted at the familiarity. "I am sorry to leave you. No, do not be astonished! No protestations, please! It is quite true. I know a man of the right sort when I meet one, the sort even I can associate with without loss of self-respect. It is a great pity you may not come with me and make a night of it."

"Another time, perhaps," Lanyard said. "The night may yet come when you and I shall meet at the Metropole or the Admiral's Palace.... Who knows?"

"Ah!" sighed the Prussian, enchanted. "What a night that will be, my friend!... But now, it is too bad, I really must ask you to step below. Such are my silly orders. I am made responsible for you. What do you think of that for a joke, eh?"

He laughed vacantly but loudly, and, attempting to poke a derisive thumb into Lanyard's ribs, lost his balance.

"What a responsibility!" said Lanyard gravely, holding him up.

"Nonsense, that's what it is. You have no possible chance to escape."

"Suppose I make one--tip you overboard, take to my heels--?"

"You would be shot like a rabbit before you got half way to the shore."

"Ah, but grant, for the sake of argument, that these brave fellows, the guards, aim poorly in this gloom?"

"Where would you go? Into the forest, naturally. But how far? You may believe me when I tell you, not a hundred yards. It's a true wilderness, scrub-oak and cedar and second growth choked with underbrush, almost trackless. In five minutes you would be helplessly lost, in this blackness, with no stars to steer by. We need only wait till daylight to find you walking in a circle."

"You can't mean," Lanyard pursued, learning something helpful every moment, "there is no communicating road?"

"The main woods road, yes: but that is far too well patrolled. Without the countersign, you would be caught or shot a dozen times before you reached the end of it."

"Ah, well!"--with the sigh of a philosopher--"then I presume there's no way out but by swimming."

"Over to the beach you mean? Well, what then? You have got a twenty-mile walk either way through deep sand sure to betray your footprints. At dawn we follow and bag you at our leisure."

"You are discouraging!" Lanyard complained. "I see I may as well go below and be good. It's a dull life."

"Tell you what," giggled the lieutenant, leading his prisoner to the conning-tower hatch and lowering his voice: "do just that, go below and be nice, and presently I will come back and we'll split a bottle. What do you say to that, eh?"

"Colossal!"

"Not a bad notion, is it? I like it myself. One gets weary for the society of a gentleman, you've no idea.... As soon as my commander is drunk enough, I will slip away. How's that?"

"Grossartig!" Lanyard approved, turning to descend.

"Wait. You shall see for yourself what it means to have the friendship of a man of my stamp." The lieutenant raised his voice, addressing the anchor watch: "Attention. Heed with care: this gentleman is my friend. He is detained merely as a matter of form. I do not wish him to be annoyed. Do you understand? You are to leave him to himself as long as he remains quietly below. But he is not to come on deck again till I return. Is all that clear, imbeciles?"

The imbeciles, saluting mechanically, indicated glimmerings of comprehension.

"Then below you go, Dr. Rodiek. And don't get impatient: I will rejoin you as soon as possible."

"Don't be long," Lanyard implored.

As he lowered himself through the hatch he saw the Prussian stumble down the gangplank and reel shoreward.

Well satisfied with his diplomacy, Lanyard lingered a while in the conning tower, closely studying and memorising the more salient features of the Island of Martha's Vineyard and its adjacent waters and mainland as delineated on a most comprehensive large-scale chart published by the German Admiralty from exhaustive soundings and surveys of its own navigators and typographers, with corrections of as recent date as the first part of the year 1917.

Here the breach in the south coast line which permitted the utilisation of what had formerly been an extensive fresh-water pond as this secret submarine base, was clearly shown. And a single glance confirmed the lieutenant's statement concerning its remote isolation from settled sections of the island.

Somewhat dismayed, Lanyard descended to the central operating compartment and scouted through the hold from bow bulkhead to stern, making certain he enjoyed undisputed privacy. And it was so; every man-jack of the U-boat's personnel--jaded to the marrow with its cramped accommodations, unremitting toil and care, unsanitary smells and forbidding associations--having naturally seized the earliest opportunity to escape so loathsome a prison.

Lanyard, however, was anything but resentful of condemnation to this solitary confinement. His interest in the interior arrangements of submersibles seemed all but feverish, as intense as sudden; witness the minute attention to detail which marked his second tour of inspection. On this round he took his time. He had all night in which to work out his salvation; the wildest schemes were revolving in his mind, the least fantastic utterly impracticable without accurate knowledge of many matters; and such knowledge might be gained only through patient investigation and ungrudging expenditure of time.

It was now something past ten by the chronometers. He could hardly do much before dawn, lacking the instinct of a red Indian to guide him through that night-bound waste of woodland. So he felt little need to slight his researches through haste, except in anticipation of his lieutenant's return. And as to that, Lanyard was moderately incredulous: he expected to see nothing more of this new-found friend, unless the infatuation of the Prussian proved far stronger than his head.

Turning first to the private quarters of the commander, a somewhat more commodious cubicle than that across the alleyway in which Lanyard had been berthed, his interest was attracted by a small safe anchored to the deck beneath the desk.

To this Lanyard addressed himself without hesitation, solving the secret of its combination readily through exercise of the most rudimentary of professional principles. The problem it offered, indeed, was child's play to such cunning of touch and hearing as had made the reputation of the Lone Wolf.

Open, the safe discovered to him a variety of articles of interest: some five thousand dollars in English and American banknotes of large denomination, several hundred in American gold; three distinct cipher codes, one of these wholly novel in Lanyard's experience and so, he believed, in the knowledge of the Allied secret services; the log of the U-boat and the intimate diary of its commander, both in cryptograph; a compact directory of German agents domiciled in Atlantic coast ports; a very considerable accumulation of German Admiralty orders; together with many documents of lesser moment.

Rapidly sorting out the more valuable of these, Lanyard disposed them about his person, then confiscated the banknotes as indemnity for his stolen money-belt, replaced the rejections, and reclosed and locked the safe.

His next interest was to arm himself. After several disappointments he discovered arms-lockers beneath the berths for the crew in the forward compartment just aft of that devoted to torpedo tubes. Here he selected a latest pattern German navy automatic pistol with three extra cartridge clips and, after some hesitation, a peculiarly devilish magazine rifle firing explosive bullets. The latter he placed handily, yet out of sight, near the foot of the companion ladder. The pistol fitted snugly a trousers pocket, its bulk hidden by the sag of his sweater....

Some time later the lieutenant, slipping down the ladder, found Lanyard studying with a convincing aspect of childlike bewilderment the complicated combinations of machinery which crowded the central operating compartment.

Fresh from a bath and shave and wearing a clean uniform, the Prussian showed vast improvement in looks if not in equilibrium. But his mouth twitched fitfully, his eyes wandered and disclosed a disquieting superabundance of white, and his tongue was noticeably thicker than before.

"Well, my friend!" he said--"you are truly disappointing. The watch said you had made no sound since going below. I was afraid of another of those famous naps of yours."

"With the prospect of a bottle with you? Impossible! I have been waiting and waiting, with my tongue hanging out."

"Too bad. Why did you not look around, help yourself? Why not?" the lieutenant demanded. "Have I not given you freedom of ship? It is yours, everything here 'yours!"

"I want nothing but an end to this great thirst," Lanyard protested.

"Then--God in Heaven!--why we standing here? Come!"

Releasing the handrail the Prussian took careful aim for the alleyway door, launched himself toward it, slipped on the greasy metal grating, and would have fallen heavily but for Lanyard.

Cursing pettishly, he stood up, threw off Lanyard's arms without thanks, and made a new attempt, this time shooting headlong through the alleyway, to bring up against the wing table in the third forward compartment, the kitchen and mess-room in one.

"A great pity," he muttered, opening a locker and fumbling in its depths-- "rotten pity...."

"What?"

"Keep you waiting so long. Not my fault." The lieutenant brought forth two bottles of champagne and one of brandy. "You open them, Herr Doctor, like 'good fellow," he said, placing the three on the table. "I just wish you 'understand no discourtesy meant ... unavoidably detained ... beastly commander ... drunk. Give 'my word, hopelessly drunk. Poor fool...."

"If my judgment is sound," Lanyard said, "this noble vessel will soon need a new commander."

"True. Quite true." The Prussian placed two aluminium cups upon the table and half filled one with brandy, then brimmed it with champagne. "Try that," he said thickly, "That will keep your tail up, my friend."

"Many thanks," Lanyard protested, filling another cup with undiluted champagne. "I prefer one thing at a time."

"Unfortunate ... don't know what is good ... King's peg ... wonderful drink. No matter. To 'new commander--prosit!"

He drained his cup at a gulp.

"To the new commander!" Lanyard echoed, and drank judiciously. "Excellent.... How long can he last, do you think, at this pace?"

"No telling--not long--too long for my liking. Shall I tell 'something?" He filled his cup again, half and half, and sat down, his wicked, rat-like face more than ever pale and repulsive. "Not 'whisper of this, mind--though I think 'crew sometimes suspects: he's going mad!"

"Not that Bavarian?"

The lieutenant nodded wisely. "If 'knew him as I know him, 'never be surprised, my friend. You think too much drink. Yes, but not entirely. He keeps seeing things, hearing them, especially by night."

"What sort of things?"

"Faces." The Prussian licked his lips, glanced furtively over his shoulder, and drank. "Dead faces, eyes eaten out, seaweed in their hair.... And voices--he's forever hearing voices ... people trying to talk, 'can't make him understand because 'mouths 'full of water, you know. But they understand one another, keep discussing how to get at him.... He tells me about it ... I tell you, it is Hell to hear him talk ... especially when submerged, as last night. Then he hears them fumbling all over the hull with their stumpy fingers, trying to find 'way in, talking about him. And he tells me, and keeps insisting, till sometimes I seem to hear them, too. But I don't. Before God, I don't! You don't believe I do, do you?"

His eyes rolled wildly.

"Why should you?"

"Just so: why should I?" The lieutenant's accents rose to a shrill pitch. "I have not his record ... still in training when he sent *Lusitania* to the bottom. Yes: it was he, second-in-command, in charge of torpedo tubes. His own hand fired that tor- pedo...."

He fell silent, staring moodily into his cup, perhaps thinking of the number of torpedoes it had been his own lot to discharge upon errands of slaughter.

And the dead silence of the ship was made audible by a stealthy drip-drip of water from the seams, and the furtive slaver of the tide on the outer plates.

A shiver ran through the body of the Prussian. He pulled himself together with obvious effort, looked up with an uncertain grin, and passed a shaking hand across his writhing lips.

"All foolishness, of course, but 'gets on one's nerves ... constant association with man like that.... 'Know what he's doing now, or was, when I came away? Sitting up with doors and windows locked and blinds drawn, drinking brandy neat. He can't sleep by night if sober, or without 'light in the room. If he does, he knows they will get him ... people he hears crawling up from the sea, slopping round the house, mumbling, whimpering in the dark--"

He broke off abruptly, with a whisper more dreadful than a shriek--" *God*!"--and jumped to his feet, whipping the automatic from his belt.

A footfall sounded in one of the after compartments. Others followed.

Someone was coming slowly down the alleyway, someone with dragging, heavy feet.

The lieutenant waited motionless, as one petrified with terror.

The bulkhead doorway framed the figure of the commander. He paused there, louring at his subaltern with haunted eyes ablaze in a face like parchment.

"So!" he said, nodding. "As I thought. It is thus I find you, fraternising with one who may be, for all we know, an enemy to the Fatherland. You drunken, babbling fool! Get ashore!" His angry foot thumped the grating. "Get ashore, and report yourself under arrest!"

With no more warning than a strangled snarl, the lieutenant shot him through the head.

XI
UNDER THE ROSE

Vague stupefaction replaced the scowl upon the countenance of the commander. He swayed, a hand faltering to his forehead, where dark blood was beginning to well from a cleanly drilled puncture. Then he collapsed completely, falling prone across the raised sill of the bulkhead opening. A convulsive tremor shook savagely his huge frame.

Thereafter he was quite still.

The report of that one shot had reverberated stunningly within those narrow walls of steel. Momentarily Lanyard looked to see the alarmed anchor watch appear; so too, apparently, the lieutenant, who remained immobile, pistol poised in a hand for the moment strangely steady, gaze fixed upon the mouth of the alleyway.

But through a long minute no other sounds were audible than that ceaseless dripping from frames and seams, with that muted, terrible mouthing of waters on the plates.

Unable either to fathom or forecast the workings of the drink-maddened mentality masked by that rat-like face, Lanyard waited with a hand covertly grasping the automatic in his pocket. There was no telling; at any moment that murderous mania might veer his way. And he was not content to die, not yet, not in any event by the hand of a decadent little beast of a Boche.

Slowly the arm of the lieutenant dropped, lowering the pistol till its muzzle chattered on the top of the table: a noise that broke the spell upon his senses. He looked down in dull brutish wonder, then roused and with a gesture of horror let the weapon fall clattering.

His glance shifting to the body of his commander, he started violently, backing up against the plates to put all possible distance between himself and his handiwork.

His lips moved, framing phrases at first incoherent, presently articulate in part:

"... ***done it at last!... Knew I must soon***...."

Abruptly he looked up at Lanyard.

"Bear witness," he cried: "I was provoked beyond human endurance. He insulted me in your presence ... me!... that scum!"

Lanyard said nothing, but met his gaze with a blank, non-committal stare, under which the eyes of the lieutenant wavered and fell.

Then with a start he realised anew the significance of that still figure at his feet, and tried to shake some of the swagger back into his wretched, fear-racked being.

"A good job!" he muttered defiantly. "And you will stand by me, I know.... Only there is nothing in that, of course, no justification possible before a court martial. Even your testimony could not save me ... I am done for, utterly...."

He hung his head. Lanyard heard whispered words: "***degraded,*" "*dishonour,*" "*firing squad*"....

A chronometer in the central operating compartment tolled eight bells.

With a sharp cry the lieutenant dropped to his knees. "He can't be dead!" he shrilled. "It is all play-acting, to frighten me!"

Frantically he sought to turn the body over.

Lanyard's hand shot swiftly out, capturing the automatic on the table. With rapid and sure gestures he extracted and pocketed the clip, drew back the breech, ejecting into his palm the one shell in the barrel, and replaced the weapon, all before the Prussian gave over his insane efforts to resurrect the dead.

"He is dead enough," he announced, eyeing Lanyard morosely--"beyond helping.... Look here; are you with me or against me?"

"Need you ask?"

"I count on you, then. Good. I think we can cover this up."

He checked and stood for a while lost in thought.

"How?" Lanyard roused him.

"Simply enough: I go on deck, send the watch ashore on some trumped-up errand. They suspect nothing, thinking the commander and I have you in charge. If they heard that shot, I will say one of us dropped a bottle of champagne, and it exploded.... When they are gone, I bring the dory alongside; and with your help it should be an easy matter to carry this body up, weight it, row it out to the middle of the lagoon, dump it overboard. Then we return. Our story is, the commander followed the anchor watch ashore; if later he wandered off, got lost in the woods in his alcoholic delirium, that is no affair of ours. Do you understand?"

"Perfectly," said Lanyard with a look of fatuous innocence. "But how about the water--is it deep enough?"

The Prussian took no pains to dissemble his scorn of this question, seemingly so witless. "To cover the body? Why, even here there is sufficient depth at low tide for us to submerge completely, barring the periscopes. And it is deeper yet in the middle."

"Thanks," Lanyard replied meekly.

"Have another drink? No?" The Prussian tossed off a half cupful of undiluted brandy, and shuddered. "Then stop here. I'll be back in a--"

"Half a minute." The lieutenant halted in the act of stepping across the body. Lanyard levelled a hand at the automatic. "Do you mind taking that with you? I have no desire to be found here with it and a dead man, should anything prevent your return."

With a sickly grimace the murderer snatched up the weapon, thrust it in its holster, and hurriedly departed.

Lanyard watched him pass through the alleyway and turn toward the companion ladder, then followed quietly.

As the lieutenant climbed out on deck, Lanyard ascended to the conning tower and waited there, listening. He could not quite make out what was said; but after a few brusque words of command two pair of boots rang on the gangplank and thumped away down the stage. At the same time Lanyard let himself noiselessly out through the hatch.

As soon as his vision grew reconciled to the change from light to darkness, he discovered the slender figure of the lieutenant skulking on tip-toe after the retreating anchor watch; about midway on the landing stage, however, he paused and bent over one of the piles, apparently fumbling with the painter of a small boat moored in the black shadows below.

At this Lanyard began to move along the deck, one by one working the mooring lines clear of their cleats and dropping them gently overboard, till but two were left to hold the U-boat in place.

Throughout he kept watch upon the manoeuvres of the lieutenant--saw him drop over the side of the stage, heard a thump of feet as he landed in a boat, and a subsequent creak of oar-locks.

The small boat was rounding the bows of the submarine when the adventurer ducked back through conning tower to hold.

He was standing where he had been left when the lieutenant came below.

"It's all right," this last announced with shabby bravado as he stepped over the body in the doorway. "We are rid of that damned watch for a time. They won't return within half an hour at least. I have the dory moored amidships. If we are lively, this dirty job will be over in no time at all."

Lanyard nodded. "I am ready."

"No need to hurry--plenty of time for one more drink." The Prussian splashed brandy into the cup, filling it to the brim. "And God knows I need it!"

Lanyard watched critically as, with head well back, he drained that staggering dose of raw spirit gulp by gulp without once removing the cup from his lips. No mortal man could drink like that and stand up under it: it was now a mere question of time....

Hardly that: the hand of the murderer shook and wavered widely as he put down the cup. For a moment he swayed with eyes fixed and glazing, features visibly losing plasticity, then lurched forward, knocking the brandy bottle to the floor, swung around a full half turn in blind effort to re-establish equilibrium, fell backward upon the table, and lay racked from head to foot with savage spasms, hands clawing empty air, chest labouring vainly to win sufficient oxygen to combat the poison with which his system was saturated.

Moving to his side, Lanyard laid a hand upon the left breast. The man's heart was hammering his ribs with agonizing blows, at first rapid, by degrees more slow and feeble.

No power on earth could save him now: he had committed suicide as surely as murder.

Wasting not another glance or thought upon him Lanyard hurried aft to the central operating room.

The time he had spent there, an hour earlier, was by no means lost in purposeless marvelling. He boasted a certain aptitude for mechanics, perhaps legitimately inherited from that obscure origin of his, largely fostered by the requirements of his craft; into the bargain, he had been privileged ere now to gain some slight insight into the principles of submersible operation. If obliged to work swiftly and in some instances upon the advice of intuition rather than practical knowledge, he went not unintelligently about his task, made few false moves.

Turning first to the diving controls, he adjusted the hydroplanes to their extreme downward inclination, then made the rounds of the vent valves, opening all wide. With a sharp hissing and whistling the air from the auxiliary tanks was driven inboard, and as Lanyard manipulated the wheels operating the forward and aft groups of Kingston valves, to the hissing was added the suck and gurgle of water flooding the main and auxiliary ballast and adjusting tanks.

Immediately the U-boat began to sink. Lanyard delayed only to close the switches which controlled the electric motors. As their drone gained volume he grasped the rifle and swarmed up the companion-ladder, passing through the conning tower to deck with little or nothing to spare--with, in fact, barely time to throw off the two mooring lines and jump into the small boat before water, sweeping hungrily up over deck and bridge, began to cascade through conning tower and torpedo hatchways.

Constrained to cut the painter lest the dory be drawn down with the fast-sinking submarine, he fitted oars to locks and put his back to them, swinging the small boat hastily clear of whirlpools which formed as the waves closed over the spot where the U-boat had rested.

From first to last less than five minutes' activity had been needed for the task of scotching this water-moccasin of the salt seas and putting its keepers at the mercy of the country whose hospitality they had too long abused.

Well content, after a little, Lanyard lay on his oars and contemplated with much interest what the night permitted to be visible: the landing stage, no more than a dark, vague mass in the darkness; the land picked out with but few lights, mainly at windows of the base buildings, painting dim ribbons upon the polished floor of the lagoon.

Methodically these were eclipsed as a moving figure passed before them.

Listening intently, Lanyard could distinguish the slow footfalls of an unsuspecting sentry--no other sounds, more than gentle voices of the night: murmurs of blind wavelets, the plaintive whisper of a little breeze belated amid the tree-tops of that dark forest, and a slow, weary soughing of swells upon the distant ocean shore.

Perceiving as yet not the slightest indication of an alarm ashore, Lanyard ventured to continue rowing, but with utmost caution, lifting and dipping his blades as gingerly as though they were fashioned of brittle glass, and for want of a better guide keeping the stern of the dory square to the shank of the T-stage.

In time the bows grounded lightly on sand. The melancholy voice of the sea now seemed a heavier sighing in the stillness. He pushed off and rowed on parallel with a dark shore line, so close in that his starboard oar touched bottom at each stroke.

At intervals he paused and rested, striving vainly to garner some clue to his bearings. Inexorably the blackness forbade that. He might have failed ere dawn to grope a way out of that trap had not the disappearance of the submarine been discovered within the hour.

A sudden clamour rose in the quarter of the landing stage, first one great shout of dismay, then two voices bellowing together, then others. Several rifle-shots were fired in the air. More lights broke out in windows ashore. Many feet drummed resoundingly upon the stage, and the confusion of voices attained a pitch of wild, hysteric uproar. Of a sudden a flare was lighted and tossed far out upon the bosom of the lagoon.

Surprised by that sharp and merciless blue glare, Lanyard instinctively shipped oars and picked up the rifle. He could see so clearly that huddle of figures upon the head of the landing stage that he confidently apprehended being fired upon at any moment; but minutes lengthened and he was not. Either the Germans were looking for bigger game than a dory adrift, or the dazzling flare hindered more than aided their vision.

At length persuaded that he had not been detected, Lanyard put aside the rifle and resumed the oars. Now his course was made beautifully clear to him: the blue light showed him that outlet to the sea which he sought within a hundred yards' distance.

Presently the flare began to wane. It was not renewed. Altogether unseen, unsuspected, Lanyard swung the dory into the breach, and drove it seaward with all his might.

Swiftly the lagoon was shut out by narrow closing banks. The blue glare died out behind a black profile of rounded dunes. Lanyard turned the bow eastward, rowing broadside to the shore.

After something more than an hour of this mode of progress, he struck in toward the beach, disembarked in ankle-deep waters, slung the rifle over his shoulder by its strap and, pushing the dory off, abandoned it to the whim of the sea.

Then again he set his face to the east, following the contour of the beach just within the wash of the tide: thereby making sure that there should be no trail of footprints in the sand to guide a possible pursuit in the morning.

The rising sun found him purposefully splashing on, weary but enheartened by the discovery that he had left behind the more thickly wooded section of the island.

Presently, turning in to the dry beach for the first time, he climbed to the summit of a dune somewhat higher than its fellows, and took observations, finding that he had come near to the eastern extremity of the island.

At some distance to his right a wagon road, faintly rutted in sand and overgrown with beach grass, struck inland.

Following this at a venture, he came, at about eight o'clock, upon the outskirts of a waterside community.

Before proceeding he hid the magazine rifle in a thicket, then made a wide detour, and picked up a roadway which entered the village from the north.

If his disreputable appearance was calculated to excite comment, readiness in disbursing money to remedy such shortcomings made amends for Lanyard's taciturnity. Within two hours, shaved, bathed, and inconspicuously dressed in a cheap suit of ready-made clothing, he was breakfasting famously upon the plain fare of a commercial tavern.

The town, he learned, was the one-time important whaling port of Edgartown. He would be able to leave for the mainland on a ferry steamer sailing early in the afternoon.

Ten minutes before going abroad he filed a long telegram in code addressed to the head of the British Secret Service in New York....

Consequences manifold and various ensued.

When the telegram had been delivered and decoded--both transactions being marked by reasonable promptitude--the head of the British Secret Service in New York called the British Embassy in Washington on the long distance telephone.

Shortly thereafter an attache of the British Embassy jumped into a motor-car and had himself driven to one of the cardinal departments of the Federal Government.

When he had kicked his heels in an antechamber upward of an hour, he was received, affably enough, by the head of the department, a smug, open-faced gentleman whose mood was largely preoccupied with illusions of grandeur, who was, in short, interested far more in considering how splendid it was to be himself than in hearing about any mare's-nest of a German U-boat base on the south shore of Martha's Vineyard.

He was, however, indulgent enough to promise to give the matter his distinguished consideration in due course.

He even went so far as to have his secretary make a note of what alleged information this young Englishman had to impart.

During the night he chanced to wake up and recall the matter, and concluded that, all things considered, it would do no harm to give the United States Navy a little amusement and exercise, even if it should turn out that the rumour of this submarine base was a canard.

So, the next morning, he went to his desk some time before noon, and issued a lot of orders. One of them had to do with the necessity for absolute secrecy.

During the day several minor officials of the department might have been, and indeed were, observed going about their business with painfully tight-lipped expressions.

Also many messages were transmitted by wireless, telephone, and telegraph, to various persons charged with the defense of the Atlantic Coast; some of these were code messages, some were not.

That same night a great forest fire sprang up on the south shore of Martha's Vineyard, both preceded and accompanied by a series of heavy explosions.

The first United States vessel to reach the lagoon found only charred remains of a landing stage and several buildings and, at the bottom of the lagoon, an incoherent mass of wreckage, a twisted and shattered chaos of steel plates and framework that might possibly have been a perfectly sound submarine, though sunken, had somebody not been warned in ample time to permit its destruction through the agency of trinitrotoluene, that enormously efficient modern explosive nicknamed by British military and naval experts "T.N.T.," and by the Germans "Trotyl."

XII
RESURRECTION

The early editions of those New York evening newspapers which Lanyard purchased in Providence, when he changed trains there en route from New Bedford to New York, carried multi-column and most picturesque accounts of the *Assyrian* disaster.

But the whole truth was in none.

Lanyard laid aside the last paper privately satisfied that, for no-doubt praise-worthy reasons of its own, Washington had seen fit to dictate the suppression of a number of extremely pertinent circumstances and facts which could hardly have escaped governmental knowledge.

Already, one inferred, a sort of censorship was at work, an effective if comparatively modest precursor to that noble volunteer committee which was presently with touching spontaneity to fasten itself upon an astonished Ship of State before it could gather enough way to escape such cirripede attachments.

Presumably it was not thought wise to disconcert a great people, in the complacence of its awakening to the fact that it was remotely at war with the Hun, with information that a Boche submersible was, or of late had been, operating in the neighbourhood of Nantucket.

Unanimously the sinking of the *Assyrian* was ascribed to an internal explosion of unknown origin. No paper hinted that German secret agents might possibly have figured incogniti among her passengers. There was mention neither of the flare which had burned on her after deck to make the *Assyrian* a conspicuous target in the night, nor of any of the other untoward events which had led up to the explosion. Nothing whatever was said of the shot fired at the submerging U-boat by a United States torpedo-boat destroyer speeding to the rescue.

Still, the bare facts alone were sufficiently appalling. Reading what had been permitted to gain publication, Lanyard experienced a qualm of horror together with the thought that, even had he drowned as he had expected to drown, such a fate had almost been preferable to participation in those awful ten minutes precipitated by that pale messenger of death which had so narrowly missed Lanyard himself as he rested on the bosom of the sea.

Within ten minutes after receiving her coup de grace the *Assyrian* had gone under; barely that much time had been permitted a passenger list of seventy-two and a personnel of nearly three hundred souls in which to rouse from dreams of security and take to the lifeboats.

Thanks to the frenzied haste compelled by the swift settling of the ship, more than one boat had been capsized. Others had been sunk--literally driven under--by masses of humanity cascading into them from slanting decks. Others, again, had never been launched at all.

The utmost efforts of the destroyer, fortuitously so near at hand, had served to rescue but thirty-one passengers and one hundred and eighty of the crew.

In the list of survivors Lanyard found these names:

Becker, Julius--New York
Brooke, Cecelia--London
Crane, Robert T.--New York
Dressier, Emil--Geneva
O'Reilly, Edmund--Detroit
Putnam, Bartlett--Philadelphia
Velasco, Arturo--Buenos Aires

Among the injured, Lieutenant Lionel Thackeray, D.S.O., was listed as suffering from concussion of the brain, said to have been contracted through a fall while attempting to aid the launching of a lifeboat.

In the long roster of the drowned these names appeared:

Bartholomew, Archer--London
Duchemin, Andre--Paris

Von Harden, Baron Gustav--Amsterdam
Osborne, Captain E. W.--London

Of all the officers, Mr. Sherry was a solitary survivor, fished out of the sea after going down with his ship.

No list boasted the name "Karl."

Lacking accommodations for the rescued, it was stated, the destroyer had summoned by wireless the east-bound freight steamship ***Saratoga***, which had transshipped the unfortunates and turned back to New York....

Throughout the best part of that journey from Providence to New York Lanyard sat blankly staring into the black mirror of the window beside his chair, revolving schemes for his immediate future in the light of information derived, indirectly as much as directly, from these newspaper stories.

Retrospective consideration of that voyage left little room for doubt that the designs of the German agents had been thoughtfully matured. They had been quiet enough between their first stroke in the dark and their last, between the burglary of Cecelia Brooke's stateroom the first night out and those murderous attacks on Bartholomew and Thackeray. Unquestionably, had they bided their time pending that hour when, according to their information, the submersible would be off Nantucket, awaiting their signal to sink the ***Assyrian***--a signal which would never have been given had their plans proved successful, had they not made the ship too hot to hold them, and finally had they not made every provision for their own escape when the ship went down.

Lanyard was confident that all of their company had been warned to hold themselves ready, and consequently had come off scot free--all, that is, save that victim of treachery, the unhappy Baron von Harden.

If the number of that group which Lanyard had selected as comprising a majority of his enemies, those nine who had discussed the Lone Wolf in the smoking room, was now reduced to five--Becker, Dressier, O'Reilly, Putnam, and Velasco--or four, eliminating Putnam, of whose loyalty there could be no question--Lanyard still had no means of knowing how many confederates among the other passengers these four might not have had.

And even four men who appreciated what peril to their plans inhered in the

Lone Wolf, even four made a ponderable array of desperate enemies to have at large in New York, apt to be encountered at any corner, apt at any time to espy and recognise him without his knowledge.

This situation imposed upon him two major tasks of immediate moment: he must hunt down those four one by one and either satisfy himself as to their innocence of harmful intent or put them permanently **hors de combat**; and he must extinguish utterly, once and for all time, that amiable personality whose brief span had been restricted to the decks of the **Assyrian**, Monsieur Andre Duchemin.

That one must be buried deep, beyond all peradventure of involuntary resurrection.

Fortunately the last step toward the positive metamorphosis indicated had been taken that very morning, when the Gallic beard of Monsieur Duchemin was erased by the razor of a New England barber, whose shears had likewise eradicated every trace of a Continental mode of hair-dressing. There remained about Lanyard little to remind of Andre Duchemin but his eyes; and the look of one's eyes, as every good actor knows, is something far more easy to disguise than is commonly believed.

But it was hardly in human nature not to mourn the untimely demise of so useful a body, one who carried such beautiful credentials and serviceable letters of introduction, whose character boasted so much charm with a solitary fault--too facile vulnerability to the prying eyes of those to whom Paris meant those days and social strata in which Michael Lanyard had moved and had his being. Witness--according to Crane--the demoniac cleverness of the Brazilian in unmasking the Duchemin incognito.

Suspicion was taking form in Lanyard's reflections that he had paid far too little attention to Senor Arturo Velasco of Buenos Aires, whose avowed avocation of amateur criminologist might easily be synonymous with interests much less innocuous.

Or why had Velasco been so quick to communicate recognition of Lanyard to an employee of the United States Secret Service?

For that matter, why had he felt called so publicly to descant upon the natural history of the Lone Wolf? In order to focus upon that one the attentions of his enemies? Or to put him on guard?

It was altogether perplexing. Was one to esteem Velasco friend or foe?

Lanyard could comfort himself only with the promise he should one day know, and that without undue delay.

Alighting in Grand Central Terminus late at night, he made his way to Forty-second Street and there, in the staring headlines of a "Late Extra," read the news that the steamship **Saratoga** had suffered a crippling engine-room accident and was limping slowly toward port, still something like eighteen hours out.

Wondering if it were presumption to construe this as an omen that the stars in their courses fought for him, Lanyard went west to Broadway afoot, all the way beset with a sense of incredulity; it was difficult to believe that he was himself, alive and at large in this city of wonder and space, where people moved at leisure and without fear on broad streets that resembled deep-bitten channels for rivers of light. He was all too wont with nights of dread and trembling, with the mediaeval gloom that enwrapped the cities of Europe by night, their grim black streets desolate but for a few, infrequent, scurrying shapes of fright.... While here the very beggars walked with heads unbowed, and men and women of happier estate laughed and played and made love lightly in the scampering taxis that whisked them homeward from restaurants of the feverish midnight.

A people at war, actually at grips with the Blond Beast, arrayed to defend itself and all humanity against conquest by that loathsome incubus incarnate, a people heedless, carefree, irresponsible, refusing to credit its peril....

Here and there a recruiting poster, down the broad reaches of Fifth Avenue a display of bunting, no other hint of war-time spirit and gravity....

Longacre Square, a weltering lake of kaleidoscopic radiance, even at this late hour thronged with carnival crowds, not one note of sobriety in the night....

Lanyard lifted a wondering gaze to the livid sky whose far, clear stars were paled and shamed by the up-flung glare, like eyes of innocence peering down into a pit of hell.

Inscrutable!

Yet one could hardly be numb to the subtle, heady intoxication of those cool, immaculate, sea-sweet airs which swept the streets, instilling self-confidence and lightness of spirit even in heads shadowed with the woe of war-worn Europe.

Lanyard had not crossed the Avenue before he found himself walking with a brisker stride, holding his own head high....

On impulse, despite the lateness of the hour, albeit with misgivings justified in the issue, he hailed a taxicab and had himself driven to the headquarters of the British Secret Service in America, an unostentatious dwelling on the northwest corner of West End Avenue at Ninety-fifth Street.

Here a civil footman answered the door and Lanyard's enquiries with the information that Colonel Stanistreet had unexpectedly been called out of town and would not return before evening of the next day, while his secretary, Mr. Blensop, had gone to a play and might not come home till all hours.

More impatient than disappointed, Lanyard climbed back into his cab, and in consequence of consultation with its friendly minded chauffeur, eventually put up for the night in an Eighth Avenue hotel of the class that made Senator Raines famous, a hostelry brazenly proclaiming accommodations "for gentlemen only," whereas it offered entertainment for both man and beast and catered rather more to beast than to man.

However, it served; it was inconspicuous and made no demands upon a shabby traveller sans luggage, more than payment in advance.

Early abroad, Lanyard breakfasted with attention fixed to the advertising columns of the *Herald*, and by mid-morning was established as sub-tenant of a furnished bachelor apartment on Fifty-eighth Street near Seventh Avenue, a tiny nest of few rooms on the street level, with entrances from both the general lobby and the street direct: an admirable arrangement for one who might choose to come and go without supervision or challenge.

Lacking local references as to his character, Lanyard was obliged to pay three months' rent in advance in addition to making a substantial deposit to cover possible damage to the furnishings.

His name, a spur-of-the-moment selection, was recorded in the lease as Anthony Ember.

At noon he brought to his lodgings two trunks salvaged from a storage warehouse wherein they had been deposited more than three years since, on the eve of his flight with his family from America, an affair of haste and secrecy forbidding the handicap of heavy impedimenta.

Thus Lanyard became once more possessor of a tolerably comprehensive wardrobe.

But, those trunks released more than his personal belongings; intermingled were possessions that had been his wife's and his boy's. As he unpacked, memories peopled those perfunctorily luxurious lodgings of the transient with melancholy ghosts as sweet and sad as lavender and rue.

For hours on end the man sat idle, head bowed down, hands plucking aimlessly at small broidered garments.

And if in the sweep and turmoil of late events he seemed to have forgotten for a little that feud which had brought him overseas, he roused from this brief interlude of saddened dreaming with the iron of deadly purpose newly entered into his soul, and in his heart one dominant thought, that now his hour with Ekstrom could not, must not, be long deferred.

In the street there rose an uproar of inhuman bawling. Lanyard went to the private door, hailed one of the husky authors of the din, an itinerant news-vendor, and disbursed a nickel coin for one cent's worth of spushul uxtry and four cents' worth of howling impudence.

He found no more of interest in the newspaper than the information that the **Saratoga** had been sighted off Fire Island and was expected to dock in New York not later than eight o'clock that night.

This, however, was acceptable reading. Lanyard had work to do which were better done before "Karl" and his crew found opportunity to communicate directly with their collaborators ashore, work which it were unwise to initiate before night-fall lent a cloak of shadows to hoodwink the ever-possible adventitious German spy.

Nor was he so fatuous as to fancy it would profit him to call before nine o'clock at the house on West End Avenue. No earlier might he hope to find Colonel the Honourable George Fleetwood-Stanistreet near the end of his dinner, and so in a mood approachable and receptive.

But there could be no harm in reconnaissance by daylight.

He whiled away the latter part of the afternoon in taxicabs, by dint of frequent changes contriving in the most casual fashion imaginable to pass the Seventy-ninth Street branch of the Wilhelmstrasse no less than four times.

Little rewarded these tactics other than a fairly accurate mental photograph of the building and its situation--and a growing suspicion that the United States Government had profited nothing by England's lessons of early war days in respect of the one way to cope with resident enemy aliens.

The house stood upon a corner, occupying half of an avenue block--the northern half of which was the site of a towering apartment house in course of construction--and loomed over its lesser neighbours a monumental monstrosity of architecture, as formidable as a fortress, its lower tiers of windows barred with iron, substantial iron grilles ready to bar its main entrance, even heavier gates guarding the carriage court in the side street. In all a stronghold not easy for the most accomplished house-breaker to force; yet the heart of it was Lanyard's goal; for there, he believed, Ekstrom (under whatever *nom de guerre*) lay hidden, or if not Ekstrom, at least a clear lead to his whereabouts.

Certainly that one could not be far from the powerful wireless station secretly maintained on the roof of this weird jumble of architectural periods, its aerials cunningly hidden in the crowning atrocity of its minaret: a station reputedly so powerful that it could receive Berlin's nightly outgivings of news and orders, and, in emergency, transmit them to other secret stations in Cuba, Mexico, and Venezuela.

Yet the shrewdest scrutiny of eyes trained to detect police agents at sight, however well disguised, failed to espy one sign of any sort of espionage upon this nest of rattlesnakes.

Apparently its tenants came and went as they willed, untroubled by and contemptuous of governmental surveillance.

A handsome limousine car pulled up at its carriage block as Lanyard drove by, one time, and a pretty woman, exquisitely gowned, alighted and was welcomed by hospitable front doors that opened before she could ring: a woman Lanyard knew as one of the most daring, diabolically clever, and unscrupulous creatures of the Wilhelmstrasse, one whose life would not have been worth an hour's purchase had she ventured to show herself in Paris, London, or Petrograd at any time since the outbreak of the war.

He drove on, deep in amaze.

Indications were not wanting, on the other hand, that enemy spies maintained close watch upon the movements of those who frequented the house on West End Avenue. A German agent whom Lanyard knew by sight was strolling by as his taxi rounded its corner and swung on down toward Riverside Drive.

This more modest residence possessed a brick-walled garden at the back, on the Ninety-fifth Street side. And if the top of the wall was crusted with broken glass in a fashion truly British, it had a door, and the door a lock. And Lanyard made a note thereon.

And when he went home to dress for dinner, he opened up the false bottom of one of his trunks and selected from a store of cloth-wrapped bundles therein one which contained a small bunch of innocent-looking keys whose true *raison d'etre* was anything in the world but guileless.

Later he did himself very well at Delmonico's, enjoying for the first time in many years a well-balanced dinner faultlessly cooked and served amid quiet surroundings that carried memory back half a decade to the Paris that was, the Paris that nevermore will be....

At nine precisely he paid off a taxicab at the corner of Ninety-fifth Street.

While waiting on the doorstep of the corner house, he raked the street right and left with searching glances, and was somewhat reassured. Apparently he called at an hour when the Boche pickets were off duty; at the moment there was no pedestrian visible within a block's distance on either hand, nobody that he could see skulked in the areas of the old-fashioned brownstone houses across the way.

The neighbourhood was, indeed, quiet even for an upper West Side residential quarter. A block over to the east Broadway was strident in the flood of its nocturnal traffic; a like distance to the west Riverside Drive hummed with pleasure cars taking advantage of the first bland night of that belated spring. But here, now that the taxi had wheeled away, there was never a car in sight, nor even a strolling brace of sidewalk lovers.

The door opened, revealing the same footman.

"Colonel Stanistreet? I will see, sir."

Lanyard entered.

"If you will be kind enough to be seated," the footman suggested, indicating a small waiting room. "And what name shall I say?"

It had been Lanyard's intention to have himself announced simply as the author of that telegram from Edgartown. Obscure impulse made him change his mind, some premonition so tenuous as to defy analysis.

"Mr. Anthony Ember."

"Thank you, sir."

After a little the footman returned.

"If you will come this way, sir...."

He led toward the back of the house, introducing Lanyard to a spacious apartment, a library uncommonly well furnished, rather more than comfortably yet without a trace of ostentation in its complete luxury, a warm room, a room intimately lived in, a room, in short, characteristically British in atmosphere.

Waist-high bookcases lined the walls, broken on the right by a cheerful fireplace with a grate of glowing cannel coal, in front of it a great club lounge upholstered, like all the chairs, in well-used leather. Opposite the chimney-piece, a handsome thing in carved oak, a door was draped with a curtain that swung with it. In the back of the room two long and wide French windows stood open to the night, beyond them that garden whose wall had attracted Lanyard's attention. There were a number of paintings, portraits for the most part, heavily framed, with overhead picture-lights. In the middle of the room was a table-desk, broad and long, supporting a shaded reading lamp. On the far side of the table a young man sat writing, with several dockets of papers arranged before him.

As Lanyard entered, this one put down his pen, pushed back his chair, and came round the table: a tallish, well-made young man, dressed a shade too foppishly in spite of an unceremonious dinner coat, his manner assured, amiable, unconstrained, perhaps a little over-tolerant.

"Mr. Ember, I believe?" he said in a voice studiously musical.

"Yes," Lanyard replied, vaguely annoyed with himself because of an unreasoning resentment of this musical quality. "Mr. Blensop?"

"I am Mr. Blensop," that one admitted gracefully. "And how may I have the pleasure of being of service?"

He waved a hand toward an easy chair beside the table, and resumed his own. But Lanyard hesitated.

"I wished to see Colonel Stanistreet."

Mr. Blensop looked up with an indulgent smile. His face was round and smooth but for a perfectly docile little moustache, his lips full and red, his nose delicately chiselled; but his eyes, though large, were set cannily close together.

"Colonel Stanistreet is unfortunately not at home. I am his secretary."

"Yes," said Lanyard, still standing. "In that case I'd be glad if you would be good enough to make an appointment for me with Colonel Stanistreet."

"I am afraid he will not be home till very late to-night, but--"

"Then to-morrow?"

Mr. Blensop smiled patiently. "Colonel Stanistreet is a very busy man," he uttered melodiously. "If you could let me know something about the nature of your business...."

"It is the King's," said Lanyard bluntly.

The secretary went so far as to betray well-bred surprise. "You are an Englishman, Mr. Ember?"

"Yes."

And for all he knew to the contrary, so Lanyard was.

"I am Colonel Stanistreet's secretary," the young man again suggested hopefully.

"That is precisely why I ask you to make an appointment for me with your employer," Lanyard retorted politely.

"You won't say what you wish to see him about?"

A trace of asperity marred the music of those tones; Mr. Blensop further indicated distaste of the innuendo inherent in Lanyard's use of the word "employer" by delicately wrinkling his nose.

"I am sorry," Lanyard replied sufficiently.

The door behind him opened, and the footman intruded.

"Beg pardon, Mr. Blensop...."

"Yes, Walker?"

The servant advanced to the table and proffered a visiting card on a tray. Mr. Blensop took it, arched pencilled brows over it.

"To see me, Walker?"

"The gentleman asked for Colonel Stanistreet, sir."

"H'm.... You may show him in when I ring."

The footman retired. Mr. Blensop looked up brightly, bending the card with nervous fingers.

"You were saying your business was...?"

"I was not," Lanyard replied with disarming good humour. "I'm afraid that is something much too important and confidential to reveal even to Colonel Stanistreet's secretary, if you don't mind my saying so."

Mr. Blensop did mind, and betrayed vexation with an impatient little gesture which caused the card to fly from his fingers and fall face uppermost on the table. Almost instantly he recovered it, but not before Lanyard had read the name it bore.

"Of course not," said the secretary pleasantly, rising. "But you understand my instructions are rigid ... I'm sorry."

"You refuse me the appointment?"

"Unless you can give me an inkling of your business--or perhaps bring a letter of introduction."

"I can do neither, Mr. Blensop," said Lanyard earnestly. "I have information of the gravest moment to communicate to the head of the British Secret Service in this country."

The secretary looked startled. "What makes you think Colonel Stanistreet is connected with the British Secret Service?"

"I don't think so; I know it."

After a moment of hesitation Mr. Blensop yielded graciously. "If you can come back at nine to-morrow morning, Mr. Ember, I'll do my best to persuade Colonel Stanistreet--"

"I repeat, my business is of the most pressing nature. Can't you arrange for me to see your employer to-night?"

"It is utterly impossible."

Lanyard accepted defeat with a bow.

"To-morrow at nine, then," he said, turning toward the door by which he had entered.

"At nine," said Mr. Blensop, generous in triumph. "But do you mind going out this way?"

He moved toward the curtained door opposite the chimney-piece. Lanyard paused, shrugged, and followed. Mr. Blensop opened the door, disclosing a vista of Ninety-fifth Street.

"Thank *you*, Mr. Ember. *Good*-night," he intoned.

The door closed with the click of a spring latch.

Lanyard stood alone in the street, looking swiftly this way and that, his hand closing upon that little bunch of keys in his pocket, his humour lawless.

For the name inscribed on that card which Mr. Blensop had so carelessly dropped was one to fill Lanyard with consuming anxiety for better acquaintance with its present wearer.

Written in pencil, with all the individual angularity of French chirography, the name was Andre Duchemin.

XIII
REINCARNATION

It took a little time and patience but, on his third essay, Lanyard found a key which agreed with the lock. He permitted himself a sigh of relief; Ninety-fifth Street was bare, the door set flush with the outside of the wall afforded no concealment to the trespasser, while the direct light of a street lamp at the corner made his lonely figure uncomfortably conspicuous.

Apparently, however, he had not been observed.

Gently pushing the door open, he slipped in, as gently closed it, then for a full minute stood stirless, spying out the lay of the land.

Fitting precisely his anticipations, the garden discovered a fine English flavour; it was well-kept, modest, fragrant and, best of all, quite dark, especially so in the shadow of the street wall. Only a glimmer of starlight enabled him to pick out the course of a pebbled footpath. A border of deep turf between this and the wall muffled his footsteps as he moved toward the back of the house.

The library windows, deeply recessed, opened on a low, broad stoop of concrete, with a pergola effect above, and a few wicker pieces upon a grass mat underfoot.

Noiselessly Lanyard stepped across the low sill and paused in the cover of heavy draperies, commanding a tolerably full view of the library if one somewhat unsatisfactory, since the light within was by no means bright. Still, this circumstance had its advantages for him; with his dark topcoat buttoned to the throat and its collar turned up to hide his linen, he was confident he would not be detected unless he gave his presence away by an abrupt movement--something which the Lone Wolf never made.

At the moment Mr. Blensop seemed to be engaged in the surprising occupation of discoursing upon art to his caller.

The latter occupied that chair which Lanyard had refused, on the far side of the table. Thus placed, the lamplight masked more than revealed him, throwing a dull glare into Lanyard's eyes. His man sat in a pose of earnest attention, bending forward a trifle to follow the exposition of Mr. Blensop, who stood beneath a portrait on the wall between the chimney-piece and the windows, his attitude incurably graceful, a hand on the switch controlling the picture-light. Apparently he had just finished speaking, for he paused, looking toward his guest with a quiet and intimate smile as he turned off the light.

"And that's all there is to it," he declared, moving back to the table.

"I see," said the other thoughtfully.

Lanyard felt himself start almost uncontrollably: rage swept through him, storming brain and body, like a black squall over a hill-bound lake. For the moment he could neither see or hear clearly nor think coherently.

For the voice of this latest incarnation of Andre Duchemin was the voice of "Karl."

When the tumult of his senses subsided he heard Blensop saying, "I'll write it out for you," and saw him pick up a pad and pencil and jot down a memorandum.

"There you are," he added, ripping off the sheet and passing it across the table. "Now you can't go wrong."

"I precious seldom do," his caller commented drily.

"I think--" Blensop began, and checked sharply as the man Walker came into the room.

"Beg pardon, Mr. Blensop--"

There was an accent of impatience in those beautifully modulated tones: "Well, what is it now?"

"A lady to see you, sir."

Blensop took the card from the proffered salver. "Never heard of her," he announced brusquely at a glance. "She asked for Colonel Stanistreet or for me?"

"Colonel Stanistreet, sir. But when I said he was not at home, she asked to see his secretary."

"Any idea what she wants?"

"She didn't say, sir--but she seemed much distressed."

"They always are. H'm.... Young and good-looking?"

"Quite, sir."

"Dessay I may as well see her," said Mr. Blensop wearily. "Show her in when I ring."

Walker shut himself out of the room.

"It's just as well," Blensop added to his caller. "You understand, my clear fellow--?"

"Assuredly." The man got up; but Blensop contrived exasperatingly to keep between him and the windows. "I'm to be back at midnight?"

"Twelve sharp; you'll be sure to find him here then. Mind leaving by this emergency exit?"

"Not in the least."

"Then *good*-night, my dear Monsieur Duchemin!"

Was there a hint of irony in Blensop's employment of that style? Lanyard half fancied there was, but did not linger to analyse the impression. Already the secretary had opened the side door.

In a bound Lanyard cleared the stoop, then ran back to the door in the wall. But with all his quickness he was all too slow; already, as he emerged to Ninety-fifth Street, his quarry was rounding the Avenue corner.

Defiant of discretion, Lanyard gave chase at speed but, though he had not thirty yards to cover, again was baffled by the swiftness with which "Karl" got about.

He had still some distance to go when the peace of the quarter was shattered by a door that slammed like a pistol shot, and with roaring motor and grinding gears a cab swung away from the curb in front of the Stanistreet residence and tore off down the Avenue.

Swearing petulantly in his disappointment, Lanyard pulled up on the corner. The number on the license plate was plainly revealed as the vehicle showed its back to the street lamp. But what good was that to him? He memorised it mechanically, in mutinous appreciation of the fact that the taxi was setting a pace with which he could not hope to compete afoot.

The rumble of another motor-car caught his ear, and he looked round eagerly. A second taxicab--undoubtedly that which had brought the young woman now presumably closeted with Mr. Blensop--was moving up into the place vacated by the first.

In two strides Lanyard was at its side.

"Follow that taxi!" he cried--"number seventy-six, three-eighty-five. Don't lose sight of it, but don't pass it--don't let them know we're following!"

"Engaged," the driver growled.

"Hang your engagement! Here"--Lanyard pressed a golden eagle into the fellow's palm--"there will be another of those if you do as I say!"

"Le's go!" the driver agreed with resignation.

If the cab was moving before Lanyard could hop in and shut the door, the other had already established a killing lead; and though Lanyard's man demonstrated characteristic contempt for municipal regulations governing the speed of motor-driven vehicles, and racketed his own madly down the Avenue, he was wholly helpless to do more than keep the tail-lamp of the first in sight.

More than once that dull red eye seemed sardonically to wink.

Still, Lanyard did not think "Karl" knew he was pursued. His conveyance had passed the corner before Lanyard emerged from the side street. There being no reason that Lanyard knew of why the spy should believe himself under suspicion, his haste seemed most probably due to natural desire to avoid adventitious recognition, coupled with, no doubt, other urgent business.

At Seventy-second Street the chase turned east, with Lanyard two blocks behind, and for a few agonizing moments was altogether lost to him. But at Broadway the tide of southbound traffic hindered it momentarily, and it swung into that stream with its pursuer only a block astern.

Thereafter through a ride of another mile and a half, the distance between the two was augmented or abbreviated arbitrarily by the rules of the road.

At one time less than two cab-lengths separated them; then a Ford, driven Fordishly, wandered vaguely out of a crosstown street and hesitated in the middle of the thoroughfare with precisely the air of a staring yokel on a first visit to the city; and Lanyard's driver slammed on the emergency brake barely in time to escape committing involuntary but justifiable flivvercide.

When he was able once more to throw the gears into high, the chase was a long block ahead.

They were entering Longacre Square before he made up that loss.

And at Forty-fourth Street, again, a stream of east-bound cars edged in between the two, reducing Lanyard's driver to the verge of gibbering lunacy.

A car resembling "Karl's" was crossing Broadway at Forty-second Street when Lanyard was still on Seventh Avenue north of the Times Building.

But only a minute later his driver pulled up in front of the Hotel Knickerbocker, and Lanyard, peering through the forward window, saw the number 76-385 on the license plate of a taxicab drawing away, empty, from the curb beneath the hotel canopy.

He tossed the second gold piece to the driver as his feet touched the sidewalk, and shouldered through a cluster of men and women at the main entrance to the lobby.

That rendezvous of Broadway was fairly thronged despite the slack mid-evening hour, between the dinner and the supper crushes; but Lanyard reviewed in vain the little knots of guests and loungers; if "Karl" were among them, he was nobody whom Lanyard had learned to know by sight on board the *Assyrian*.

With as little success he searched unobtrusively all public rooms on the main floor.

It was, of course, both possible and probable that "Karl," himself a guest of the hotel, had crossed directly to the elevators and been whisked aloft to his room.

With this in mind, Lanyard paused at the desk, asked permission to examine the register and, being accommodated, was somewhat consoled; if his chase had failed of its immediate objective, it now proved not altogether fruitless. A majority of the *Assyrian* survivors seemed to have elected to stop at the Knickerbocker. One after another Lanyard, scanning the entries, found these names:

Edmund O'Reilly--Detroit
Arturo Velasco--Buenos Aires
Bartlett Putnam--Philadelphia
Cecelia Brooke--London
Emil Dressier--Geneve

Half inclined to commit the imprudence of sending a name up to Miss Brooke--any name but Andre Duchemin, Michael Lanyard, or Anthony Ember--together with a message artfully worded to fix her interest without giving comfort to the enemy, should it chance to go astray, the adventurer hesitated by the desk; and of a sudden was satisfied that such a move would be not only injudicious but waste of time; for, now that he paused to think of it, he surmised that the young woman--"young and good-looking", on Walker's word--who had called to see Colonel Stan-istreet was none other than this same Cecelia Brooke.

What more natural than that she should make early occasion to consult the head of the British Secret Service in America?

A pity he had not waited there in the window! If he had, no doubt the mystery with which the girl had surrounded herself would be no more mystery to Lanyard; he would have learned the secret of that paper cylinder as well as the part the girl had played in the intrigue for its possession, and so be the better advised as to his own future conduct.

But in his insensate passion for revenge upon one who had all but murdered him, he had forgotten all else but the moment's specious opportunity.

With a grunt of impatience Lanyard turned away from the desk, and came face to face with Crane.

The Secret Service man was coming from the direction of the bar in company with Velasco, O'Reilly, and Dressier.

Of the three last named but one looked Lanyard's way, O'Reilly, and his gaze, resting transiently on the countenance of Andre Duchemin minus the Duchemin beard, passed on without perceptible glimmer of recognition.

Why not? Why should it enter his head that one lived and had anticipated his own arrival in New York by twenty hours whom be believed to be buried many fathoms deep off Nantucket?

As for Crane, his cool gray, humorous eyes, half-hooded with their heavy lids, favoured Lanyard with casual regard and never a tremor of interest or surprise; but as he passed his right eye closed deliberately and with a significance not to be ignored.

To this Lanyard responded only with a look of blankest amaze.

Chatting with an air of subdued self-congratulation pardonable in such as have come safe to land through many dangers of the deep, the quartet strolled round the desk and boarded one of the elevators.

Not till its gate had closed did Lanyard stir. Then he went away from there with all haste and cunning at his command.

The route through the cafe to Broadway offered the speediest and least conspicuous of exits. From the side door of the hotel he plunged directly into the mouth of the Subway kiosk and, chance favouring him, managed to purchase a ticket and board a southbound local train an instant before its doors ground shut.

Believing Crane would take the next elevator down, once he had seen the others safely in their rooms, Lanyard was content to let him find the lobby destitute of ghosts, to let him fume and wonder and think himself perhaps mistaken.

The last thing he desired was entanglement with the American Secret Service. For Crane he entertained personal respect and temperate liking, thought the man socially an amusing creature, professionally a deadly peril to one who had a feud to pursue.

Leaving the train at Grand Central, the adventurer passed through the back ways of the Terminus, into the Hotel Biltmore, upstairs to its lobby, thence out by the Vanderbilt Avenue entrance, walking through Forty-fourth Street to Fifth Avenue, where he chartered a taxicab, gave the address of his lodgings, and lay back in the corner of its seat satisfied he had successfully eluded pursuit and very, very grateful to the Subway system for the facilities it afforded fugitives like himself through its warren of underground passages.

One thing troubled him, however, without respite: the Brooke girl was on his conscience. To her he owed an accounting of his stewardship of that trust which she had reposed in him. It was intolerable in his understanding that she should be permitted to go one unnecessary hour in ignorance of the truth about that business- -the truth, that is, as far as he himself knew it.

If through Crane or in some unforseeable fashion she were to learn that Andre Duchemin lived, she would think him faithless. If she knew that Duchemin had been one with Michael Lanyard, the Lone Wolf, she would not be surprised. But that, too, was intolerable; even the Lone Wolf had his code of honour.

Again, if she remained in ignorance of the fact that Lanyard had escaped drowning, she would continue to believe her secret at the bottom of the sea with him; whereas, in the hands of the enemy, in the possession of "Karl" and his, confederates, it was potentially Heaven only knew how dangerous a weapon.

Abruptly Lanyard reflected that at least one doubt had been eliminated by that encounter in the Knickerbocker. It was barely possible that "Karl" had gone to the bar on entering and added himself to Crane's party, but it was hardly creditable in Lanyard's consideration. He was convinced that, whether or not Velasco, O'Reilly, and Dressier were parties to the Hun conspiracy, none of these was "Karl."

As for the Brooke matter, he felt it incumbent upon him immediately to find some safe means of communicating with the girl. She could be trusted not to betray him to the police, however much she might at first incline to doubt him. But he would persuade her of his sincerity, never fear!

The telephone offered one solution of his difficulty, an agency non-committal enough, provided one were at pains not to call from one's private station, to which the call might be traced back.

With this in mind he stopped and dismissed his taxicab at Fifty-seventh Street and Sixth Avenue, and availed himself of a coin-box telephone booth in the corner druggist's.

The experience that followed was nothing out of the ordinary. Lanyard, connected with the Knickerbocker promptly, with the customary expenditure of patience laboriously spelled out the name B-r-double-o-k-e, and was told to hold the wire.

Several minutes later he began to agitate the receiver hook and was eventually rewarded with the advice that the Knickerbocker operator, being informed his party was in the rest'runt, was having her paged.

Still later the central operator told him his five minutes was up and consented to continue the connection only on deposit of an additional nickel.

Eventually, in sequel to more abuse of the hook, he received this response from the Knickerbocker switchboard: "Wait a min'te, can't you? Here's your party."

Lanyard was surprised at the eagerness with which he cried: "Hello!"

A click answered, and a bland voice which was not the voice he had expected to hear: "Hello? That you, Jack?"

He said wearily: "I am waiting to speak with Miss Cecelia Brooke."

"Oh, then there *must* be some mistake. This is Miss *Crooke* speaking."

Lanyard uttered a strangled "Sorry!" and hung up, abandoning further effort as hopeless.

That matter would have to stand over till morning.

Time now pressed: it was nearly eleven; he had a rendezvous with Destiny to keep at midnight, and meant to be more than punctual.

Walking to his apartment house, he proceeded to establish an alibi by entering through the public hallway and registering with the telephone attendant a call for seven o'clock the next morning.

In the course of the next half hour Lanyard let himself quietly out of the private door, slipped around the block and boarded a Riverside Drive bus.

Alighting at Ninety-third Street, he walked two blocks north on the Drive, turned east, and without misadventure admitted himself a second time to the Stanistreet garden.

XIV
DEFAMATION

It was hardly possible to watch Mr. Blensop functioning in his vocational capacity without reflecting on that cruel injustice which Nature only too often practises upon her offspring in secreting most praiseworthy qualities within fleshy envelopes of hopelessly frivolous cast.

The flowing gestures of this young man, his fluting accents, poetic eyes, and modestly ingratiating moustache, the preciosity of his taste in dress, assorted singularly with an austere devotion to duty rare if unaffected.

Beyond question, whether or not naturally a man of studious and conscientious temper, Mr. Blensop figured to admiration in the role of such an one.

Seated, the shaded lamplight an aureole for his fair young head, he wrought industriously with a beautiful gold-mounted fountain pen for fully five minutes after Lanyard had stolen into the draped recess of the French window, pausing only now and again to take a fresh sheet of paper or consult one of the sheaves of documents that lay before him.

At length, however, he hesitated with pen lifted and abstracted gaze focussed upon vacancy, shook a bewildered head, and rose, moving directly toward the windows.

For as long as thirty breathless seconds Lanyard remained in doubt; there was the barest chance that in his preoccupation Blensop might pass through to the garden without noticing that dark figure flattened against the inswung half of the window, in the dense shadow of the portiere. Otherwise the game was altogether up; Lanyard could see no way to avoid the necessity of staggering Blensop with a blow, racing for freedom, abandoning utterly further effort to learn the motive of "Karl's" impersonation of Duchemin.

He gathered himself together, waited poised in readiness for any eventuality-- and blessed his lucky stars to find his apprehensions idle.

Three paces from the windows, Mr. Blensop made it plain that he was after all not minded to stroll in the garden. Pausing, he swung a high-backed wing chair round to face the corner of the room, switched on a reading lamp, sat down and selected a volume of some work of reference from the well-stocked book shelves.

For several minutes, seated within arm's length of the trespasser, he studied intently, then with a cluck of satisfaction replaced the volume, extinguished the light, and went back to his writing.

But presently he checked with a vexed little exclamation, shook his pen impatiently, and fixed it with a frown of pained reproach.

But that did no good. The cussedness of the inanimate was strong in this pen: since its reservoir was quite empty it mulishly refused more service without refilling.

With a long-suffering sigh, Mr. Blensop found a filler in one of the desk drawers, and unscrewed the nib of the pen.

This accomplished, he paused, listened for a moment with head cocked intelligently to one side, dropped the dismembered implement, and got up alertly. At the same moment the door to the hallway opened, and two women entered, apparently sisters: one a lady of mature and distinguished charm, the other an equally prepossessing creature much her junior, the one strongly animated with intelligent interest in life, the other a listless prey to habitual ennui.

To these fluttered Mr. Blensop, offering to relieve them of their wraps.

"Permit me, Mrs. Arden," he addressed the elder woman, who tolerated him dispassionately. "And Mrs. Stanistreet ... I say, aren't you a bit late?"

"Frightfully," assented Mrs. Stanistreet in a weary voice. "It must be all of midnight."

"Hardly that, Adele," said Mrs. Arden with a humorous glance.

"Dinner, the play, supper, and home before twelve!" commented Blensop, shocked. "I say, that is going some, you know."

"George would insist on hurrying home," the young wife complained. "Frightfully tiresome. We were so comfy at the Ritz, too...."

"The Crystal Room?" Dissembled envy poisoned Blensop's accents.

"Frightfully interestin'--everybody was there. I did so want to dance--missed you, Arthur."

"I say, you didn't, did you, really?"

"Poor Mr. Blensop!" Mrs. Arden interjected with just a hint of malice. "What a pity you must be chained down by inexorable duty, while we fly round and amuse ourselves."

"I must not complain," Blensop stated with humility becoming in a dutiful martyr, a pose which he saw fit quickly to discard as another man came briskly into the room. "Ah, good evening, Colonel Stanistreet."

"Evening, Blensop."

With a brusque nod, Colonel Stanistreet went straightway to the desk, stopping there to take up and examine the work upon which his secretary had been engaged: a gentleman considerably older than his wife, of grave and sturdy cast, with the habit of standing solidly on his feet and giving undivided attention to the matter in hand.

"Anything of consequence turned up?" he enquired abstractedly, running through the sheets of pen-blackened paper.

"Three persons called," Blensop admitted discreetly. "One returns at midnight."

Stanistreet threw him a keen look. "Eh!" he said, making swift inference, and turned to his wife and sister-in-law. "It is nearly twelve now. Forgive me if I hurry you off."

"Patience," said Mrs. Arden indulgently. "Not for worlds would I hinder your weighty affairs, dear old thing, but I sleep more sound o' nights when I know my trinkets are locked up securely in your safe."

With a graceful gesture she unfastened a magnificent necklace and deposited it on the desk.

"Frightful rot," her sister commented from the doorway. "As if anybody would dare break in here."

"Why not?" Mrs. Arden enquired calmly, stripping her fingers of their rings.

"With a watchman patrolling the grounds all night--"

"Letty is sensible," Stanistreet interrupted. "Howson's faithful enough, and these American police dependable, but second-storey men happen in the best-guarded neighbourhoods. Be advised, Adele: leave your things here with Letty's."

"No fear," his wife returned coolly. "Too frightfully weird...."

She drifted across the threshold, then hesitated, a pretty figure of disdainful discontent.

"But really, Colonel Stanistreet is right," Blensop interposed vivaciously. "What do you imagine I heard to-night? The Lone Wolf is in America!"

"What is that you say?" Mrs. Arden demanded sharply.

"The Lone Wolf ... Fact. Have it on most excellent authority."

"The Lone Wolf!" Mrs. Stanistreet drawled. "If you ask me, I think the Lone Wolf nothing in the world but a scapegoat for police stupidity."

"You wouldn't say that," Mrs. Arden retorted, "if you had lived in Paris as long as I. There, in the dear old days, we paid that rogue too heavy a tax not to believe in him."

"Frightful nonsense," insisted the other. "I'm off. 'Night, Arthur. Shall you be long, George?"

"Oh, half an hour or so," her husband responded absently as she disappeared.

With a little gesture consigning her jewellery, heaped upon the desk, to the care of her brother-in-law, Mrs. Arden uttered good-nights and followed her sister.

Blensop bowed her out respectfully, shut the door and returned to the desk.

"What's this about the Lone Wolf?" Stanistreet enquired, sitting down to con the papers more intently.

"Oh!" Blensop laughed lightly. "I was merely repeating the blighter's own assertion. I mean to say, he boasted he was the Lone Wolf."

"Who boasted he was the Lone Wolf?"

"Chap who called to-night, giving the name of Duchemin--Andre Duchemin. Had French passports, and letters from the Home Office recommending him rather highly. Useful creature, one would fancy, with his knowledge of the right way to go about the wrong thing. What? Ought to be especially helpful to us in hunting down the Hun over here."

"Is this the man who returns at midnight?"

"Yes, sir. I thought it best to make the appointment."

"Why?"

"He said he had crossed on the *Assyrian*, said it significantly, you know. I fancied he might be the person you have been expecting."

Stanistreet looked up with a frown. "Hardly," he said--"if, that is, he is really what he claims to be. I wonder how he came by those letters."

"Does seem odd, doesn't it, sir? A confessed criminal!"

"An extraordinary man, by all accounts.... Those other callers--?"

"Nobody of importance, I should say. A man who gave his name as Ember and got a bit shirty when I asked his business. Told him you might consent to see him at nine in the morning."

"And the other?"

"A young woman--deuced pretty girl--also reticent. What was her name? Brooke--that was it: Cecelia Brooke."

"The devil!" Stanistreet exclaimed, dropping the papers. "What did you say to her?"

"What could I say, sir? She refused to divulge a word about her business with us. I told her--"

Warned by a gesture from Colonel Stanistreet, Blensop broke off. Walker was opening the door.

"Well, Walker?"

"A Mr. Duchemin, sir, says Mr. Blensop made an appointment with you for twelve to-night."

"Show him in, please."

The footman shut himself out. Blensop clutched nervously at Mrs. Arden's jewels.

"Hadn't I better put these in the safe first?"

"No--no time." Stanistreet opened a drawer of the desk--"Here!"--and closed it as Blensop hastily swept the jewellery into it. "Safe enough there--as long as he doesn't know, at all events. But don't forget to put them away after he goes."

"No, sir."

Again the door opened. Walker announced: "Mr. Duchemin." Stanistreet rose in his place. A man strode in with the assurance of one who has discounted a cordial welcome.

Through the gap which he had quietly created between the portiere and the side of the window, Lanyard stared hungrily, and for the second time that night damned heartily the inadequate light in the library.

The impostor's face, barely distinguishable in the up-thrown penumbra of the lampshade, wore a beard--a rather thick, dark beard of negligent abundance, after a mode popular among Frenchmen--above which his features were an indefinite blur.

Lanyard endeavoured with ill success to identify the fellow by his carriage; there was a perceptible suggestion of a military strut, but that is something hardly to be termed distinctive in these days. Otherwise, he was tall, quite as tall as Lanyard, and had much the same character of body, slender and lithe.

But he was "Karl" beyond question, confederate and murderer of Baron von Harden, the man who had thrown the light bomb to signal the U-boat, the brute with whom Lanyard had struggled on the boat deck of the *Assyrian*--though the latter, in the confusion of that struggle, had thought the German's beard a masking handkerchief of black silk.

Now by that same token he was no member of that smoking-room coterie upon which Lanyard's suspicions had centered.

On the other hand, any number of passengers had worn beards, not a few of much the same mode as that sported by this nonchalant fraud.

Vainly Lanyard cudgelled his wits to aid a laggard memory, haunted by a feeling that he ought to know this man instantly, even in so poor a light. Something in his habit, something in that insouciance which so narrowly escaped insolence, was at once strongly reminiscent and provokingly elusive....

Pausing a little ways within the room, the fellow clicked heels and bowed punctiliously in Continental fashion, from the hips.

"Colonel Stanistreet, I believe," he said in a sonorous voice--"Karl's" unmistakable voice--"chief of the American bureau of the British Secret Service?"

"I am Colonel Stanistreet," that gentleman admitted. "And you, sir--?"

"I have adopted the name of Andre Duchemin," the impostor stated. "With permission I retain it."

Colonel Stanistreet inclined his head slightly. "As you will. Pray be seated."

He dropped back into his chair, while "Karl" with a murmur of acknowledgment again took the armchair on the far side of the desk, where the lamp stood between him and the secret watcher.

"My secretary tells me you have letters of introduction...."

"Here." Calmly "Karl" produced and offered those purloined papers.

"You will smoke?" Stanistreet indicated a cigarette-box and leaned back to glance through the letters.

During a brief pause Blensop busied himself with collecting together the documents which had occupied him and began reassorting them, while "Karl," helping himself to a cigarette, smoked with manifest enjoyment.

"These seem to be in order," Stanistreet observed. "I note from this code letter that your true name is Michael Lanyard, you were once a professional French thief known as 'The Lone Wolf', but have since displayed every indication of desire to reform your ways, and have been of considerable use to the Intelligence Office. I am desired to employ your services in my discretion, contingent--pardon me--upon your continued good behaviour."

"Precisely," assented "Karl."

"Proceed, Monsieur Duchemin."

"It is an affair of some delicacy.... Do we speak alone, Colonel Stanistreet?"

"Mr. Blensop is my confidential secretary...."

"Oh, no objection. Still--if I may venture the suggestion--those windows open upon a garden, I take it?"

"Yes. Blensop, be good enough to close the windows."

"Certainly, sir."

Stepping delicately, Blensop moved toward the end of the room.

Again Lanyard was confronted with the alternatives of incontinent flight or attempting to remain undetected through the adoption of an expedient of the most desperate audacity. He had prepared against such contingency, he did not mean to go; but the feasibility of his contemplated manoeuvre depended entirely upon chance, its success in any event was forlornly problematic.

"Karl" remained hidden from him by the lamp, so he from "Karl." Colonel Stanistreet, facing his caller, sat half turned away from the windows. Everything rested with Blensop's choice, which of the two windows he would elect first to close.

A right-handed man, he turned, as Lanyard had foreseen, to the right, and momentarily disappeared in the recess of the farther window.

In the same instant Lanyard slipped noiselessly from behind the portiere, and dropped into that capacious wing chair which Blensop had thoughtfully placed for him some time since.

Thus seated, making himself as small and still as possible, he was wholly concealed from all other occupants of the library but Blensop; and even this last was little likely to discover him.

He did not. He closed and latched the farther window, then that wherein Lanyard had lurked, and ambled back into the room with never a glance toward that shadowed corner which held the wing chair.

And Lanyard drew a deep breath, if a quiet one. Behind him the conversation had continued without break. It was true, he could see nothing; but he could hear all that was said, he had missed no syllable, and now every second was informing him to his profit....

"Your secretary, no doubt, has told you I am a survivor of the *Assyrian* disaster."

"Yes...."

"You were, I believe, expecting a certain communication of extraordinary character by the *Assyrian*, to be brought, that is, by an agent of the British Secret Service."

After an almost imperceptible pause Stanistreet said evenly: "It is possible."

"A communication, in fact, of such character that it was impossible to entrust it to the mails or to cable transmission, even in code."

"And if so, sir...?"

"And you are aware that, of the two gentlemen entrusted with the care of this document, one was drowned when the *Assyrian* went down, and the other so seriously injured that he has not yet recovered consciousness, but was transferred directly from the pier to a hospital when the *Saratoga* docked."

"What then, Monsieur Duchemin?"

"Colonel Stanistreet," said the impostor deliberately, "I have that communication. I will ask you not to question me too closely as to how it came into my possession. I have it: that is sufficient."

"If you possess any document which you conceive to be so valuable to the British Government, monsieur, and consequently to the Allied cause, I have every confidence in your intention to deliver it to me without delay."

A note of mild derision crept into the accents of "Karl."

"I have every intention of so doing, my dear sir.... But you must appreciate I have incurred considerable personal danger, hardship, and inconvenience in taking good care of this document, in seeing that it did not fall into the wrong hands; in short, in bringing it safely here to you to-night."

A slightly longer pause prefaced Stanistreet's reply, something which he delivered in measured tones: "I am able to promise you the British Government will show due appreciation of your disinterested services, Monsieur--Duchemin."

"Not disinterested--not that!" the cheat protested. "Gentlemen of my kidney, sir, seldom put themselves out except in lively anticipation of favours to come."

"Be good enough to make yourself more clear."

"Cheerfully. I possess this document. I understand its character is such that Germany would pay a round price for it. But I am a good patriot. In spite of the fact that nobody knew I possessed it, in spite of the fact that I need only have quietly taken it to Seventy-ninth Street to-night--"

"Monsieur Duchemin!" Stanistreet's voice was icy. "Your price?"

"Sorry you feel that way about it," said "Karl" with ill-concealed insincerity. "You must know thieving is no more what it once was. Even I, too, often am put to it to make both ends--"

"If you please, sir--how much?"

"Ten thousand dollars."

Silence greeted this demand, a lull that to Lanyard seemed endless. For in his fury he was trembling so that he feared lest his agitation betray him. The very walls before his eyes seemed to quake in sympathy. He was aware of the ache of swollen veins in his temples, his teeth hurt with the pressure put upon them, his breath came heavily, and his nails were digging painfully into his palms.

"Blensop?"

"Sir?"

"How much have we on hand, in the emergency fund?"

"Between ten and twelve thousand dollars, sir."

"Intuition, monsieur, is an indispensable item in the equipment of a successful *chevalier d'Industrie*. So, at least, the good novelists tell us...."

"Open the safe, Blensop, and fetch me ten thousand dollars."

"Very good, sir."

"I presume you won't object to satisfying me that you really have this document, before I pay you your price."

"It is this which makes it a pleasure to deal with an Englishman, monsieur: one may safely trust his word of honour."

"Indeed...."

"Permit me: here is the document. Use that magnifying glass I see by your elbow, monsieur; take your time, satisfy yourself."

"Thanks; I mean to."

Another break in the dialogue, during which the eavesdropper heard an odd sound, a sort of muffled swishing ending in a slight thud, then the peculiar metallic whine of a combination dial rapidly manipulated, finally the dull clank of bolts falling back into their sockets.

"Your *coffre-fort*--what do you say?--strong-box--safe--is cleverly concealed, Colonel Stanistreet."

There was no direct reply, but after a moment Stanistreet announced quietly: "This seems to be an authentic paper.... Monsieur Duchemin, what knowledge precisely have you of the nature of this document?"

"Surely monsieur cannot have overlooked the circumstance that its seals were intact."

"True," Stanistreet admitted. "Still...."

"I trust Monsieur does not question my good faith?"

"Why not?" Stanistreet enquired drily.

"Monsieur!"

"Oh, damn your play-acting, sir! If you can be capable of one infamy, you are capable of more. None the less, you are right about an Englishman's word: here is your money. Count it and--get out!"

"Thanks"--the impostor's tone was an impertinently exact imitation of Stanistreet's--"I mean to."

"Permit me to excuse myself," Stanistreet added; and Lanyard heard the muffled scrape of chair-legs on the rug as the Englishman got up.

"Gladly," the spy returned--"and ten thousand thanks, monsieur!"

The secretary intoned melodiously: "This way, Monsieur Duchemin, if you please."

"Pardon. Is it material which way I leave?"

"What do you mean?" Stanistreet demanded.

"I should be far easier in my mind if monsieur would permit me to go by way of his garden, rather than run the risk of his front door."

"What's this?"

"In these little affairs, monsieur, I try to make it a rule to avoid covering the same ground twice."

"You have the insolence to imply I would lend myself to treachery!"

"I beg monsieur's pardon very truly for suggesting such a thing. Nevertheless, one cannot well be overcautious when one is a hunted man."

"Blensop ... be good enough to see this man out through the garden."

"Yes, sir."

"Again, monsieur, my thanks."

"Good-night," said Stanistreet curtly.

Blensop passed Lanyard's chair, unlatched and opened the window and stood aside. An instant later "Karl" joined him, swung on a heel, facing back, clicked heels again and bowed mockingly. Apparently he got no response, for he laughed quietly, then turned and went out through the window, Blensop mincing after.

With a struggle Lanyard mastered the temptation to dash after the spy, overtake and overpower him, expose and give him up to justice. Only the knowledge that by remaining quiescent, by biding his time, he might be enabled to redeem his word to the Brooke girl, gave him strength to be still.

But he suffered exquisitely, maddened by the defamation imposed upon his nick-name of a thief by this brazen impostor.

Nor was wounded *amour-propre* mended by an exclamation in the room behind his chair, the accents of Colonel Stanistreet thick with contempt:

"The Lone Wolf! Faugh!"

XV
RECOGNITION

Presently Blensop came back, closed the window, and passed blindly by Lanyard, his reappearance saluted by Stanistreet in tones that shook with contained temper.

"You saw that animal outside the walls?"

Mildly injured surprise was indicated in the reply: "Surely, sir!"

"And locked the door after him?"

"Yes, sir--securely."

"Howson anywhere about?"

"I didn't see him. Daresay he's prowling somewhere within call. Do you wish to speak to him?"

"No.... But you might, if you see anything of him, tell him to keep an extra eye open to-night. I don't trust this self-styled Lone Wolf."

"Naturally not, sir, under the circumstances."

Stanistreet acknowledged this with an irritated snort. "No matter," he thought aloud; "if it has cost us a pretty penny, we have got this safe in hand at last. I've not had too much sleep, I can promise you, since the report came through of Bartholomew's death and Thackeray's disablement. Nor am I satisfied that this Monsieur Duchemin came by the document fairly--confound his impudence! If he hadn't put me on honour, tacitly, I'd not hesitate an instant about informing the police."

"Rather chancy course to take in this business, what?"

"I don't know.... That Yankee invention known as the 'frame-up' would easily make America too small for the Lone Wolf without the British Secret Service ever being mentioned in the matter."

"Yes; but suppose the beast knows the contents of this paper, suspects the authorship of the 'frame-up'--as he instinctively would--and blabs? Messages have been unsealed and copied and resealed before this."

"That one consideration ties my hands.... Here, my boy: take this and put it in the safe--and don't forget Mrs. Arden's things, of course. Good-night."

"Trust me, sir. Good-night."

A door closed with a slight jar, and for half a minute the room was so positively quiet that Lanyard was beginning to wonder if Blensop himself had gone out with his employer, when he heard a low and musical chuckle, followed by a soft clashing as the secretary scooped Mrs. Arden's jewellery out of the desk drawer.

Itching with curiosity, Lanyard turned with infinite care and peered round the wing of the chair, thus gaining a view of the wall farthest from the street.

Blensop remaining invisible, Lanyard's interest centred immediately upon the safe the ingenuity of whose concealment had excited "Karl's" favourable comment, and with much excuse.

One of the portraits--that upon whose merits Blensop had descanted to "Karl" earlier in the night--was, Lanyard saw, so mounted upon a solid panel of wood that, by means of hidden mechanism, it could be moved sidelong from its frame, uncovering the face of a safe built into the wall.

This last now stood open, its door, swung out toward Lanyard, showing a simple arrangement of dials and locks with which he was on terms of contemptuous familiarity; only the veriest tyro of a cracksman would want more than a good ear and a subtle sense of touch in order to open it without knowledge of the combination.

With all its reputation for efficiency and astuteness the British Secret Service entrusted its mysteries to an antiquated contraption such as this!

Humming a blithe little air, Blensop moved into Lanyard's field of vision and stopped between him and the safe, deftly pigeonholing therein the docketed papers and Mrs. Arden's jewels. Then, closing the door, he shot its bolts, gave the dial a brisk twirl, located a lever in the side of the frame and thrust it into its socket.

With the same swish and thud which had puzzled Lanyard at first hearing, the portrait slipped back into place.

Rounding on a heel, Blensop paused, head to one side, a slight frown shadowing his bland countenance, and stood briefly rooted in some perplexity of obscure origin. Twice he shook a peevish head, then smiled radiantly and brought his hands together in an audible clap.

"I have it!" he cried in delight and, dancing briskly toward the desk, once more disappeared.

Now what was this which Mr. Blensop so spontaneously had, and from the having of which he derived so much apparently innocent enjoyment? Wanting an answer, Lanyard settled back in disgust, then sat sharply forward, gaze riveted to the near sash of the adjacent window.

In showing "Karl" out, Blensop had moved the portieres, exposing more glass than previously had been visible. Now this mirrored darkly to the adventurer a somewhat distorted vision of Blensop standing over the desk, seemingly employed in no more amusing occupation than filling his fountain-pen. But undoubtedly he was in the highest spirits; for the lilt of his humming rose sweet and clear and ever louder.

To this accompaniment he pocketed his pen, two-stepped to the windows, drew the portieres jealously close, returned to the desk, switched off the reading lamp, and left the room completely dark but for a dim glow from the ash-filmed embers of the fire.

But before he went out the secretary interrupted his humming to laugh with a mischievous elan which completely confounded Lanyard. He was not unacquainted with the Blensop type, but the secret glee which seemed to animate this specimen was something far beyond his comprehension.

As the door softly closed Lanyard moved silently across the room and bent an ear to its panels, meanwhile drawing over his hands a pair of thin white kid gloves.

From beyond came no sound other than a faint creaking of stair-treads quickly silenced.

Opening the door, Lanyard peered out, finding the hallway deserted and dimly lighted by a single bulb of little candle-power at its far end, then scouted out as far as the foot of the stairs, listened there for a little, hearing no sounds above, and reconnoitred through the other living rooms, at length returning to the library persuaded he was alone on the ground floor of the house.

A Yale lock was fixed to the library side of the door. Lanyard released its catch, insuring freedom from interruption on the part of anybody who lacked the key, crossed to the other side door, left this on the latch and, having thus provided an avenue for escape, turned attention to business, in brief, to the safe.

Turning on the picture-light he found and operated the lever, with his other hand so restraining the action of the panel that it moved aside without perceptible jar.

Then with an ear to that smooth, cold face of enamelled steel, he began to manipulate the combination. From within the door a succession of soft clicks and knocks punctuated the muted whine of the dial, speaking a language only too intelligible to the trained hearing of a thief; synchronous breaks and resistance in the action of the dial conveyed additional information through the medium of supersensitive finger tips. Within two minutes he had learned all he needed to know, and standing back twirled the knob right and left with a confident hand. At its fourth stop he heard the dull bump of released tumblers, grasped the handle, and twisted it strongly. The door swung open.

Systematically Lanyard searched the pigeonholes, emptying all but one, examining minutely their contents without finding that slender roll of paper.

Mystified, he hesitated. The thing, of course, was somewhere there, only hidden more cunningly than he had hoped. It was possible, even probable, that Blensop had stowed the cylinder away in a secret compartment.

But the interior arrangement was disconcertingly simple. Lanyard saw no sign of waste space in which such a drawer might be secreted. Unless, to be sure, one of the pigeonholes had a false back....

He began a fresh examination, again emptying each pigeonhole and sounding its rear wall without result till there remained only that in which Blensop had placed the Arden jewels.

It was necessary to move these, but Lanyard long withheld his hand, reluctant to touch them, for that same reason which had influenced him to avoid them in his first search.

Jewels such as these he both worshipped and desired with the passionate adoration of connoisseur and lover in one. He feared violently the temptation of physical contact with such stuff.

For his was no thief's errand to-night, but a matter, as he conceived it, of his private honour, something apart and distinct from the code of rogue's ethics which guided his professional activities. He had pledged his word to Cecelia Brooke to keep safe for her that cylinder of paper, to return it upon her demand for whatsoever disposition she might choose to make of it. It was no concern of his what that choice might turn out to be, any more than it was his affair if the document were a paper of international importance. But she must and should, if act of his could compass it, be given opportunity to redeem her word of honour if, as one believed, that likewise were involved in the fate of the document.

He had stolen into this house like a thief because he had given his pledge and perforce had been made false to that pledge, because he had been despoiled of the concrete evidence of the trust reposed unasked in him, and because he had learned that his spoiler was to meet Stanistreet in this room at midnight.

He was here solely to make good his word, to take away that cylinder, could he find it, and to return it to the girl ... not to thieve....

Never that!...

Slowly, reluctantly, inevitably he put forth his hand and selected from among those brilliant symbols of his soul's profound damnation the necklace, a rope of diamonds consummately matched, a rivulet of frozen fire, no single stone less lovely than another.

"Admirable!" he whispered. "Oh, admirable!"

Hesitant to do this thing which to him, by the strange standard of his warped code, spelled dishonour, he would and he would not; and while he paltered, was visited by an oddly vivid memory of the clear and candid eyes of Cecelia Brooke, seemed veritably to see them searching his own with their look of grieving wonder ... the eyes of one woman who had reckoned him worthy of her trust....

Almost he won victory in this fight he was foredoomed to lose. Under the level and steadfast regard of those eyes his hand went out to replace the necklace, moved unsteadily, faltered....

Beyond the windows an incautious footfall sounded. In the darkness out there someone blundered into a piece of wicker furniture and disturbed it with a small scraping sound, all but inaudible, but to the thief as loud as the blast of a police whistle.

Instantly and instinctively, in two simultaneous gestures, Lanyard dropped the necklace into an inner pocket of his coat and switched off the picture-light.

With hands now as steady and sure as they had been vacillant a moment since, he closed the safe door noiselessly, shot its bolts, and was yards away, crouching behind an armchair, before the man outside had ceased to fumble with the window fastenings.

If this were the watchman Howson, doubtless he would be satisfied with finding the room dark and apparently untenanted, and would go off upon his rounds unsuspecting. If he did not, or if he noticed the displaced panel, then would come Lanyard's time to break cover and run for it.

With a faint creak one of the windows swung inward. Curtain-rings clashed dully on their poles. Someone came through the portieres and paused, pulling them together behind him. The beam of an electric flash-lamp lanced the gloom and its spotlight danced erratically round the walls.

Now there was no more thought of flight in Lanyard's humour, but rather a firm determination to stand his ground. This was no night watchman, but a house-breaker, one with no more title to trespass upon those premises than himself; and at that an unskilled hand at such work, the rawest of amateurs practising methods as clumsy and childish as any actor playing at burglary on a stage before a simple-minded audience.

The noise he made on entering alone proved that, then this fatuous business with the flash-lamp. And as he moved inward from the windows it became evident that he had not even had the wit to close the portieres completely; a violet glimmer of starlight shone in through a deep triangular gap between them at the top.

For all that, the intruder seemed to know what he wanted and where to seek it, betrayed a nice acquaintance with the room, proceeding directly to the safe picked out by his lamp.

Arrived beneath it he uttered a low sound which might have been interpreted as surprise due to finding the panel already out of place. If so, surprise evidently roused in him no suspicion that all might not be well. On the contrary, he quite calmly located and turned the switch controlling the picture-light.

Immediately, as its rays gushed down and disclosed the man, Lanyard rose boldly from his place in hiding. Now there was no more need for concealment; now was his enemy delivered into his hands.

The man was "Karl."

His back to Lanyard, unconscious of that one's catlike approach, the spy put up his flash-lamp, searched in a waistcoat pocket and produced a slip of paper, and bent his face close to the combination dial, studying its figures; but abruptly, like a startled animal, whirled round to face the windows.

One of the sashes was thrown back roughly, and a figure clad in the gray livery of a private watchman parted the portieres and entered the library.

"Everything all right in here, Mr. Blensop?"

Lanyard saw the sheen of blue steel in the hands of "Karl," and leaped too late: even as he fell upon the spy's shoulders, the pistol exploded.

The watchman reeled back with a choking cry, caught wildly at the portieres, and dragged them down with him as he fell.

His screams of agony made hideous the night. And the second cry was no more than uttered when Lanyard, even in the heat of his struggle, heard sounds indicating that already the household was alarmed.

But the door would hold for a while; it was not probable that the first to come downstairs would think to bring with him the key. Time enough to think of escape when Lanyard had settled his score with this one: no light undertaking; not only was the score a long one, longer than Lanyard then dreamed, but, as he had learned to his cost, the man was an antagonist of skill and strength not to be despised.

Nevertheless, aided by the surprise of his onslaught, Lanyard succeeded in disarming the spy, forcing him to drop the pistol at the outset, and through attacking from behind had him at a further disadvantage. For all that he found his hands full till, by a trick of jiu-jitsu, he wrenched one of the fellow's arms behind him so roughly as almost to dislocate it at the shoulder and, forcing the forearm up toward his shoulder blades, held him temporarily helpless.

"Be still, you murderous canaille!" he growled--"or must I tear your arm from its socket? Still, I say!"

"Karl" uttered a grunt of pain and ceased to struggle.

Pinning him against the bookcase, Lanyard hastily rifled his pockets, at the first dip bringing forth a thin sheaf of American bank-notes with the figures $1000 conspicuous on the uppermost.

"Ten thousand dollars," he said grimly--"precisely my fee for the use of my name--to say nothing of its abuse!"

A torrent of untranslatable German blasphemy answered him. Intelligible was the half-frantic demand: "Who the devil are you?"

"Take a look, assassin--see for yourself!" Lanyard twisted the spy around to face him, holding him helpless against the wall with a knee in his middle and a hand gripping his throat inexorably. "Do you know me now--the man you thought you'd drowned a hundred fathoms deep?"

Blows thundered on the hallway door. Neither heeded. The spy was staring into Lanyard's face, his eyes starting with horror and affright.

"Lanyard!" he gasped. "Good God! will you never die?"

"Never by your hand--" Lanyard began, but stopped sharply.

For a moment he glared incredulously, and in that moment knew his enemy.

"Ekstrom!" he cried; and the man at his mercy winced and quailed.

The din in the hallway grew louder. Voices cried out for the key. Somebody threw himself against the door so heavily that it shook.

The emergency forced itself upon Lanyard's consciousness, would not be denied. Its dilemma seemed calculated to unseat his reason. If he lingered, he was lost. Either he must grant this creature new lease of life, or be caught and pay the penalty of murder for an execution as surely just as any in the history of mankind.

It was bitter, too bitter to have come to this his hour so long desired, so long deferred, so arduously sought, and have the fruits of it snatched from his craving grasp.

He could not bring himself to this renunciation; slowly his fingers tightened on the other's throat.

Driven to desperation by the light of madness that began to flicker in Lanyard's eyes, the Prussian abruptly put all he had of might and fury into one final effort, threw Lanyard off, and in turn attacked him, fighting like a lunatic for footroom, for space enough to turn and make for the windows.

In spite of all he could do Lanyard saw the man work away from the wall and manoeuvre his back toward the windows; then he flew at him with redoubled fury, driving home blow after blow that beat down Ekstrom's guard and sent him staggering helplessly, till an uppercut, swinging in under his uplifted forearms, put an end to the combat. Ekstrom shot backward half a dozen feet, stumbled over the prostrate body of the watchman, and crashed headlong into the windows, going down in a shower of shattered glass.

In one and the same instant Lanyard darted back and dropped upon his knees in the shadow of the club lounge, and the door to the hallway slammed open. A knot of men, to the number of half a dozen, tumbling into the library, saw that figure floundering amid the ruins of the window, and made for it, passing on the other side of the lounge, between it and the fireplace.

Unseen, Lanyard rose, ran crouching across the room; found the side door, opened it just far enough to permit the passage of his body, and drew it to behind him.

Ninety-fifth Street was a lonely lane of midnight quiet. He sped across it like the shadow of a cloud wind-hunted.

XVI
AU PRINTEMPS

In those days New York nights were long; this was still young when Lanyard sauntered sedately from a side street and stopped on a corner of Broadway in the Nineties; he had not long to wait ere a southbound taxicab hove in sight and sheered over to the curb in answer to his signal.

It was still something short of one o'clock when he was set down at his door.

Wearily he let himself in by the private entrance, made a light, and without troubling even to discard his overcoat threw himself into a chair. Leaden depression weighed down his heart, and the flavour of failure was as aloes in his mouth. Thrice within an hour he had fallen short of his promises, to Cecelia Brooke, to himself, to his *idee fixe*. His three chances, to redeem his word to the girl, to measure up to his queer criterion of honour, to rid his world of Ekstrom, all had slipped through fingers seemingly too infirm to profit by them.

He felt of a sudden old; old, and tired, and lonely.

The uses of his world, how weary, stale, flat, and unprofitable! What was his life? An emptiness. Himself? A shuttlecock, the helpless sport of his own failings, a vain thing alternately strutting and stumbling, now swaggering in the guise of an avenger self-appointed, now sneaking in the shameful habiliments of a felon self-condemned.

What had prevented his dealing out to Ekstrom the punishment he had so well earned? That insatiable lust for loot of his. But for that damning evidence against him of the stolen necklace in his pocket he might have had his will of Ekstrom, and justified himself when discovered by proving that he had merely done justice to a thief who sold what he had stolen and stole back to steal again what he had sold.

Self-contempt attacked self-conceit like an acid. He saw Michael Lanyard a sorry figure, sitting stultified with self-pity ... crying over spilt milk....

Impatiently he shook himself. What though he had to-night forfeited his chances? He could, nay, would, make others. He must....

To what end? Would life be sweeter if one found a way to restore to Cecelia Brooke her precious document and to smuggle back to Mrs. Arden her pilfered diamonds? Would this deadly ache of loneliness be less poignant with Ekstrom dead?

With lack-lustre eyes he looked round that cheerless room, reckoning its perfunctory pretense of comfort the forlornest mockery. To lodgings such as this he was condemned for life, to an interminable sequence of transient quarters, sordid or splendid, rich or mean, alike in this common quality of hollow loneliness....

His aimless gaze wandered toward the door opening on the public hallway, and became fixed upon a triangular shape of white paper, the half of an envelope tucked between door and sill.

Presently he rose and got the thing, not until he touched it quite persuaded he was not the victim of an optical hallucination.

A square envelope of creamy paper, it was superscribed simply in a hand strange to him, ***Anthony Ember, Esq.***, with the address of his apartment house.

Tearing the envelope he found within a double sheet of plain notepaper bearing a message of five words penned hastily:

"***Au Printemps*--
"***one o'clock*--   "***Please*!"

Nothing else, not another word or pen-scratch....

Opening the door Lanyard hailed the hall-attendant, a sleepy and not over-intelligent negro.

"When did this come for me?"

"'Bout anour ago, Mistuh Embuh."

"Who brought it?"

"A messenger boy done fotch it, suh--look lak th' same boy."

"What same boy?"

"Same as come in when you do, 'bout 'leven o'clock--remembuh?"

Lanyard nodded, recalling that on his way up the street from Sixth Avenue he had been subconsciously irritated by the shrill, untuneful whistling of a lout-ish youth in Western Union uniform, who had followed him into the house and become engaged in some minor altercation with the attendants while Lanyard was unlocking the door to his apartment.

"What of him?"

"Why, he bulge in heah an' say we done send a call, an' we tell him we don' know nuffin' 'bout no call, an' he sweah an' carry on, an' aftuh you done gone in he ast whut is yo' name, an' somebody tell him an' he go away. An' then 'bout haf-fanour aftuhwuds he come back with that theah lettuh--say to stick it undeh yo' do, ef yo' ain't home. Leastways he look to me lak th' same boy. Ah dunno fo' suah."

Repeated efforts failing to extract more enlightenment from this source, Lan-yard again shut himself in with the puzzle.

Somebody had set a messenger boy to dog him and find out his name and ad-dress. Not Crane: Lanyard had seen that one disappear in the elevator of the Knick-erbocker and had thereafter moved too quickly to permit of Crane's returning to the lobby, calling a messenger boy, and pointing out Lanyard.

For that matter, Lanyard was prepared to swear nobody had followed him from the Knickerbocker to the Biltmore.

Vaguely he seemed to recall a first impression of the boy at the time when he emerged from the drug store after his unprofitable effort to telephone Cecelia Brooke, an indefinite memory of a shambling figure with nose flattened against the druggist's window, apparently fascinated by the display of a catch-penny corn cure.

Was there a link between that circumstance and the long delay which Lanyard had suffered in the telephone booth? Had the Knickerbocker operator been less stupid and negligent than she seemed? Was the truth of the matter that Crane had surmised Lanyard would attempt communication with the Brooke girl and had set a watch on the switchboard for the call?

Assuming that the Secret Service man had been clever enough for that, it was not difficult to understand that Lanyard had purposely been kept dangling at the other end of the wire till the call could be traced back to its source and a messenger despatched from the nearest Western Union office with instructions to follow the man who left the booth, and report his name and local habitation.

Sharp work, if these inferences were reasonable. And, satisfied that they were, Lanyard inclined to accord increased respect to the detective abilities of the American.

But this note, this hurried, unsigned scrawl of five unintelligible words: what the deuce did it mean?

On the evidence of the handwriting a woman had penned it. Cecelia Brooke? Who else? Crane might well have been taken into her confidence, subsequent to the sinking of the *Assyrian*, and on discovering that Lanyard had survived have used this means of relieving the girl's distress of mind.

But its significance?... "Au Printemps" translated literally meant "in the springtime," and "in the springtime at one o'clock" was mere gibberish, incomprehensible. There is in Paris a department store calling itself "Au Printemps"; but surely no one was suggesting to Lanyard in New York a rendezvous in Paris!

Nevertheless that "Please!" intrigued with a note at once pleading and imperative which decided Lanyard to answer it without delay, in person.

"Au Printemps--one o'clock--please!"

Upon the screen of memory there flashed a blurred vision of an electric sign emblazoning the phrase, "Au Printemps," against the facade of a building with windows all blind and dark save those of the street level, which glowed pink with light filtered through silken hangings; a building which Lanyard had already passed thrice that night without, in the preoccupation of his purpose, paying it any heed; a building on Broadway somewhere above Columbus Circle, if he were not mistaken.

Already it was one o'clock. Fortunately he was still in evening dress, and needed only to change collar and tie to repair the disarray caused by his encounter with Ekstrom.

In two minutes he was once more in the street.

Within five a cab deposited him in front of the Restaurant Au Printemps, an institution of midnight New York whose title for distinction resided mainly in the fact that it opened its upper floors for the diversion of "members" about the time when others put up their shutters.

Lanyard's advent occurred at the height of its traffic. The dining rooms on the street level were closed and unlighted: but men and women in pairs and parties were streaming across the sidewalk from an endless chain of motor-cars and being ground through the revolving doors like grist in the hopper of an unhallowed mill, the men all in evening dress, the women in garments whose insolence outrivalled the most Byzantine nights of L'Abbaye Theleme.

Drawn in with the current through the turnstile door, Lanyard found himself in an absurdly little lobby thronged to suffocation, largely with people of the half-world--here and there a few celebrities, here and there small tight clusters of respectabilities making a brave show of feeling at ease--all waiting their turn to be lifted to delectable regions aloft in an elevator barely big enough to serve in a private residence.

For a moment Lanyard lingered unnoticed on the outskirts of this assemblage, searching its pretty faces for the prettier face he had come to find and wondering that she should have chosen for her purpose with him a resort of this character. His memory of her was sweet with the clean smell of the sea; there was incongruity to spare in this atmosphere heady with the odours of wine, flesh, scent, and tobacco. Perplexing....

A harpy with a painted leer and predacious eyes pounced upon him, tore away his hat and coat, gave him a numbered slip of pasteboard by presenting which he would be permitted to ransom his property on extortionate terms.

And still he saw no Cecelia Brooke, though his aloof attitude coupled with an intent but impersonal inspection of every feminine face within his radius of vision earned him more than one smile at once furtively provocative and unwelcome.

By degrees the crowd emptied itself into the toy elevator--such of it, that is, as was passed by a committee on membership consisting of one chubby, bearded gentleman with the look of a French diplomatist, the empressement of a head waiter and the authority of the Angel with the Flaming Sword. ***Personae non gratae*** to the management--inexplicably so in most instances--were civilly requested to produce membership cards and, upon failure to comply, were inexorably rejected, and departed strangely shamefaced. Others of acceptable aspect were permitted to mingle with the upper circles of the elect without being required to prove their "membership."

In the person of this suave but inflexible arbiter Lanyard identified a former maitre d'hotel of the Carlton who had abruptly and discreetly fled London soon after the outbreak of war.

He fancied that this one knew him and was sedulous both to keep him in the corner of his eye and never to meet his regard directly.

And once he saw the man speak covertly with the elevator attendant, guarding his lips with a hand, and suspected that he was the subject of their communication.

The lobby was still comfortably filled, a constant trickle of arrivals replacing in measure the losses by election and rejection, when Lanyard, watching the revolving doors, saw Cecelia Brooke coming in.

She was alone, at least momentarily; and in his sight very creditably turned out, remembering that all her luggage must have been lost with the *Assyrian*. But what Englishwoman of her caste ever permitted herself to be visible after nightfall except in an evening gown of some sort, even though a shabby sort? Not that Miss Brooke to-night was shabbily attired: she was much otherwise; from some mysterious source of wardrobe she had conjured wraps, furs, and a dancing frock as fresh and becoming as it was, oddly enough, not immodest. And with whatever cares preying upon her secret mind, she entered with the light step and bright countenance of any girl of her age embarked upon a lark.

All that was changed at sight of Lanyard.

He bowed formally at a moment when her glance, resting on him, seemed about to wander on; instead it became fixed in recognition. Instantly her smile was erased, her features stiffened, her eyes widened, her lips parted, the colour ebbed from her cheeks. And she stopped quite still in front of the door till lightly jostled by other arrivals.

Then moving uncertainly toward him, she said, "Monsieur Duchemin!" not loudly, for she was not a woman to give excuse for a scene under any circumstances, but in a tone of complete dumbfounderment.

Covering his own dashed contenance with a semblance of unruffled amiability, he bowed again, now over the hand which the girl tentatively offered, letting it rest lightly on his fingers, touching it as lightly with his lips.

"It is such a pleasant surprise," he said at a venture, then added guardedly: "But my name--I thought you knew it was now Anthony Ember."

Her eyes were blank. "I don't understand," she faltered. "I thought you ... I never dreamed.... Is it really you?"

"Truly," he averred, lips smiling but mind rife with suspicion and distrust.

This was not acting; he was convinced that her surprise was absolutely unfeigned.

So she had not expected to find him "Au Printemps" at one o'clock in the morning, till that very moment had believed him as dead as any of those poor souls who had perished with the *Assyrian*!

Therefore that note had not come from her, therefore Lanyard had complimented Crane without warrant, crediting him with another's cleverness. Then whose...?

And while Lanyard's head buzzed with these thoughts, an independent chamber of his mind was engaged in admiring the address with which the girl was recovering from what must have been, what plainly had been, a staggering shock. Already she had begun to grapple with the situation, to take herself in hand and dissemble; already her face was regaining its accustomed cast of self-confidence, composure, and intelligent animation. Throughout she pursued without a break the thread of conventional small talk.

"It is a surprise," she said calmly. "Really, you are a most astonishing person, Mr. Ember. One never knows where to look for you."

"That is my good fortune, since it provides me with unexpected pleasures such as this. You are with friends?"

"With a friend," she corrected quietly--"with Mr. Crane. He stopped outside to pay our taxi-driver. How odd it seems to find any place in the world as much alive as this New York!"

"It seems almost impossible," Lanyard averred--"indeed, somehow wrong. I've a feeling one has no right to encourage so much frivolity. And yet...."

"Yes," she responded quickly. "It is good to hear people laugh once more. That is why Mr. Crane suggested coming here to-night, to cheer me up. He said Au Printemps was unique, promised I'd find it most amusing."

"I'm sure...." Lanyard began as Crane entered, breezing through the turnstile and comprehending the situation in a glance.

"Hello!" he cried. "Didn't I tell you everybody alive would be here?"

Nor was Cecelia Brooke less ready. "But fancy meeting Mr. Ember here! I had no idea he was in New York--had you?"

"Perhaps a dim suspicion," Crane admitted with a twinkle, taking Lanyard's hand. "Howdy, Ember? Glad to see you, gladder'n you'd think."

"How is that?" Lanyard asked, returning the cordiality of his grasp.

Crane's penetrating accents must have been audible in the remotest corner of the ground-floor rooms: he made no effort to modulate them to a quieter pitch.

"You can help me out of a fix if you feel like it. You see, I promised Miss Brooke if she'd take me for her guide, she'd see life to-night; and now, just when we're going good, I've got to renig. Man I know held me up outside, says I'm wanted down town on special business and must go. I might be able to toddle back later, but can't bank on it. Do you mind taking over my job?"

"Chaperoning Miss Brooke's investigations into the seamy side of current social history? That will be delightful."

"Attaboy! If I'm not back in half an hour you'll see her safely home, of course?"

"Trust me."

"And you'll excuse me, Miss Brooke? I hope you don't think--"

"What I do think, Mr. Crane, is that you have been most kind to a lonely stranger. Of course I'll excuse you, not willingly, but understanding you must go."

"That makes me a heap easier in my mind. But I' got to run. So it's good-night, unless maybe I see you later. So long, Ember!"

With a flirt of a raw-boned hand, Crane swung about, threw himself spiritedly into the revolving door, was gone.

"Amazing creature," Lanyard commented, laughing.

"I think him delightful," the girl replied, surrendering her wraps to a maid. "If all Americans are like that--"

"Shall we go up?"

She nodded--"Please!"--and turned with him.

The committee on membership himself bowed them into the elevator. Several others crowded in after them. For thirty seconds, while the car moved slowly upward, Lanyard was free to think without interruption.

But what to think now? That Crane, actuated by some motive occult to Lanyard, had engineered this apparently adventitious ***rencontre*** for the purpose of throwing him and the Brooke girl together? Or, again, that Crane was innocent of guile in this matter--that other persons unknown, causing Lanyard to be traced to his lodgings, had framed that note to entice him to this place to-night? In the latter event, who was conceivably responsible but Velasco, Dressier, O'Reilly--any one of these, or all three working in concert? The last-named had looked Lanyard squarely in the face without sign of recognition, back there in the lobby of the Knickerbocker, precisely as he should, if implicated in the conspiracies of the Boche; though it might easily have been Velasco or Dressier who had recognized the adventurer without his knowledge....

The car stopped, a narrow-chested door slid open, a gush of hectic light coloured morbidly the faces of alighting passengers, a blare of syncopated noise singularly unmusical saluted the astonished ears of Lanyard and Cecelia Brooke. She met his gaze with a smiling *moue* and slightly lifted eyebrows.

"More than we bargained for?" he laughed. "But there is always something new in this America, I promise you. Au Printemps itself is new, at all events did not exist when I was last in New York."

Following her out, he paused beside the girl in a constricted space hedged about with tables, waiting for the maitre d'hotel to seat those who had been first to leave the elevator.

The room, of irregular conformation, held upward of two hundred guests and habitues seated at tables large and small and so closely set together that waiters with difficulty navigated narrow and tortuous channels of communication. In the middle, upon a small dancing floor, rudely octagonal in shape, made smaller by tables crowded round its edge to accommodate the crush, a mob of couples danced arduously, close-locked in one another's arms, swaying in rhythm with the over-emphasized time beaten out by a perspiring little band of musicians on a dais in a far corner, their activities directed by an antic conductor whose lantern-jawed, sallow face peered grotesquely out through a mop of hair as black and coarse and lush as a horse's mane.

Execrable ventilation or absence thereof manufactured an atmosphere that reeked with heat animal and artificial and with ill-blended effluvia from a hundred sources. Perhaps the odour of alcohol predominated; Lanyard thought of a steam-heated wine-cellar. He observed nothing but champagne in any glass, and if food were being served it was done surreptitiously. Sweat dripped from the faces of the dancers, deep flushes discoloured all not so heavily enamelled as to preserve an inalterable complexion, the eyes of many stared with the fixity of hypnosis. Yet when the music ended with an unexpected crash of discord these dancers applauded insatiably till the jaded orchestra struck up once more, when they renewed their curious gyrations with quenchless abandon.

The Brooke girl caught Lanyard's eye, her lips moved. Thanks to the din, he had to bend his head near to hear.

She murmured with infinite expression: "Au Printemps!"

The maitre d'hotel was plucking at his sleeve.

"Monsieur had made reservations, no?" Startled recognition washed the man's tired and pasty countenance. "Pardon, monsieur: this way!" He turned and began to thread deviously between the jostling tables.

Dubiously Lanyard followed. He likewise had known the maitre d'hotel at sight: a beastly little decadent whose cabaret on the rue d'Antin, just off the avenue de l'Opera, had been a famous rendezvous of international spies till war had rendered it advisable for him to efface himself from the ken of Paris with the same expedition and discretion which had marked the departure from London of his confrere who now guarded the lower gateway to these ethereal regions of Au Printemps.

The coincidence of finding those two so closely associated worked with the riddle of that note further to trouble Lanyard's mind.

Was he to believe Au Printemps the legitimate successor in America of that less pretentious establishment on the rue d'Antin, an overseas headquarters for Secret Service agents of the Central Powers?

He began to regret heartily, not so much that he had presented himself in answer to that note, but the responsibility which now devolved upon him of caring for Miss Brooke. Much as he had wished to see her an hour ago, now he would willingly be rid of her company.

Why had he been lured to this place, if its character were truly what he feared? Conceivably because he was believed--since it now appeared he had cheated death--still to possess either that desired document or knowledge of its whereabouts.

Naturally the enemy would not think otherwise. He must not forget that Ekstrom was playing double; as yet none but Lanyard knew he had stolen the document and done a murder to cover the theft from his associates and leave him free to sell to England without exciting their suspicion.

Consequently, Lanyard believed, he had been invited to this place to be sounded, to be tempted, bribed, intimidated--if need be, and possible--somehow to be won over to the uses of the Prussian spy system.

Leading them to the farther side of the room, the maitre d'hotel paused bowing and mowing beside a large table already in the possession of a party of three.

Lanyard's eyes narrowed. One of the three was Velasco, another a young man unknown to him, a mannerly little creature who might have been written by the author of "What the Man Will Wear" in the theatre programmes. The third was Sophie Weringrode, the Wilhelmstrasse agent whom he had only that afternoon observed entering the house in Seventy-ninth Street.

He stopped short, in a cold rage. Till that moment a mirror-sheathed pillar had hidden from him Velasco and the Weringrode; else Lanyard had refused to come so far; for obviously there were no unreserved tables, indeed few vacant chairs, in that part of the room.

Not that he minded the cynical barefacedness of the dodge; that was indeed amusing; he was sanguine as to his ability to dominate any situation that might arise, and to a degree indifferent if the upshot should prove his confidence misplaced; and he did not in the least object to letting the enemy show his cards. But he did enormously resent what was, after all, something quite outside the calculations of these giddy conspirators, the fact that he must either beat incontinent retreat or introduce Cecelia Brooke to the company of Sophie Weringrode.

His face darkened, a stinging reproof for the maitre d'hotel trembled on his tongue's tip; but that one was busily avoiding his eye on the far side of the table, drawing out a chair for "mademoiselle," while Velasco and the Weringrode were alert to read Lanyard's countenance and forestall any steps he might contemplate in defiance of their designs.

At first glimpse of the Brooke girl Velasco jumped up and hastened to her, with eager Latin courtesy expressing his unanticipated delight in the prospect of her consenting to join their party. And she was suffering with quiet graciousness his florid compliments.

At the same time the Weringrode was greeting Lanyard in the most intimate fashion--and damning him in the understanding of Cecelia Brooke with every word.

"My dear friend!" she cried gayly, extending a bedizened hand. "I had begun to despair of you. Is it part of your system with women always to be a little late, always to keep us wondering?"

Schooling his features to a civil smile, Lanyard bowed over the hand.

"In warfare such as ours, my dear Sophie," he said with meaning, "one uses all weapons, even the most primitive, in sheer self-defense."

The woman laughed delightedly. "I think," she said, "if you rose from the dead at the bottom of the sea, *Tony*, it would be with wit upon your lips.... And you have brought a friend with you? How charming!" She shifted in her chair to face Cecelia Brooke. "I wish to know her instantly!"

Velasco was waiting only for that opening. "Dear princess," he said, instantly, "permit me to present Miss Cecelia Brooke ... Princess de Alavia...."

Completely at ease and by every indication enjoying herself hugely, the girl bowed and took the hand the Weringrode thrust upon her. Her eyes, a-brim with excitement and mischief, veered to Lanyard's, ignored their warning, glanced away.

"How do you do?" she said simply. "I didn't understand Mr. Ember expected to meet friends here, but that only makes it the more agreeable. May we sit down?"

XVII
FINESSE

The person in the educated evening clothes was made known as Mr. Revel. For Lanyard's benefit and his own he vacated the chair beside Sophie Weringrode, seating himself to one side of Cecelia Brooke, who had Velasco between her and the soi-disant princess.

Already a waiter had placed and was filling glasses for Lanyard and the girl.

With the best grace he could muster the adventurer sat down, accepted a cigarette from the Weringrode case, and with openly impertinent eyes inspected the intrigante critically.

She endured that ordeal well, smiling confidently, a handsome creature with a beautiful body bewitchingly gowned.

Time, he considered, had been kind to Sophie--time, the mysteries of the modern toilette, and the astonishing adaptability of womankind. Splendidly vital, like all of her sort who survive, she seemed mysteriously able to renew that vitality through the very extravagance with which she squandered it. She had lived much of late years, rapidly but well, had learned much, had profited by her lessons. To-night she looked legitimately the princess of her pretensions; the manner of the grande dame suited her type; her gesture was as impeccable as her taste; prettier than ever, she seemed at worst little more than half her age.

And her quick intelligence mocked the privacy of his reflections.

"Fair, fast, and forty," she interpreted smilingly.

He pretended to be stunned. "Never!" he protested feebly.

The woman reaffirmed in a series of rapid nods. "Have I ever had secrets from you? You are too quick for me, monsieur: I do not intend to begin deceiving you at this late day--or trying to."

"Flattery," he declared, "is meat and drink to me. Tell me more."

She laughed lightly. "Thank you, no; vanity is unbecoming in men; I do not care to make you vain."

Aware that Cecelia Brooke was listening all the while she seemed to be enchanted with the patter of Mr. Revel and the less vapid observations of Velasco, Lanyard sought to shunt personalities from himself.

"And now a princess!"

"Did you not know I had married? Yes, a princess of Spain--and with a castle there, if you must know."

"Quite a change of atmosphere from Berlin," he remarked. "But it has done you no perceptible harm."

That won him a black look. "Oh, Berlin!" she said with contemptuous lips. "I haven't been there since the beginning of the war. I wish never to see the place again. True: I was born an Austrian; but is that any reason why I should love Germany?"

She leaned forward, her fan gently tapping the knuckles of his hand.

"Pay less attention to me," she insisted, with a nod toward the middle of the room. "You are missing something. Me, I never tire of her."

The floor had been cleared. A drummer on the dais was sounding the long-roll crescendo. At the culminating crash the lights were everywhere darkened save for an orange-coloured spot-light set in the ceiling immediately above the dancing floor. Into that circular field of torrid glare bounded a woman wearing little more than an abbreviated kirtle of grass strands with a few festoons of artificial flowers. Applause roared out to her, the orchestra sounded the opening bars of an Americanised Hawaiian melody, the woman with extraordinary vivacity began to perform a denatured hula: a wild and tawny animal, superbly physical, relying with warrant upon the stark sensuality of her body to make amends for the censored phrases of the primitive dance. The floor resounded like a great drum to the stamping of her bare feet, till one marvelled at such solidity of flesh as could endure that punishment.

Sophie Weringrode lounged negligently upon the table, bringing her head near Lanyard's shoulder.

"Play fair," she said between lips that barely moved.

Without looking round Lanyard answered in the same manner: "Why ask more than you are prepared to give?"

"The police ran you out of America once. We need only publish the fact that Mr. Anthony Ember is the Lone Wolf...."

"Well?"

"Leave Berlin out of it before this girl."

Lanyard shrugged and laughed quietly. "What else?"

"We can't talk now. Ask me for the next dance."

The woman sat back in her chair, attentive to the posturing of the dancer, slowly fanning herself.

Lanyard's semblance of as much interest was nothing more; furtively his watchfulness alternated between two quarters of the room.

On the farther edge of the circle of tropical radiance he had marked down a table at which two men were seated, Dressier and O'Reilly. No more question now as to the personnel of the conspiracy; even Velasco had thrown off the mask. The enemy had come boldly into the open, indicating a sense of impudent assurance, indicating even more, contempt of opposition. No longer afraid, they no longer skulked in shadows. Lanyard experienced a premonition of events impending.

In addition he was keeping an eye on the door to the elevator shaft. Once already it had opened, letting a bright window into the farther wall of the shadowed room, discovering the figure of the maitre d'hotel in silhouette, anxiety in his attitude. He was waiting for somebody, waiting tensely. So were the others waiting, all that crew and their fellow workers scattered among the guests. Lanyard told himself he could guess for whom.

Only Ekstrom was wanting to complete the circle. When he appeared--if by chance he should--things ought to begin to happen.

If tolerably satisfied that Ekstrom would not come--not that night, at all events--Lanyard, none the less, continued to be jealously heedful of that doorway.

But the hula came to an end without either his vigilance or the impatience of the maitre d'hotel being rewarded. Writhing with serpentine grace to the edge of the illuminated area, the dancer leaped back into darkness and the folds of a wrap held by a maid, in which garment she was seen, bowing and laughing, when the lights again blazed up.

Without ceasing to play, changing only the time of the tune, the orchestra swung into a fox-trot. Lanyard glanced across the table to see Cecelia Brooke rising in response to the invitation of dapper Mr. Revel.

In his turn, he rose with Sophie Weringrode. "Be patient with me," he begged. "It is long since I danced to music more frivolous than a cannonade."

"But it is simple," the woman promised--"simple, at least, to one who can dance as you could in the old days. Just follow me till you catch the step. It doesn't matter, anyway; I desire only the opportunity to converse."

Yielding to his arms, she shifted into French when next she spoke.

"You do admirably, my friend. Never again depreciate your dancing. If you knew how one suffers at the feet of these Americans--!"

"Excellent!" he said. "Now that is settled: what is it you are instructed to propose to me?"

She laughed softly. "Always direct! Truly you would never shine as a secret agent."

"Not as they shine," Lanyard countered--"in the dark."

"Don't be a fraud. We are what we are, and so are you. Let us not begin to be censorious of one another's methods of winning a living."

"Agreed. But when do we begin to talk business?"

"Why do you continue so persistently antagonistic?"

"I am French."

"That is silly. You are an outlaw, a man without a country. Why not change all that?"

"And how does one effect miracles?"

"Germany offers you a refuge, security, freedom to ply your trade unhindered--within reasonable limits."

"And in exchange what do I give?"

"Your services, as and when required, in our service."

"Beginning when?"

"To-night."

"With what specific performance?"

"We want, we must without fail have, that document you took from the Brooke girl."

"Perhaps we had better continue in English. You are speaking a tongue un-known to me."

"Don't talk rot. You know well what I mean. We know you have the thing. You didn't steal it to turn it over to England or the States. What is your price to Germany?"

"Whatever you have in mind, believe me when I say I have nothing to sell to the Wilhelmstrasse."

"But what else can you do with it? What other market--?"

"My dear Sophie, upon my word I haven't got what you want."

"Then why so keen to get the Brooke girl on the telephone as soon as you found out where she was stopping?"

"How did you learn about that, by the way?"

"Let the credit go to Senor Velasco. He saw you first."

"One thought as much.... Nevertheless, I haven't what you want."

"You gave it back to Miss Brooke?"

"Having nothing to give her, I gave her nothing."

The woman was silent throughout a round of the floor; then, "Tell me some-thing," she requested.

"Can I keep anything from you?"

"Are you in love with the English girl?"

Lanyard almost lost step, then laughed the thought to derision. "What put that into your pretty head, Sophie?"

"Do you not know it yourself, my friend?"

"It is absurd."

She laughed maliciously. "Think it over. Possibly you have not stopped to think as yet. When you know the truth yourself, you will be the better qualified to fib about it. Also, you will not forget...."

"What?" he demanded bluntly as she paused with intention.

"That as long as she possesses the document--since you have it not--her life is endangered even more than yours."

"She hasn't got it!" Lanyard declared, as nearly in panic as he ever was.

"Ah!" the woman jeered. "So you confess to some knowledge of it after all!"

"My dear," he said, teasingly, "do you really want to know what has become of that paper?"

"I do, and mean to."

"What if I tell you?"

Her eyes lifted to his in childlike candour. "Need you ask?"

"You are irresistible.... Ask Karl."

She demanded sharply: "Whom?"

"Ekstrom."

"Ah!" Again the adventuress was silent for a little. "What does he know?"

"Ask him, enquire why he murdered von Harden, then what business took him to Ninety-fifth Street twice this evening--once about nine o'clock, again at midnight."

"You must be mad, monsieur. Karl would not dare...."

"You don't know him--or have forgotten he was trained in the International Bureau of Brussels, and there learned how to sell out both parties to a business that won't bear publicity."

"I wonder," the woman mused. "Never have I wholly trusted that one."

"Shall I give you the key?"

"If you love Karl as little as I...."

"But where do you suppose the good man is, this night of nights?"

"Who knows? He was not here when I arrived at midnight. I have seen nothing of him since."

"When you do--if he shows himself at all--look him over carefully for signs of wear and tear."

"Yes, monsieur? And in what respect?"

"Look for cuts about his head and hands, possibly elsewhere. And should he confess to an affair with a wind-shield in a motor accident, ask him what happened to the study window in the house at Ninety-fifth Street."

Impish glee danced in the woman's eyes. "Your handiwork, dear friend?"

"A mere beginning.... You may tell him so, if you like."

He was subjected to a convulsive squeeze. "Never have I felt so kindly disposed toward an enemy!"

"It is true, I were a better foe to Germany if I kept my counsel and let Ekstrom continue to play double."

The music ceasing, to be followed by the inevitable clamour for more, Lanyard offered an arm upon which Sophie rested a detaining hand.

"No--wait. We dance this encore. I have more to say."

He submitted amiably, the more so since not ill-pleased with himself. And when again they were moving round the floor, she bore more heavily upon his shoulder and was thoughtful longer than he had expected. Then--

"Attention, my friend."

"I am listening, Sophie."

"If what you hint is true--and I do not doubt it is--Karl's day is done."

"More nearly than he dreams," Lanyard affirmed grimly.

"I shan't be sorry. I am German through and through; what I do, I do for the Fatherland, and in that find absolution for many things I care not to remember. If through what you tell me I may prove Karl traitor, I owe you something."

"Always it has been my fondest hope, Sophie, some day to have you in my debt."

Her fingers tightened on his. "Do not jest in the shadow of death. Since you have been unwise enough to venture here to-night, you will not be permitted to leave alive--unless you pledge yourself to us and prove your sincerity by producing that paper."

"That sounds reasonable--like Prussia. What next?"

"I have warned you, so paid off my debt. The rest is your affair."

"Do you imagine I take this seriously?"

"It will turn out seriously for you if you do not."

"How can I be prevented from leaving when I will, from a public restaurant?"

"Is it possible you don't know this place? It is maintained by the Wilhelm-strasse. Attempt to leave it without coming to a satisfactory understanding, and see what happens."

"What, for instance?"

"The lights would be out before you were half across the room. When they went up again, the Lone Wolf would be no more, and never a soul here would know who stabbed him or what became of the knife."

"Are you by any chance amusing yourself at my expense?"

Once more the woman showed him her handsome eyes: he found them frankly grave, earnest, unwavering.

"If you will not listen, your blood be on your own head."

"Forgive me. I didn't mean to be rude...."

"Still, you do not believe!"

"You are wrong. I am merely amused."

"If you understood, you could never mock your peril."

"But I don't mock it. I am enchanted with it. I accept it, and it renews my youth. This might be Paris of the days when you ran with the Pack, Sophie--and I alone!"

The woman moved her pretty shoulders impatiently. "I think you are either mad or ... the very soul of courage!"

The encore ended; they returned to the table, Sophie leaning lightly on Lanyard's arm, chattering gay inconsequentialities.

Dropping into her chair, she bent over toward Cecelia Brooke.

"He dances adorably, my dear!" the intrigante declared. "But I dare say you know that already."

The English girl shook her head, smiling. "Not yet."

"Then lose no time. You two should dance well together, for you are more of a size. I think the next number will be a waltz. We get altogether too few of them; these American dances, these one-steps and foxtrots, they are not dances, they are mere romps, favourites none the less. And there is always more room on the floor; so few waltz nowadays. Really, you must not miss this opportunity."

This playful insistence, the light stress she laid upon her suggestion that Cecelia Brooke dance with him, considered in conjunction with her recent admonition, impressed Lanyard as significantly inconsistent. Sophie was no more a woman to make purposeless gestures than she was one sufficiently wanting in finesse to signal him by pressures of her foot. There was sheer intention in that iteration: "... *lose no time ... you must not miss this opportunity*." Something had happened even since their dance; she had observed something momentous, and was warning him to act quickly if he meant to act at all.

With unruffled amiability, amused, urbane, Lanyard bowed his petition across the table, and was rewarded by a bright nod of promise.

Lighting another cigarette, he lounged back, poised his wine glass delicately, with the eye of a connoisseur appraised its pale amber tint, touched it lightly to his lips, inhaling critically its bouquet, sipped, and signified approval of the vintage by sipping again: all without missing one bit of business in a scene enacted on the far side of the room, directly behind him but reflected in a mirror panel of the wall he faced.

The diplomatist charged with the task of discriminating the sheep from the goats in the lower lobby had come up to confer with his colleague, the maitre d'hotel of the upper storey. When Lanyard first saw the man he was standing by the elevator shaft, none too patiently awaiting the attention of the other, who, caught by inadvertence at some distance, was moving to join him, with what speed he could manage threading the thick-set tables.

Was this what Sophie had noticed? Had she likewise, perhaps, received some secret signal from the guardian of the lower gateway?

A signal possibly indicating that Ekstrom had arrived

They met at last, those two, and discreetly confabulated, the maitre d'hotel betraying welcome mitigation of that nervous tension which had heretofore so palpably affected him; and, as the other stepped back into the elevator, Lanyard saw this one's glance irresistibly attracted to the table dedicated to the service of the Princess de Alavia. Something much resembling satisfaction glimmered in the fellow's leaden eyes: it was apparent that he anticipated early relief from a distasteful burden of responsibility.

Then, at ease in the belief that he was unobserved, he turned to a near-by table round which four sat without the solace of feminine society--four men whose stamp was far from reassuring despite their strikingly quiet demeanour and inconspicuously correct investiture of evening dress.

Two were unmistakable sons of the Fatherland; all were well set up, with the look of men who would figure to advantage in any affair calling for physical competence and courage, from coffee and pistols at sunrise in the Parc aux Princes to a battle royal in a Tenderloin dive.

Their table commanded both ways out, by the stairs and by the elevator, much too closely for Lanyard's peace of mind.

And more than one looked thoughtfully his way while the maitre d'hotel hovered above them, murmuring confidentially.

Four nods sealed an understanding with him. He strutted off with far more manner than had been his at any time since the arrival of Lanyard, and vented an excess of spirits by berating bitterly an unhappy clown of a waiter for some trivial fault.

The first bars of another dance number sang through the confusion of voices: truly, as Sophie had foretold, a waltz.

XVIII
DANSE MACABRE

Trained in the old school of the dance, Lanyard was unversed in that grace-less scamper which to-day passes as the waltz with a generation largely too indolent or too inept of foot to learn to dance.

His was that flowing waltz of melting rhythm, the waltz of yesterday, that dance of dances to whose measures a civilization more sedate in its amusements, less jealous of its time, danced, flirted, loved, and broke its hearts.

Into the swinging movement of that antiquated waltz Lanyard fell without a qualm of doubt, all ignorant as he was of his benighted ignorance; and instantly, with the ease and gracious assurance of a dancer born, Cecelia Brooke adapted her-self to his step and guidance, with rare pliancy made her every movement exqui-sitely synchronous with his.

No need to lead her, no need for more than the least of pressures upon her yielding waist, no need for anything but absolute surrender to the magic of the mo-ment....

Effortless, like creatures of the music adrift upon its sounding tides, they cir-cled the floor once, twice, and again, before reluctantly Lanyard brought himself to shatter the spell of that enchantment.

Looking down with an apologetic smile, he asked:

"Mademoiselle, do you know you can be an excellent actress?"

As if in resentment the girl glanced upward sharply, with clouded eyes.

"So can most women, in emergency."

"I mean ... I have something serious to say; nobody must guess your thoughts."

She said simply: "I will do my best."

"You must--you must appear quite charmed. Also, should you catch me smirking like an infatuated ninny, remember I am only doing my own indifferent best to act."

Laughter trembled deliciously in her voice: "I promise faithfully to bear in mind your heartlessness!"

"I am an ass," he enunciated with the humility of conviction. "But that can't be helped. Attend to me, if you please--and do not start. This place turns out to be a nest of Prussian spies. I was brought here by a trick. I understand the order is I may not leave alive."

Playing her part so well as almost to embarrass Lanyard himself, the girl smiled daringly into his eyes.

"Because of that packet?" she breathed.

"Because of that, mademoiselle."

"Where is it?"

For an instant Lanyard lost countenance absolutely. Through sheer good fortune the girl was now dancing with face averted, her head so nearly touching his shoulder that it seemed to rest upon it.

Nevertheless, it was at cost of an heroic struggle that he fought down all signs of that shock with which it had been borne in upon him that he dared not assure the girl her packet was in safe hands.

If he had failed in his efforts to restore the thing to her, that she might consign it as she saw fit and so discharge her personal trust, till now Lanyard had solaced himself with a hazy notion that she would in turn be comforted when she learned the document was in the keeping of her country's Secret Service.

Impossible to tell her that: his own act had rendered it impossible, that act the outcome of wilful trifling with his infirmity, his itch for thieving.

Of a sudden the pilfered necklace secreted in an inner pocket of his waistcoat, above his heart, seemed to have gained the weight of so much lead. The hideous consciousness of the thing stung like the bite of live coals.

This woman was in distress; he yearned to lighten her burden; he could do that with half a dozen words; his guilt prohibited.

A thief!

Now indeed the Lone Wolf tasted shame and realized its bitterness....

Puzzled by his constraint, the girl's eyes again sought his; and warned in time by the movement of her head, he mustered impudence to meet their question with the look of tenderness that went with the role she suffered him to play.

"What is the matter?"

"I am ashamed that I have failed you...."

"Don't think of that. I know you did your best. Only tell me what became of it."

"It was stolen; when I returned to my stateroom that night I was held up and robbed. The thief shot at me, killed his confederate, decamped by way of the port. I pursued. Another aided him to overpower and cast me overboard."

"Yet you escaped...!"

Strange she should seem more intrigued by that than concerned about her loss!

"I escaped, no matter how...."

"You don't know who stole the packet?"

"I don't recall the man among the passengers, but he may have been in one of the boats, a fellow of about my stature, with a flowing beard...."

He sketched broadly Ekstrom as he had seen him in the Stanistreet library.

Her eyes quickened.

"One such escaped in our boat, the second steward; I think his name was Anderson."

"Doubtless the same."

"Then it is gone!"

For once in his acquaintance with her, that brave spirit seemed to falter: she became a burden, bereft for a little of all grace and spontaneity.

He was constrained to swing her forcibly into time.

Almost instantly she recollected herself, covered her lapse with a little laugh innocent of any hint of its forced falsity, and showed him and the room as well a radiant countenance: all with such address and art that the incident might well have escaped notice, otherwise have passed for a bit of natural by-play.

Yet distress was too eloquent in the broken query: "What *am* I to do?"

Heartsick, self-sick to boot, he essayed to suggest that she consult Colonel Stanistreet, but lacking so much effrontery, stammered and fell silent.

Perhaps misinterpreting, she cried in quick contrition: "I am forgetting! Forgive me. I should have said: what are you to do?"

He whipped his wits together.

"Look down, turn your face aside, smile.... I have a plan, a desperate remedy, but the best I can contrive. When next the lift comes up, we must try to be near it. There is one row of tables which we must break through by main force. Leave that to me, follow as I clear a way, go straight into the lift. If anything happens, run down the stairway on the left. The ground floor is two flights below. If I am any way detained, don't stop--go on, get your wraps, take the first taxi you see, return directly to the Knickerbocker. I will telephone you later."

"If you live," she breathed.

"Never fear for me...."

"But if I do? Do you imagine I could rest if I thought you had sacrificed yourself for me?"

"You must not think that. I am far too selfish--"

"That is not so. And I refuse positively to do as you wish unless you tell me how I may communicate with you."

Resigned to humour her, he recited his address and the number of the house telephone, and when she had memorized both by iteration, resumed:

"Once outside, if anybody tries to hinder you, don't let them intimidate you into keeping quiet, but scream, scream at the top of your lungs. These beasts abominate a screaming woman, or any other undue noise. Not only will that frighten them off, but it will fetch the nearest policeman."

The music ceased. She stood flushed, smiling, adorably pretty, eyes star-like for him alone.

"We are not far from the lift now," she said just audibly.

"But the door is shut. Hush. Here comes the encore. Once more around...."

They drifted again into that witching maze of melody and movement made one.

"You are silent," she said, after a little. "Why?"

Lanyard answered with a warning pressure on her hand.

The elevator was stationary at the floor, its door wide, the maitre d'hotel engaged in a far quarter of the room, while those four formidable guardians of the exit were gossiping with animation over their glasses.

"Steady. Now is our time."

Abruptly they stopped. A couple that had been following them avoided colli-sion by a close margin. Over his partner's head the man scowled portentously--and dissipated his display of temper on Lanyard's indifferent back.

Upon those guests who sat between the dancing floor and elevator, Lanyard wasted no consideration. Pushing roughly between two adjoining tables, he lifted one chair with its astonished occupant bodily out of the way, then turned, swung an arm round the girl's waist, all but threw her through the lane he had created, followed without an instant's pause.

It was all so quickly accomplished that the girl was in the car before another person in the room appreciated what was happening. And Lanyard, in the act of slamming the door shut without heed for the protesting operator, saw only a room full of amazed faces with gaping mouths and rounded eyes--and one man of the four at the near-by table in the act of rising uncertainly, with a stupefied look.

Elbowing the boy aside, he seized the operating lever and thrust it to the notch labelled "Descend." An instant of pause followed: like its attendant the elevator seemed stalled in inertia of stupefaction.

Beyond the door somebody loosed an infuriated screech. Angry hands drummed on the glass panel. With a premonitory shudder the car started spasmodically, moved downward at first gently, then with greater speed, coming to an abrupt stop at the street level with a shock that all but threw its passengers from their feet.

Up the shaft that senseless punishment of the panel continued. Some other intelligence conceived the notion for ringing for the car to return: its annunciator buzzed stridently, continuously.

Unlatching the lower door, Lanyard threw it back, stepped out, finding the lobby deserted but for a simpering group of coat-room girls, to one of whom he flipped a silver dollar.

"Find this lady's wraps--be quick!"

Deftly catching the coin, the girl snatched the check from Cecelia Brooke, and darted into the women's dressing room.

Throughout a wait of agonising suspense, the elevator boy remained cower-ing in a corner of the car, staring at Lanyard as at some shape of terror, while the ignored buzzer droned without cessation to persistent pressure from above.

Out of the dark entrance to the lower dining room the bearded diplomatist popped with the distracted look of a jack-in-the-box about to be ravished of its young.

"Monsieur is not leaving?" he expostulated shrilly, darting forward.

Lanyard stopped him with a look whose menace was like a kick.

"I am seeing this lady to her cab," he said in a cold and level voice.

The coat-room girl emerged from her lair with an armful of wraps and furs.

Again the bearded one made as if to block the doorway.

"But, monsieur--mademoiselle--!"

Lanyard caught the fellow's arm and sent him spinning like a top.

"Out of the way, you rat!" he snapped; then to the girl: "Be quick!"

As she shouldered into a compartment of the revolving door incoherent yells began to echo down the staircase well. At length it had occurred to those above to utilize that means of descent.

Wedged in the wheeling door, a final glimpse of the lobby showed Lanyard the startled, putty-like mask of the maitre d'hotel at the head of the stairway with, beyond him, the head of one who, though in shadow, uncommonly resembled Ekstrom--but Ekstrom as he was in the old days, without his beard.

That picture passed like a flash on a cinema screen.

They were on the sidewalk, and the girl was running toward a taxicab, the only vehicle of its sort in sight, at the curb just above the entrance.

Coatless and bareheaded, Lanyard swung to face the door porter, a towering, brawny animal in livery, self-confident and something more than keen to interfere; but his mouth, opening to utter some sort of protest, shut suddenly without articulation when Lanyard displayed for his benefit a .22 Colt's automatic. And he fell back smartly.

Jerking open the cab door, the girl stumbled into the far corner of the seat. The motor was churning in promising fashion, the chauffeur settling into place at the wheel. Into his hand Lanyard thrust a ten-dollar bill.

"The Knickerbocker," he ordered. "Stop for nobody. If followed steer for the nearest policeman. There'll be no change."

He closed the door sharply, leaned over it, dropped the little pistol into the girl's lap.

"Chances are you won't want that--but you may."

She bent forward quickly, eyes darkly lustrous with alarm, and placed a hand upon his arm.

"But you?"

"It is I whom they want, not you. I won't subject you to the hazard of my company."

Gently Lanyard lifted the hand from his sleeve, brushed it gallantly with his lips, released it.

"Good-night!" he laughed, then stepped back, waved a hand to the chauffeur--"Go!"

The taxicab shot away like a racing hound unleashed. With a sigh of relief Lanyard gave himself wholly to the question of his own salvation.

The rank of waiting motor-cars offered no hope: all but one were private town cars and limousines, operated by liveried drivers. A solitary roadster at the head of the line tempted and was rejected; even though it had no guardian chauffeur, something of which he could not be sure, he would be overhauled before he could start the motor and get the knack of its gear-shift mechanism. Even now Au Printemps was in frantic eruption, its doors ejecting violently a man at each wild revolution.

Down Broadway an omnibus of the Fifth Avenue line lumbered, at no less speed than twenty miles an hour, without passengers and sporting an illuminated "Special" sign above the driver's seat.

Dashing out into the roadway, Lanyard launched himself at the narrow platform of the unwieldy vehicle and, in spite of a yell of warning from the guard, landed safely on the step and turned to repel boarders.

But his manoeuvre had been executed too swiftly and unexpectedly. The group before Au Printemps huddled together in ludicrous inaction, as if stunned. Then one raged through it, plying vicious elbows. As he paused against the light Lanyard identified unmistakably the silhouette of Ekstrom.

So that one had, after all, escaped the net of his own treachery!

The 'bus guard was shaking Lanyard's arm with an ungentle hand.

"Here, now, you got no business boardin' a Special."

From his pocket Lanyard whipped the first bank-note his fingers encountered.

"Divide that with the chauffeur," he said crisply--"tell him to drive like the devil. It's life or death with me!"

The protruding eyeballs of the guard bore witness to the magnitude of the bribe.

"You're on!" he breathed hoarsely, and ran forward through the body of the conveyance to advise the driver.

Swarming up the curved stairway to the roof, Lanyard dropped into the rear seat, looking back.

The group round the doorway was recovering from its stupefaction. Three struck off from it toward the line of waiting cars. Of these the foremost was Ekstrom.

Simultaneously the 'bus, lumbering drunkenly, lurched into Columbus Circle, and the roadster left the curb carrying in addition to the driver two passengers-- Ekstrom on the running-board.

Tardily Lanyard repented of that impulse which had moved him to bestow his one weapon upon Cecelia Brooke.

The night air had a biting edge. A chill rain had begun to drizzle down in minute globules of mist, which both lent each street light its individual nimbus of gold and dulled deceitfully the burnished asphaltum, rendering its surface greasy and treacherous. More than once Lanyard feared lest the 'bus skid and overturn; and before the old red brick building between Broadway and Eighth Avenue shut out the western sector of the Circle, he saw the roadster, driven insanely, shoot crabwise toward the curb, than answer desperate work at the wheel and whirl madly, executing a volte-face so violent that Ekstrom's hold was broken and he was hurled a dozen feet away. And Lanyard's chances were measurably advanced by the delay required in order to pick up the sprawling one, start the engine anew, and turn more cautiously to resume the pursuit.

Striking diagonally across Broadway the 'bus swung into Fifty-seventh Street at the moment when the roadster turned the corner of Columbus Circle.

The head of the guard lifted above the edge of the roof. Clinging to the supports of the stairway, he addressed Lanyard in accents of blended suspicion and respect.

"Lis'n, boss: is this all right, on the level, now?"

"Absolutely, unless that racing-car catches up with us, in which case you'll have a dead man--myself--on your hands."

"Well ... we don't wanna lose our jobs, that's all."

"You won't unless I lose my life."

"Anything you'd like me to do?"

"Go down, wait on the platform, if anybody attempts to get aboard kick him in the act."

"Sure I will!"

The guard disappeared.

Wallowing like a barge in a strong seaway, the omnibus crossed Seventh Avenue and sped downhill toward Sixth with dangerous momentum. Shortly, however, this began to be modified by the brakes, a precaution against mishap which even the fugitive must approve. Ahead loomed the gaunt structure of the Sixth Avenue "L," bridging the roadway at so low an elevation as to afford the omnibus little more than clear headroom. Once beneath it a single bounce up from the surface-car tracks must mean a wreck.

But the pursuit was less than half a block astern and gaining swiftly, even as the speed of the omnibus was growing less and desperately less.

At what seemed little better than a snail's pace it began to pass beneath the span of the Elevated.

Like a racing thoroughbred the roadster swept up alongside, motor chanting triumphantly, running-board level with the platform step.

Ekstrom, poised to leap aboard, hesitated; a pistol in his hand exploded; a shattered window fell crashing.

There was a yell from the guard, not of pain but of fright. Apparently he executed a von Hindenburg retreat. Without more opposition Ekstrom gained the platform.

In the same breath Lanyard stood up. The lowermost girder of the "L" was immediately overhead. He grasped it, doubled his legs beneath him, swung clear. The omnibus shot from under him, the roadster convoying.

Drawing himself up, he seized a round iron upright of guard-rail and heaved his body in over the edge of the platform round the switching-tower, which was at this hour dark and untenanted.

In the street below a police whistle shrieked, and a fusillade of pistol shots woke scandalised echoes.

Bending almost double Lanyard moved rapidly northward on the footway beside the western tracks, and so gained the old station on the west side of Fifty-eighth Street, for years dedicated to the uses of desuetude. Through this he crept, then down the stairs, encountering at the lower landing an iron gate which obliged him to climb over and jump.

Not a soul paid the least attention to this matter of a gentleman in evening dress without hat or top coat dropping from the stairway of a disused elevated station at two o'clock in the morning.

In New York anything can happen, and most things do, without stirring up meddlesome impulses in innocent bystanders.

XIX
FORCE MAJEURE

This visit to his rooms was the briefest of the several Lanyard made that night, considerations of mortal urgency dictating its drastic abbreviation. If the events of the last few hours had meant anything whatever they had demonstrated two truths which shone like beacon lights: that Manhattan Island was overpopulated as long as both he and Ekstrom remained on it; that Ekstrom had been goaded to the verge of aberration by the discovery that Lanyard had come safely through the *Assyrian* debacle to take up anew his self-appointed office of Nemesis to the Prussian spy system in general and to the genius of its American bureau in particular.

Henceforth that one would know no more rest while Lanyard lived.

Thus that little street-level apartment forfeited whatever attractions it originally had possessed in the adventurer's estimation. Not only was the address known to Ekstrom's associates, and so open to him, but its peculiar characteristics, its facilities for access from the street direct, rendered it a highly practicable death-trap for a hunted man.

Lanyard was well persuaded he need only wait there long enough to receive a deputation from Seventy-ninth Street. And with any assurance that Ekstrom would come alone, he might have been content to wait. Not only had he through too intimate acquaintance with his methods every assurance that Ekstrom would never brave alone what he could induce another to risk with him, but Lanyard was never one willing to play the passive part.

A banal axiom of all warfare applied: The advantage is with him who fights upon the offensive.

Since midnight the offensive had shifted from Lanyard's grasp to the enemy's.

He was determined to recapture it; and that was something never to be accomplished by sitting still and waiting for events to unfold, but only by carrying the war into the enemy's camp.

He delayed, then, only long enough to change his clothing and to conceal about him certain properties which it seemed unwise to expose to chance discovery on the part of Ekstrom or in the ever-possible event of police intervention.

Within five minutes from the time of his return he was closing behind him the private door.

Wearing a quiet lounge suit but no top coat, with a hat not so soft as to lack character but soft enough to stick upon one's head in time of action, and carrying a stick neither brutishly stout nor ineffectively slender, he strolled up to Seventh Avenue, turned north, entered Central Park--and strolled no more.

Kindly shadows enfolded him, engulfed him altogether. One minute after he had passed through the gateway he would have defied unaided apprehension by the most zealous officer of the peace. He went swiftly and secretly, avoiding all lighted ways.

Not till then did conscience stir and remind him of his slighted promise to call up Cecelia Brooke.

No time now for that; the errand that engaged him was of a nature to brook no more procrastination. The girl must wait. He was sorry if, as she had protested, solicitude for his welfare must interfere with her night's rest. But what must be, must: until he saw the end of this adventure he could be influenced by no minor consideration whatsoever.

Not that he seriously believed Cecelia's sleep would be uneasy because of him. That was too much.

His temper was grim and skeptical. The resentment roused by the trap that had so nearly laid him by the heels, together with the subsequent effort to assassinate him out of hand, had settled into a phase of smouldering fury whose heat consumed like misty vapours every lesser emotion, every humane consideration.

Some by-thought recalling the Weringrode's innuendo that he was in love without his knowledge, moved him to laugh outright if strangely, an unpleasant laugh that held as much of pain as of derision.

What room in that dark heart of his for love?... the heart of a thief and a potential assassin, the heart of the Lone Wolf!...

How was he to know he had hardly left his lodgings before their hush was interrupted by the grumble of the house telephone?

Intermittently for upward of three minutes that sound persisted. When at length it discontinued the quiet of the untenanted rooms reigned undisturbed for a brief time only.

An odd metallic stridor became audible, a succession of scrapings of stealthy accent at the private entrance. Its latch clicked. The door swung back against the wall with a muffled bump. Two pairs of furtive feet padded in the little private hallway. The flash of an electric hand-lamp flickered hither and yon like a searching poignard, picked out the door to the one bedchamber and vanished. There was guarded whispering, then a thud as one of the intruders gained the middle of the bedchamber in a bound. An instant later a switch snapped, and the room was flooded with light.

Beneath the chandelier stood a man in evening dress the worse for misadventure, one knee of his trousers cut open, both legs caked with a film of half-dry mud, his linen dingy with mud-stains, his top coat shockingly bedraggled. He was bareheaded, apparently having lost his hat; a black smear across one cheek added emphasis to the pallor of newly shaven jowls; and his eyes were blazing.

"Stole away!" he muttered briefly in disgust, then called: "Ed!"

As quietly as a shadow a second man joined him, greeting him with a "Hush!"

This gentleman was in far more presentable repair and a more equable frame of mind. There was even a glint of amusement in his hard blue eyes. His countenance had an Irish cast.

"Hush?" the other iterated with contempt. "What for? The hound's not here."

"No, Karl," Ed admitted; "but there are others in the house. If it's known to them that Lanyard's out, they may turn in a police alarm; and I for one have had enough of bulls for one night."

Karl grunted disdainfully. "I told you this would be a waste of time...."

"And I agreed with you entirely. But you would come."

"Lanyard's no such fool as to stick round a place he knows I know about." Karl's hands twitched and his features worked nervously. "He knows me too well, knows that if ever I lay hands on him again--"

His voice was rising to an hysterical pitch when the other checked him with a sibilant hiss. At the same time his hand darted out and switched off the light. Karl uttered a startled ejaculation.

"*Sssh*!" his companion repeated.

In the street a motor-car was rumbling, stationary before the door. Then the remote grinding of the house door-bell was heard.

"Let's get out of this," suggested the Irishman. "It's no good waiting, anyway."

"Hold hard! We won't go till we have a clear field."

The Prussian stole out into the sitting room and stood listening at the door to the public hallway, his companion standing by with a mutinous air.

"Oh, come along!" he insisted, in a stage whisper.

"Shut up! Listen...."

Shuffling footfalls traversed the hallway. The front door was opened. The clear voice of an Englishwoman was answered in the slurring patois of a negro.

"No'm, he ain't in."

The next enquiry was intelligible: the speaker had entered the hallway.

"Are you sure?"

"Yas'm. Sumbody done call him up 'bout ten min'tes ago, an' I rung an' rung an' he don' answer. He ain't in or he don' mean to answer nobody, tha's all."

"I am very anxious about him. Have you a key to his rooms?"

"Yas'm, I got a pass-key, but--"

"Please use it. Take this. Go in and make sure he is out, or if at home that he is all right."

"Yas'm, thanky ma'am, but--"

"Do as I tell you. I will see that you don't get into trouble."

"All right, ma'am." The negro chuckled, probably over his tip. "Yo' sho' has got the p'suadin'est way...."

The Irishman caught the German's arm. "Come out of this," he pleaded.

"No fear. I'll see it through. That's the Brooke girl the fool got in with on the boat. She may know something...."

"But--"

"Leave this to me. You look out for the negro. I'll take care of Miss Cecelia Brooke."

Swearing unhappily, the Irishman flattened against the wall to one side of the door. Karl waited behind it as it admitted the hall attendant, who made directly toward the central chandelier.

"Yo' jes' wait, ma'am, an' I'll mek a light an'--"

But the girl had impetuously followed him in.

The light went up, and Karl put a heavy shoulder against the door, closing it with a slam. The negro turned and stood with gaping mouth and staring eyes, dumb with terror. The girl recognised Karl with a little cry, and darted back toward the door. Immediately he caught her in his arms. Her lips opened, but their utterance was stifled by a handkerchief thrust between them with the dexterity of a practised hand.

Without one word of warning the Irishman stepped forward and struck the negro brutally in the face. The boy reeled, whimpering. Two more blows delivered with murderous ferocity silenced him altogether. He collapsed like a broken puppet, insensible on the floor, his face a curious ashen colour beneath its glossy skin of brown.

XX
RIPOSTE

The drizzle had grown thicker, the night blacker, the early morning air still more chill. But Lanyard was moving too swiftly to be affected by this last circumstance; the first he anathematised with the perfunctory bitterness of a skilled artisan who sees his work in a fair way to be obstructed by elemental depravity. Another of his trade would have termed such weather conditions ideal, and so might the Lone Wolf on an everyday job; but the prospect of a footing rendered insecure by rain trebled the hazards attending a plan of campaign that would brook neither revision nor delay.

There was only one way to break into the house on Seventy-ninth Street; this Lanyard had appreciated upon his first reconnaissance of the previous afternoon. He could have wished for more time in which to prepare and assemble tested equipment instead of relying upon chance to supply the requisite gear; but with all time at his disposal the mechanical difficulties of the problem would remain. Far from indifferent to these, Lanyard addressed himself to their conquest doggedly and with businesslike economy of motion.

Shunning the public paths he went over the park wall like a cat, sped across town through Eightieth Street, and so came to that plot of land upon which an apartment building was in process of erection, immediately to the north of the American headquarters of the Prussian spy system.

Walled in with stone two storeys deep, its gaunt skeleton of steel had been joined together as far as the seventh level. How much higher it was destined to rise was immaterial; for Lanyard's purpose it was enough that the frame had already outgrown its neighbour on the south.

A litter of lumber, huge steel girders, and other material narrowed the side street to half its normal width. The sidewalk space was trampled earth roofed with heavy planks for the protection of pedestrian heads, a passage lighted by electric bulbs widely spaced; midway in this an entrance to the structure was flanked by a wooden shanty, by day a tool house, after working hours a shelter for the night watchman. This boasted one glazed window dull with orange light.

Approaching with due precaution, Lanyard peered in. The light came from a single electric bulb and a potbellied sheet-iron stove, glowing red. Near by, in a chair tipped against the wall, sat the watchman, corncob pipe in hand, head drooping, eyes closed, mouth ajar. A snore of the first magnitude seemed to vibrate the very walls. On the floor beside the chair stood a two-quart tin pail full of arid emptiness.

Dismissing further consideration of the watchman as a factor, satisfied that the entire neighbourhood as well was sound asleep, Lanyard darted up the plank walk that led into the building, then paused to get his bearings.

Effluvia of mortar and damp lumber saluted him in an uncanny place whose darkness was slightly qualified by a faint refracted glow from the low canopy of cloud and by equally dim shafts of diffused street light. There was more or less flooring of a temporary character over a sable gulf of cellars, and overhead a sullen, weeping sky cross-hatched with stark black ironwork.

With infinite patience Lanyard groped his way through that dark labyrinth to the foot of a ladder ascending an open shaft wherein a hoisting tackle dangled.

Here he stumbled over what he had been seeking, a great coil of one-inch hempen cable, from which he measured off roughly what he would require, if his calculations were correct, and something over. This length he re-coiled and slung over his shoulder: an awkward, weighty handicap. Nevertheless he began to climb.

Above the third level there was merely steel framework; he had somewhat more light to guide him, with a view of the north wall of the Seventy-ninth Street house, bright in the glare of avenue lamps.

The wall was absolutely blank.

At the seventh level the ladders ended. He stepped off upon a foot-wide beam, paused to make sure of his poise, and began to walk the girders with a sureness of foot any aviator might have envied.

At regular intervals he encountered uprights: between these he had to depend upon his sense of direction and equilibrium to guide him safely across those narrow walks of steel made slippery by rain.

But, thanks to forethought, his footwork was faultless: he wore shoes old, well-broken, very soft, flexible, and silent.

The building was in the shape of a squat E, with two courts facing south. On this seventh level the first court was bridged by a single girder, the middle of which was Lanyard's immediate objective. Since it lacked uprights he took it cautiously on hands and knees until approximately equidistant from both ends, when he straddled it, took the cable from his shoulders, uncoiled a length and made it fast round the girder with a clove hitch: giddy work, in that darkness, on that greasy span, fashioning by simple sense of touch the knot upon which his life was to depend, half of the time prone upon the girder and fishing blindly beneath it for the rope's end, with nothing but a seventy--foot drop between him and eternity, not even another girder to break a fall....

He was now immediately opposite the minaret, at an elevation of about twenty feet above the roof he wished to reach, and as far away, or perhaps a trifle farther.

Still he detected no signs of life about that nest of spies: if the wireless were in operation its apparatus was well-housed; there was no sound of the spark, never a glimmer of its violet flash.

Laboriously--the knot completed to his satisfaction--Lanyard returned via the eastern arm of the E, paying out the coiled cable as he progressed, working round to the north side of the court.

Once again pausing opposite the minaret, he knotted the end of the cable loosely round an upright connecting with the sixth level, let it slide down, followed it, repeated the process, and rested finally on the fifth.

Now his ordeal approached a climax which he contemplated with what calmness he could while securing the rope beneath the arms.

In another sixty seconds or less it must be demonstrated whether his dead reckoning would set him down safe and sound on the roof or dash him against the walls of the Seventy-ninth Street house, to swing back and dangle impotently in mid-air till daylight and police discovered him--unless, escaping injury, he were able to pull himself up hand over hand to the girder.

With one arm round the upright to prevent the sag of rope from dragging him over prematurely, he essayed a final survey.

Either the murk deceived or Lanyard had judged shrewdly. His feet were on an approximate level with the coping round the roof, and he stood about as far from the upper girder to which the rope was hitched as that was distant from the coping.

One look up and round at those louring skies, duskily flushed by subdued city lights: with no more ceremony Lanyard released the upright and committed his body to space.

If the downward sweep was breathless, what followed was breath-taking: once past the nadir of that giant swing, he was borne upward by an impetus steadily and sensibly slackening.

Instant followed leaden-winged instant while the wall, looming like a mountainside, seemed to be toppling, insensately bent upon his annihilation; even so his momentum, decreasing with frightful swiftness, seemed possessed of demoniac desire to frustrate him.

After an age-long agony of doubt it became evident he was not destined to crash into the wall, but not that he was to gain the coping: through fractions of a second hideously protracted this last drew near, nearer, slowly, ever more slowly.

And he was twisting dizzily....

With frantic effort he crooked an arm over the coping at a juncture when, had he not acted instantly, he must have swung back. There was a racking wrench, as though his arm were being torn from its socket.

At the end of a struggle even more wearing he flung his other arm across the ledge, and for some time hung there, at the end of an almost taut rope, unable to overcome its resistance and pull himself in over the coping, stubbornly refusing to loose his grasp.

Presently, grown desperate, he let go with his right hand, holding fast only with the left, fumbled in a pocket, found his knife, opened it with his teeth, and began, to saw at the rope round his chest.

Strand after strand parted grudgingly till it fell away altogether and reaction from its tension threw him against the coping with such violence that he all but lost his hold. Dropping the knife, he swept his right arm up and once more hooked his fingers over the inside of the ledge.

Far down the knife clinked suggestively upon stone.

Breathing deep, Lanyard braced knees and feet against the wall, worried, heaved, hauled, squirmed like a mad thing, in the end rolled over the top and fell at length upon the roof, panting, trembling, bathed in sweat, temporarily tormented by impulses to retch.

By degrees regaining physical control, he sat up, took his bearings, and crept toward the foot of the minaret.

A small, narrow doorway in its base was on the latch. He passed through to the landing of a dark winding stairway with a dim light at the bottom of its circular well.

While he stood attentive, intermittent stridor troubled the stillness, originating at some point on the floors below: the proscribed wireless was at work.

Hearing no other sounds, Lanyard went on down the steps, at their foot pausing to spy out through a half-open doorway to the topmost storey.

Nobody moved in the corridor. He saw nothing but a line of closed doors, presumably to servants' quarters. Now, however, the vibrant rasp of the radio spark was perceptibly stronger and had a background of subdued noise, echoes of distant voices, deadened sounds of hasty footfalls, now and again a heavy thump or the bang of a door.

Moving out, he commanded the length of the corridor. Toward one end a door stood open. He could see no more of the room beyond than a narrow patch of wall fitfully illuminated by a play of violet light.

Then a man stepped out of this operating room, turning on the threshold to utter some parting observation; and Lanyard retired hastily to the shaft of the minaret stairway, but not before recognising Velasco.

A moment later the Brazilian passed his lurking-place, walking with bended head, a worried frown darkening his swarthy countenance; and Lanyard emerged in time to see his head and shoulders vanish down a stairway at the far end of the corridor.

Following with discretion, Lanyard leaned over the head of the main staircase well, looking down three flights to the ground floor, to which Velasco was descending.

The house seemed veritably to hum with secret and, to judge by the pitch of its rumour, well-nigh panic activity. One divined a scurrying as of rats about to desert a sinking ship. Untoward events had thrown this establishment into a state of excited confusion: their nature Lanyard could not surmise, but their conjunction with his designs was exasperatingly inopportune. To search this place and find his man--if he were there at all--without being discovered, while its inmates buzzed about like so many startled hornets, was a fair impossibility; to attempt it was to court death.

None the less he was inflexible in determination to go on, to push his luck to its extremity, by sheer force to bend fortuity to his service and suffer without complaint whatever the consequences of its recoil.

Yet even as he advanced a foot to begin the descent, he withdrew it.

On the ground floor, a door closing with a resounding crash had proved the signal for an outburst of expostulant, acrimonious voices: some half a dozen men giving angry tongue at one and the same time, their roars of polysyllabic gutturalisms fusing into utterly unintelligible clamour.

One thought of a mutiny in a German madhouse.

Moment after moment passed, the squall persisting with unmitigated viciousness. If now and again it subsided momentarily, it was only into uglier growls and swiftly to rise once more to high frenzy of incoherence.

Two of the disputants appeared in the square frame of the staircase well, oddly foreshortened figures brandishing wild arms, one of them Velasco, the other a man whom Lanyard failed to identify, seemingly united in common anger directed at the head of some person invisible.

Abruptly, with a gesture of almost homicidal fury, the Brazilian darted out of sight. The other followed.

Then the object of their wrath took to the stairs, stopping at the rail of the first landing and gesticulating savagely over the heads of his audience, Velasco and the others returning amid a knot of fellows to bay round the newel post.

His voice, full-throated, cried them all down--Ekstrom's deep and resonant voice, domineering over the uproar, hectoring one after another into sullen silence.

In the beginning employing nothing but terms and phrases of insolence and objurgation untranslatable, when he had secured a measure of attention he delivered a short address in tones of unqualified contempt.

"I will have obedience!" he stormed. "Let no one misunderstand my status here: I am come direct from His Majesty the Emperor with full power and authority to command and direct affairs which you have, individually, collectively, proved yourselves either unfit or unable to cope with. What I do, I do in my absolute discretion, with the full sanction and confidence of the Kaiser. He who questions my judgment or my actions, questions the wisdom of the All-Highest. Let it be clearly understood I am answerable to no one under God but myself and my Imperial master. Henceforth be good enough to hold your tongues or take the consequences-- and be damned to you all!"

Briefly he stood glowering down at their upturned faces, then sneered, and turned away.

"Come along, O'Reilly," he said. "Fetch the woman, and give no more heed to swine-dogs!"

His hand slipped up the rail to the first floor, vanished.

If O'Reilly followed with the woman mentioned, both kept back from the rail and so out of Lanyard's field of vision.

The group at the foot of the stairs moved away, grumbling profanely.

At once Lanyard began to descend, rapidly and without care to avoid detection.

One flight down he met face to face a manservant, evidently a footman, with an armful of clothing which he was conveying from one chamber to another. The fellow stopped short, jaw dropping, eyes popping; whereupon Lanyard paused and addressed him in German with a manner of overbearing contempt, that is to say, in character.

"You're wanted upstairs in the radio room," he said--"at once!"

The servant bleated one word of protest: "But--!"

"Be silent. Do as I bid you. It is an emergency. Drop those things and go! Do you hear, imbecile?"

Completely cowed and cheated, the man obeyed literally, letting his burden of garments fall to the floor and bounding hurriedly up the stairs.

Another flight was negotiated without misadventure; on this floor as well servants were flitting busily to and fro, but none favoured the adventurer with the least attention.

Midway down the third flight he pulled up to one side of the landing, and reconnoitred. It was on the next floor below, the first above the street, that Ekstrom had stopped. But in what quarter thereof? The exigency forbade the risk of one false turn. If Lanyard were to take Ekstrom unawares it must be at the first cast.

From the ground floor came semi-coherent snatches of surly comment, like growls of a thunderstorm passing off into the distance:

"*At a time such as this*...."

"*... Secret Service snapping at our heels* ..."

"*... base on the Vineyard discovered* ..."

"*... Au Printemps raided, Sophie Weringrode under arrest. God knows whether she will hold her tongue!*"

"*Trust her! But this ass* ..."

"*Bringing a woman here, putting all our necks into a halter* ..."

Immediately opposite the foot of the stairway, on the first storey, a door opened. O'Reilly came alertly forth, closed the door behind him, paused, fished in his pocket for a cigarette case, lighted and inhaled with deep appreciation, meantime eavesdropping on the utterances below with his head cocked to one side and a malicious smile shadowing his handsome Irish face.

In his own good time he shrugged an indifferent shoulder, thrust his hands into his pockets, and sauntered coolly on down the stairs.

The moment he disappeared, Lanyard went into action, in two bounds cleared landing and stairs, in another threw himself upon the door. It opened readily. Entering, he put his back to it, with his left hand groped for, found and turned a key, his right holding ready the automatic pistol he had taken from the lockers of the U-boat.

The room was a combination of administrative bureau and study, very handsomely if somewhat over-decorated and furnished, with an atmosphere as distinctively German as that of a Bierstube, the sombreness of its colour scheme lending weight to its array of massive desks, tables, chairs, bookcases, and lounges.

Between great draped windows and an impressive chimney-piece opposite, beside a broad, long desk, in a straight-backed chair sat a woman, gagged, bound as to her wrists, strips of cloth which had but lately bound ankles as well on the floor about her feet.

That woman was Cecelia Brooke.

Ekstrom stood behind her, in the act of loosening the knots which held the gag secure.

For a space of thirty seconds, transfixed by the apparition of his enemy, he did not stir other than to raise weaponless hands in deference to the pistol trained upon his head. But the blood ebbed from his face, leaving it a ghastly mask in which shone the eyes of a man who sees certain death closing in upon him and is powerless to combat it, even to die fighting for life. And his lips curled back in a snarl neither of contempt nor of hatred but of terror.

And for as long Lanyard remained as motionless, rooted in a despondency of thwarted hopes no less profound than the despair of the Prussian, apprehending what that one could not yet guess, that once more, and now certainly for the last time, vengeance was denied him, the fulfilment of all his labours and their sole purpose snatched from his grasp.

The instincts of a killer were not his. Barring injudicious attempt to summon aid or take the offensive, Ekstrom was safe from injury at the hands of Michael Lanyard. His cunning, his favour in the countenance of fortune, or whatever it was that had enabled him to make the girl his prisoner and bring her here, bade fair to prove his salvation.

Deep in Lanyard's consciousness an echo stirred of half-forgotten words: "***Vengeance is mine****…*"

The sense of frustration brewed a hopelessness as stark as that of a brow-beaten child. A blackness seemed to be settling down upon his faculties. A mist wavered momentarily before his eyes. He gulped convulsively, swallowing what had almost been a sob.

But he spoke in a voice positively dispassionate.

"Keep your hands up."

Lanyard removed and pocketed the key, crossed to the middle of the room without once letting his gaze waver from the face of the Prussian, passed behind him, planted the muzzle of the pistol beneath Ekstrom's shoulder-blade, and methodically searched him, finding and putting aside on the desk one automatic, nothing else.

"Stand aside!"

The almost puerile measure of his disappointment was betrayed in the thrust with which he shouldered Ekstrom out of the way, so forcibly that the man was sent staggering wildly half a dozen paces.

"Don't move, assassin!... Pardon, mademoiselle: one moment," Lanyard muttered, with his one free hand undoing the gag.

He made slow work of that, fumbling while watching Ekstrom with unremitting intentness, hoping against hope that his enemy might make one false move, one only, by some infatuate endeavour to turn the tables excuse his killing.

But Ekstrom would not. Recovery of his equilibrium had been coincident with the shock administered to his hardihood and sense of security by Lanyard's entrance. He stood now in a pose of insouciant grace, hands idly clasped before him, disdain glimmering in languid-lidded eyes, contempt in the set of his lips--an ensemble eloquent of brazen effrontery, the outgrowth of perception of the fact that Lanyard, being what he was, could neither shoot him down in cold blood nor, with the Brooke girl present, even attempt to injure him: compunctions unassembled in the make-up of the Boche, therefore when discovered in men of other races at once despicable and ridiculous....

The gag came away.

"Mademoiselle has not been injured?" Lanyard enquired, solicitous.

The girl coughed and gasped, shaking her head, enunciating with difficulty in little better than a husky whisper: "... roughly handled, nothing worse."

Lanyard's face burned as if his blood were molten mercury. "*Nothing worse*!" Appreciation of what handling she must have suffered, if she had resisted at all, before those beasts could have bound her, excited an indignation from whose light, as it blazed in Lanyard's eyes, even Ekstrom winced.

The hand was tremulous with which he sought to loose her wrists, so much so that she could not but notice.

"Don't mind me--look to that man!" she begged. "Leave me to unfasten these with my teeth. He can't be trusted for a single instant."

"Mademoiselle," Lanyard mumbled, instinctively employing the French idiom--"you have reason."

For an instant only he hesitated, swayed this way and that by the maddest of impulses, then resigned himself absolutely to their ascendancy.

"This goes beyond all bounds," he said in an undertone.

Deliberately leaving the Englishwoman to free herself according to her suggestion--forgetful, indeed, for the moment, that she was not altogether free--he moved to the desk and left his own automatic there beside Ekstrom's.

"Mademoiselle," he said mechanically, without looking at the girl, without power to perceive aught else in the world but the white, evil face of his enemy, "for what I am about to do, I beg you forgive me, of your charity. I can endure no more. It is too much...."

He strode past her.

She twisted in her chair, then rose, following him with wide eyes of alarm above her hands, whose bonds her teeth worried without rest.

Ekstrom had not stirred, though one flash of pure exultation had transfigured his countenance on comprehension of Lanyard's purpose: thanks to the silly scruples of this animal, one more chance for life was granted him.

Nor would the Prussian give an inch when Lanyard paused, confronting him squarely, within arm's length.

"Ekstrom," the adventurer began in a voice lacking perceptible inflection ... "what is between you and me needs no recounting. You know it too well--I likewise. It is my wish and my intention to kill you with my two hands. Nothing can prevent that, not even what you count upon, my reluctance--to you incomprehensible--to commit an act of violence in the presence of a woman. But because Miss Brooke is here, because you have brought her here by force, because you are what you are and so have treated her insolently ... before we come to our final accounting, you shall get down upon your knees and ask her pardon."

He saw no yielding in the eyes of the Prussian, only arrogance; and when he paused, he was answered in one phrase of the gutters of Berlin, couched in the imagery of its lowest boozing-kens, so unspeakably vile in essence and application that Lanyard heard it with an incredulity almost stupefying--almost, not altogether.

It was barely spoken when those lips that framed it were crushed by a blow of such lightning delivery that, though he must have been prepared for it, Ekstrom's guard was still lowered as he reeled back, lost footing, and went to his knees.

Panting, snarling, uttering teeth and blasphemy, the Prussian recoiled like a serpent, gathered himself together and launched headlong at Lanyard, only to be met full tilt by a second blow and a third, each more merciless than its predecessor, beating him down once more.

This time Lanyard did not wait for him to come back for punishment, but closed in, catching him as he strove to rise, meeting each fresh effort with ruthless accuracy, battering him into insanity of despair, so that Ekstrom came back again and again without thought, animated only by frenzied brute instinct to find the throat of his tormenter, and ever and ever failing; till at length he crumpled and lay crushed and writhing, then subsided into insensibility, was quite still but for heaving lungs and the spasmodic clutchings of his broken and ensanguined fingers....

With a start, a broken sigh, a slight movement of the hand interpreting a crushing sense of the futility of human passion, Lanyard relaxed, drew back from standing over his antagonist, abstractedly found a handkerchief and dried his hands, of a sudden so inexpressibly shamed and degraded in his own sight that he dared not look the girl's way, but stood with hang-dog air, avoiding her regard.

Yet, could he have mustered up heart, he might have surprised in her eyes a light to lift him out from this slough of humiliation, to obliterate chagrin in a flood of wonder and--misgivings.

When, however, he did after a moment turn to her, that look was gone, replaced by one that reflected something of his own apprehension; for a heavy hand was hammering on the study door, and more than one voice on the other side was calling on "Karl" to open.

Either the servant whom Lanyard had met and victimised on his way downstairs had given the alarm, or else the noise of the encounter within the study had brought that pack of spies to the door, wildly demanding admission.

Steadied by one swift exchange of alarmed glances with the girl, Lanyard hastily reviewed the room, seeking some avenue of escape. None offered but the windows. He ran to them, tore back their draperies, and found them closed with shutters of steel and padlocked.

Simultaneously the din at the door redoubled.

With a worried shake Lanyard crossed to the chimney-piece, ducked his head, and stepped into its huge fireplace. One upward glance sufficed to dash his hopes:

here was no way out, arduous though feasible; immediately above the fireplace the flue narrowed so that not even the most active man of normal stature might hope to negotiate its ascent.

He returned with only a gesture of disconcertion to answer the girl's look of appeal.

"Can we do nothing?" she asked, raising her voice a trifle to make it heard above the tumult in the corridor.

"There's no help for it, I'm afraid," he said, going to the desk and taking up the pistols--"nothing to do but shoot our way out, if we can. Take this," he added, offering her one of the weapons, which she accepted without spirit. "If you can't get your own consent to use it, give it to me when I've emptied the other."

She breathed a dismayed "Yes ..." and wonderingly consulted his face, since he did not stir other than thoughtfully to replace his pistol on the desk, then stood staring at his soot-smeared palms.

"What is it?" she demanded nervously. "Why do you hesitate?"

As one fretted by inconsequential questions, he merely shook his head, glancing sidelong once at the unconscious Prussian, again with calculation toward the door.

This he saw quivering under repeated blows.

With brusque decision he said: "Get a chair--brace it beneath the door-knob, please!"--and leaving her without more explanation turned back to the fireplace.

Motionless, in dumb confusion, the girl stood staring after him till roused by a blow of such splintering force as to suggest that an axe had been brought into play upon the door, then ran to a ponderous club chair and with considerable exertion managed to trundle it to the door and tip it over, wedging its back beneath the knob.

By this time it had become indisputably patent that an axe was battering the panels. But the door, in character with the room, was a substantial piece of workmanship and needed more than a few blows, even of an axe, to break down its barrier of solid oak.

She looked round to discover Lanyard kneeling beside Ekstrom, insanely--so it seemed to the girl--engaged in blackening the upper half of the man's face with a handful of soot.

Unconsciously uttering a little cry of distress she sped to his side and caught his shoulder with an importunate hand.

"In Heaven's name, Monsieur Duchemin, what are you doing? Is this a time for childishness--?"

He responded with a smile of boyish mischief so genuine that her doubts of his reason seemed all too well confirmed.

"Making up my understudy," he said simply. And brushing his hands over the rug to rid them of superfluous soot, Lanyard rose. "Please go back and stand by the door--on the side of the hinges. I'll be with you in one minute."

Resigned to humour this lunatic whim--what else could she do?--the girl retreated to the position designated, and watched with ever darker doubts of his sanity, while Lanyard hurriedly drew the shells from his automatic and carefully placed its butt in the slack grasp of Ekstrom's fingers.

Then, lifting from a near-by table a great cut-glass bowl of flowers, the adventurer inverted it over Ekstrom's body.

Expending its full force upon the man's chest, that miniature deluge splashed widely, wetting his face, half filling his open mouth. Some of the soot was washed away, but not a great deal: enough stuck fast to suit Lanyard's purpose.

Roused by that cool shock, half strangled as well, Ekstrom coughed violently, squirmed, spat out a mouthful of water, and lifted on an elbow, still more than half dazed.

Joining the girl by the door, Lanyard saw the Prussian sit up and glare blankly round the room, a figure of tragic fun, drenched, woefully disfigured, eyes rolling wildly in the wide spaces round them which Lanyard had left unblackened.

Swinging the club chair away from the door, the adventurer placed it with its back to the room.

"Get down behind that," he indicated shortly, and drew the key from his pocket. "Don't show yourself for your life. And let me have that pistol, please."

A bright triangular wedge of steel broke through one of the panels as he fitted and turned the key in the lock.

His wits clearing, Ekstrom saw him and with a howl of fury staggered to his feet, clutching the unloaded pistol and endeavouring to level it for steady aim.

Simultaneously Lanyard turned the knob and let the door fly open, remaining beside the chair that hid the girl.

A knot of spies, O'Reilly and Velasco among them, whirled into the room, pulled up at sight of that strange, grim figure, disguised beyond all recognition by its half-mask of black, facing and menacing them with a pistol.

O'Reilly fired in the next breath, his shot echoed by half a dozen so closely bunched as to resemble the rattle of a mitrailleuse.

At the first report the pistol dropped from Ekstrom's grasp. He carried a hand vaguely to his throat, staggered a single step, uttered a strangled moan, and fell forward, his body fairly riddled, his death little short of instantaneous.

While the fusillade was still resounding Lanyard, seizing the girl's wrist, unceremoniously dragged her from behind the chair and thrust her through the door, retreating after her with his face to the roomfull, his pistol ready.

None of that lot paid him any heed, the attention of all wholly absorbed by the tragedy their violent hands had wrought. Velasco, the first to stir, ran forward and dropped to his knees beside the dead man. Others followed.

Gently Lanyard drew the door to, locked it on the outside, and at the sound of a choking cry from Cecelia Brooke, whirled smartly round, prepared if need be to make good his promise to clear with gun-play a way to the street though opposed by every inmate of the establishment.

But the first face he saw was Crane's.

The Secret Service man stood within a yard. To him as to a rock of refuge Cecelia Brooke had flown, to his hand she was clinging like a frightened child, trying to speak, failing because she choked on sobs and gasps of horror.

Behind him, on the landing at the head of the staircase, running up from below, ascending to the upper storeys, were a score' or more of men of sturdy and business-like bearing and indubitably American stamp. Of these two were herding into a corner a little group of frightened German servants.

Lanyard's stare of astonishment was met by Crane's twisted smile.

"My friend," he said, as quietly as anyone could with his accent of a quizzical buzz-saw, "I sure got to hand it to you. Every time I try to pull anything off on the dead quiet you beat me to it clean. Everywhere I think you ain't and can't be, that's just where you are. But I ain't complaining; I got to admit, if you hadn't staged your act to occupy the minds of those gents in there, we might've had a lot more difficulty raiding this joint."

Quickly he wound an arm round the waist of Cecelia Brooke when, without warning, she swayed blindly and would have fallen.

"Here, now!" he protested. "That's no way to do.... Why, she's flickered out! Well, Monsieur Duchemin-Lanyard-Ember, to a man up a tree this looks like your job. You take this little lady off my hands and see her home, and I'll just naturally try and finish what I started--or what you did. For, son, I got to give you credit: you sure are one grand li'l trouble-hound!"

XXI
QUESTION

Through the breathing hush of that dark hour which foreruns the dawn, that hour in which the head that knows a wakeful pillow is prone to sudden and disquieting apprehension of its insignificance and it's soul's dread isolation, the cab sped swiftly south upon the Avenue, shadowed reaches of the park upon its right, upon its left the dull, tired faces of those homes whose tenants lay wrapped in the cotton-wool of riches.

The rain had ceased. A little wind was blowing up. There was a fresh smell in the air. Sidewalks began to be maculated with spreading areas of dryness, but the roadway was still wet and shining, the wide black mirror of a myriad lights.

Through the windows of the speeding cab an orderly procession of street lamps, marching past, threw each its fugitive and pallid glimmer. Periods of modified darkness intervened, when the face of the girl in her corner seemed a vision subtle and wraithlike. But ever the recurrent lights revealed her sweetly incarnate if deep in enervation of crushing weariness.

Once she stirred and sighed profoundly; and Lanyard, bending toward her, asked if he could be in any way of service.

She replied in an undertone scarcely better than a whisper: "Thank you, I am quite comfortable.... Please--what time is it?"

The cab was passing Sixtieth Street. Lanyard caught a fleeting glimpse of a street clock with a dial like a little golden moon.

"It's just four."

"Thank you...."

"Very tired?"

"Very...."

He had the maddest notion that her head inclined to droop toward his shoulder. Perhaps the motion of the cab.... If so, she recovered easily.

"Can I do anything?"

"No, thank you, only ..." An ungloved hand stirred from her lap and for the merest instant rested lightly above his own, or hovered rather, barely touching it with a touch tenuous and elusive, no sooner realised than gone. "I mean," she murmured, "I am a bit too overwrought, too tired, to talk."

"I quite understand," he said. "Please forget I'm here; just rest."

Perhaps she smiled drowsily. Or was that, too, a freak of his imagination? Lanyard assured himself it was, in excess of consideration even tried to persuade himself he had dreamed that ghost of a caress upon his hand. It seemed so little like her.

Not that anything had happened more than a gesture of transient inadvertence due to fatigue. It could not have been intentional, that act of intimacy, when the girl was altogether engrossed in young Thackeray.

There was something one must not forget, something that gave the lie flatly to that innuendo of the Weringrode's. Ignorant of the circumstances the intrigante had leaped blindly at conclusions, after the habit of her kind.

True, Sophie had not implied that this girl cared for him, but vice versa: either supposition, however, was as absurd as the other. As if Lanyard could love a woman who loved another! As if the name of love meant aught to him but the memory of a sweetness like a vagrant air of Spring that had breathed fitfully for a season upon the Winter of his heart!

A corner of Lanyard's mouth lifted in a sneer. That precious heart of his! the heart of a thief upon which even now the fruits of his thieving weighed....

Irritated, he wrenched his thoughts into another channel, and began to piece together inconsecutive snatches of information gained from Crane in the confusion of the quarter hour just past, while the Secret Service operatives were busy rounding up the inmates of that spy-fold and searching for evidences of their impudent activities.

It appeared that Washington had at length, however tardily, roused out of its inertia and at midnight had telegraphed instructions to arrest out of hand every enemy alien in the land against whom there was evidence of conspiracy or even a ponderable suspicion.

So unexpected was this order that Crane had volunteered to show Cecelia Brooke that midnight rendezvous of the Prussian spy system without the least notion that he might be required before morning to lead a raiding force against the establishment; and even when a messenger stopped him as he turned to enter Au Printemps, he was not advised concerning the cause of this demand for his immediate presence at headquarters.

The first cast of what Crane aptly termed the dragnet had brought in the management and service staff to a man, with a number of the restaurant's habitues, including Sophie Weringrode and her errand-boy, the exquisite Mr. Revel.

Velasco, however, had somehow mysteriously managed to slip through the meshes and had straightway hastened to spread the alarm.

As for O'Reilly and Dressier, they had left with Ekstrom in pursuit of Lanyard less than five minutes before, and so had escaped not only arrest but all knowledge of the raid prior to their return to Seventy-ninth Street.

The second cast of the net had been made at the latter place as soon as the watchers were able to assure Crane that Ekstrom and O'Reilly had returned--Dressier having anticipated them there by something like half an hour.

By daybreak, then, these gentry would be interned on Ellis Island....

And break of day impended visibly in grayish shades that stole westward through the cross-town streets like clouds of secret agents spying out the city against invasion by the serried lances of the sun.

A garish twilight washed Forty-second Street from wall to wall by the time the car swung round in front of the Knickerbocker. As yet, however, there was little evidence that the town was growing restive in its sleep with premonition of the ardour of another day.

Lanyard stepped down and offered the girl a hand in whose palm her slender fingers rested lightly for an instant ere she passed on, while he turned to bid the driver wait. Following, he overtook her in the entrance, where by tacit consent both paused and lingered in an odd constraint. There was so much to be said that was impossible to say just then.

Visibly the woman drooped, betraying physical exhaustion in every line of her pose, seeming scarcely strong enough to lift the silken lashes that trembled upon cheeks a little drawn and pale, with the faintest of bluish rings beneath the eyes.

"I must not keep you," Lanyard broke the silence. "I merely wished to say good-night and ... I am sorry."

"Sorry?" she echoed.

"That you had such an unhappy experience," he explained--"thanks to your thoughtfulness for me. I do not deserve so much consideration; and that only makes me feel all the more regretful."

"It was silly of me," she admitted with a shadowy, rueful smile. "I'm afraid my silliness makes too much trouble...."

He commented honestly: "I don't understand."

"If I had only been patient enough to wait for you to call me...."

"Forgive that oversight. I was pressed for time, as you may imagine."

"Oh, it all comes back to my own stupidity. I might have known you had come through all right."

"How should you?"

"Why not?--when you turn up here in New York safe and sound after being drowned on the *Assyrian*!--as if that were not proof enough that you bear a charmed life!"

"Charmed!" he laughed.

"And you haven't yet told me how you survived that adventure."

"You are kind to be interested, and I am unfortunate in never seeing you save under circumstances unfavourable for yarn-spinning."

"You might be more fortunate."

"Only tell me how!"

"If you cared to ask me to dine with you to-morrow--I mean, to-night--"

"You would--?"

He was distressed by consciousness that his voice had thrilled impetuously. But perhaps she had not noticed; there was no change in the even friendliness of her tone.

"I'm as inquisitive as any woman that ever lived. Even if I wished to, I'm afraid I shouldn't be able to resist an invitation to hear your Odyssey."

"Delmonico's at eight?"

"Thank you," she said primly.

"You make me too happy. May I call for you?"

"Please." She offered a hand whose touch he found cool, steady, and impersonal. "Good morning, Mr. Ember."

He stood in a stare while she went quickly through the lobby to a waiting elevator, then roused and went back to his cab.

It was by daylight that he reentered his rooms and found them tenanted by a negro boy bound and gagged, bruised and sore, and scared beyond intelligible expression.

Freeing him and salving his injuries bodily and spiritual with a liberal douceur, Lanyard exacted an oath of silence, then turned him out.

He had approximately five hours to put in somehow before his appointment with Colonel Stanistreet at nine, and was too well versed in the lore of late hours to think of giving any part of that time to sleep. By so doing he would only insure a mutinous awakening, with mind and body sluggish and unrested. If, on the other hand, he remained awake, he would go to that interview in a state of supernormal animation exceedingly to be desired if he were to round out this adventure without discredit.

For its end was not yet. He had still a part to play whose lines were not yet written, whose business remained to be invented. He neither dared shirk that appointment, for reasons of policy, nor wished to, while there remained reparation to be accomplished, a wrong to be righted, justice to be done, a question to be answered.

Only when these matters had been put in order would he feel his honour discharged of its burdens, himself free once more to drop out and go in peace his lonely ways in life, ways henceforth to be both lonely and aimless.

For, when he strove to peer into the future, only an emptiness confronted him. With Ekstrom accounted for finally and forevermore, there was nothing to come but the final accounting of the Lone Wolf with that civilization which had bred and suffered him.

One way presented itself to make that reckoning even. The Foreign Legion of France asks no embarrassing questions of its recruits, and enlistment in its ranks offers with anonymity a consoling certainty.

Thus alone might he find his way home to the heart of that enigma whence he had emerged, a nameless waif astray in grim Parisian by-ways....

This vision of his end contenting him, he began to scheme a campaign for the day that was simple enough in prospect: a little chicanery with Stanistreet, a personal appeal to Crane to restore the passports of Monsieur Andre Duchemin which must have been found on Ekstrom's body, a berth on some steamer sailing for Europe, then the last evanishment.

One detail alone troubled him, his promise to the Brooke girl that she should dine with him that night.

Reminded of this obligation, figuratively he seized Michael Lanyard by the scruff of his neck and shook him with a savage hand. What insensate folly was ever his, what want of wit and strength to keep out of temptation's ways! Why must he have fallen in so readily with her suggestion? Why this infatuate thirst for sympathy, this eagerness to violate the seals of reticence at the wish of a strange woman? Was there any reasonable explanation of the strange lack of his wonted self-sufficiency in the company of Cecelia Brooke?

No matter. If he might not contrive somehow to squirm out of that engagement, he could at all events school himself to decent reticence. He promised himself to make his account of the submarine adventure drearily bald and trite, to minimize to the last degree his part therein, above all things to refrain from painting the Lone Wolf in romantic colours.

She was much too good a sort, too straight, sincere, fair-minded, honest--the sort of girl who deserved the Thackeray sort of man, never a thief.

If she even dreamed....

Lanyard brought forth from its hiding place the necklace, weighed it in his hand, examined it minutely. Granting its marvellous perfection, he recognized no more its beauty, dispassionately reviewed in turn each stone of matchless loveliness, no more susceptible to their seductive purity, perceiving in them nothing but hard, bright, translucent pebbles, cold, soulless, cruel.

One by one they slipped through his fingers like beads of an unholy rosary.

At length, crushing them together in the hollow of his palm, he stood a while in thought, then turning to his writing-desk bundled the necklace in wrappings of white tissue secured with rubber bands, counted carefully the sheaf of bills he had taken from Ekstrom, sealed the whole amount in a plain, long envelope, and put this aside in company with the necklace.

Already two hours had passed and, since he meant to call at the house on West End Avenue well in advance of the hour when Cecelia Brooke might be there-- presuming Blensop to have given her the same appointment as he had given "Mr. Ember," that is, nine o'clock--it was now time to prepare.

Returning to his bedchamber, he laid out a carefully selected change of clothing, shaved, parboiled himself in a hot bath, chilled him to the pith in one of icy coldness, and dressed with scrupulous heed to detail, studiously effacing every sign of his sleepless night.

That experience was in no way to be surmised from his appearance when he sallied forth to breakfast at the Plaza.

At eight precisely, presenting himself at the Stanistreet residence, he desired the footman to announce him as the author of a certain telegram from Edgartown.

He was obliged to wait less than a minute, the footman returning in haste to request him to step into the library.

This apartment--which he found much as he had last seen it, eight hours ago, its window shattered, the portieres down, the furniture in some disorder--was, on his introduction, occupied by two persons, one an elderly, iron-gray gentleman of untidy dress and unobtrusive habit in spite of a discerning cool, gray eye, the other Mr. Blensop in the neatest of one-button morning-coat effects, with striped trouserings neither too smart nor too sober for that state of life unto which it had pleased God to call him, and fair white spats.

If his attire was radiant, so was the temper of the secretary sunny. He tripped forward in sprightliest fashion, offering cordial hands to the caller till he recognized him, and even then was discountenanced only for the briefest moment.

"My dear Mr. Ember!" he purred soothingly--"why didn't you tell me last night it was you who had sent that telegram? If I had for a moment suspected the truth you should have had your appointment with Colonel Stanistreet at any hour you might have cared to name, no matter how ungodly!"

Lanyard bowed gravely. "Thank you," he said. "And Colonel Stanistreet--?"

"Is just finishing breakfast. He will be down directly. Please be seated, make yourself entirely at ease. And will you excuse me--?"

"With pleasure," Lanyard assured him, his gravity unbroken.

A doubt clouded Mr. Blensop's bright eyes, but its transit was instantaneous.

He turned forthwith to join the iron-gray man before the portrait which concealed the safe.

"And now, Mr. Stone," said Mr. Blensop, with indulgence.

"Well, sir," said Mr. Stone quietly, "if you'll be good enough to show me how this contraption works, maybe I'll find out something interesting, maybe not."

Mr. Blensop proceeded to oblige by operating the lever and sliding aside the portrait.

"Thanks," said Mr. Stone, producing a magnifying glass from a waistcoat pocket and beginning to peer myopically at the face of the safe. "I take it nobody's been pawing over this since the late, as you might say, unpleasantness?"

"Not a soul has touched it. By Colonel Stanistreet's order it was covered as soon as we found it had been tampered with."

"*Um-m*," Mr. Stone acknowledged, bending close to his work.

Partially, perhaps, by way of administering an urbane rebuke to Lanyard for his readiness to dispense with his society, Mr. Blensop remained in the neighbourhood of Mr. Stone, hovering round him like a domesticated humming-bird.

"Do you find anything?" he enquired, when Stone straightened up.

"Fingerprints a-plenty," Mr. Stone admitted with a hint of temper--"a slew of the damn things. Looks like you must've called in the neighbours to help make a good show. However, we'll see what we can make of 'em."

He conjured from some recess in his clothing a squat bottle, from another a stopper in which was fitted a blowpipe, joined the two together, approached the safe with one end of the pipe between his lips and sprayed it with a thin film of white powder, the contents of the bottle.

"I say, do tell me what that's for?"

"That," said Mr. Stone patiently, "is to make the fingerprints stand out, so we can get a good likeness of 'em."

He put the bottle aside, blinked at the safe approvingly, and by further exercise of powers of legerdemain materialized a pocket kodak and a flashlight pistol.

"Can't I help you?" Blensop offered eagerly. "I used to be rather a dab at amateur photography, you know."

"Well, I'm kind of stuck on pressing the button myself," Stone confessed, adjusting the focus. "But if you want to work that flashlight, I don't mind."

"Delighted," Mr. Blensop asserted. "How does it go, now?"

"Like this." Stone set his camera down to demonstrate. "Now just stand behind me," he concluded, "and pull the trigger when I say 'now'."

"I'll do my best, but--I say--will it bang?"

Stone had taken up the camera once more. His sole answer was a grunt upon which his hearers placed two distinct interpretations--Lanyard's affording him considerable gratification.

"If you're ready," said Stone--"*now*"

Mr. Blensop squinted unbecomingly and pressed the trigger. A vivid flare lifted from the pan of the pistol, and winked out in a cloud of vapour, slowly dissipating.

"Is that all?"

"Yes, sir--that's all of that." Stone stowed the camera away about his person and from another cranny produced a small cardboard box of glass slides, one of which he offered. "Now if you'll just run your fingers through your hair and rest them on this slide, light but steady...."

"What for?" Blensop demanded with a giggle of nervous reluctance. "You don't think I'm the thief, do you?"

"No, sir, I don't. But if I haven't got your fingerprints, how am I going to tell them from the thief's?"

"Oh, I see," Blensop said with a note of allayed apprehension, and put himself on record.

The door opening to admit Colonel Stanistreet, Lanyard rose. At sight of him the Englishman checked and stared enquiringly, his eyes shadowed by careworn brows; for it was apparent that, if the events of the night had not depressed the spirits of the secretary, his employer had known little sleep or none since the burglary.

"Colonel Stanistreet," Blensop said melodiously, abandoning Stone to his unsupervised devices, "this is Mr. Ember, the gentleman who called last night before you got home. It appears he is the person who sent us that telegram from Edgartown day before yesterday."

"Indeed? Ember is not the name with which the message was signed."

"The message was purposely left unsigned," Lanyard explained.

Stanistreet nodded approval. "I am glad to meet you, Mr. Ember," he said, offering a hand. "Be seated. I am most anxious first to express our gratitude, next to learn how you came by your information."

"You will find it an interesting story."

"No doubt of that." Stanistreet took the desk chair, opened a cigar humidor, and offered it. "I shall be even more interested, however," he said with an evanescent trace of humour, "to know who the devil you are, sir."

"That is something I am prepared to prove to your satisfaction."

"If you will be so good.... But excuse me for one moment." Stanistreet turned in his chair. "Mr. Stone?"

"Yes, sir."

"Have you finished with the safe? If so, I want my secretary to check over its contents carefully and make sure nothing else is missing."

"I'm all through with it, Colonel Stanistreet. Now, if you don't mind, I'm going to mouse around and see if I can nose out anything else that's useful."

"That shall be entirely as you will. Now, Blensop"--Stanistreet nodded to the secretary--"let us make certain...."

"Yes, sir."

Blithely Mr. Blensop addressed himself to the safe.

"There has been an accident of some sort, Colonel Stanistreet?" Lanyard enquired civilly, nodding toward the shattered French window.

"A burglary, sir."

"The criminal escaped--?"

Stanistreet nodded. "Our watchman surprised him, and was shot for his pains--not seriously, I'm happy to say. The burglar got himself tangled up in that window, but extricated in time, and went over the garden wall before we could determine which way he had taken."

"I trust you lost nothing of value?"

Stanistreet shrugged. "Unhappily, we did--a diamond necklace, the property of my sister-in-law, and--ah--a document we could ill afford to part with.... But you offered to show me credentials, I believe."

"Such as they are," Lanyard replied. "My passports and letters were stolen from me. But these, I think, should serve as well to prove my bona fides."

He laid out in order upon the desk his plunder from the safe aboard the U-boat-

-all but the money--the three cipher codes, the log, the diary of the commander, the directory of German secret agents, and such other documents as he had selected.

The first Colonel Stanistreet took up with a dubious frown which swiftly lightened, yielding, as he pursued his examination into the papers and began to recognize their surpassing value to the Allied cause, to a subdued glimmer of gratulatory excitement.

But he was at pains to satisfy himself as to the authenticity of each paper in turn, providing a lull for which Lanyard was not ungrateful since it gave him a chance to adjust his understanding to an unexpected development in the affair.

He lounged at ease, smoking, his eyes, half-veiled by lowered lids, keenly reviewing the room and its tenants.

Stone, the detective (an operative, Lanyard rightly inferred, of the American Secret Service, loaned to the British in order to keep the burglary out of police records and newspapers), had wandered out into the garden that glowed with young April sunlight beyond the windows. From time to time he was to be seen stooping and inspecting the earth with the gravity of an earnest, efficient, sober-sided sleuth of the old school.

Blensop was busy before the safe, extracting the contents of each pigeonhole in turn, thumbing its dockets of papers, checking each off upon a typewritten list several pages in length.

To that lithe and debonair figure Lanyard's gaze oftenest reverted.

So not only had the necklace been stolen but "a document" which the British Secret Service "could ill afford to part with"!

Lanyard entertained no least doubt as to the identity of the document in question. There could be but one, he felt, which Stanistreet would so characterize.

That document had not been in the safe when Lanyard had opened it at midnight.

After a moment Mr. Blensop uttered a musical note of vexation. The lead of his pencil had broken. He threw it pettishly aside, came over to the desk, took up a penholder, dipped it in the ink-well, and returned to his task.

XXII
CHICANE

Colonel Stanistreet put down the last of the papers and slapped his hand upon it resoundingly.

"This is one of the most remarkable collections of data, I venture to assert, that has ever come into the hands of the British Government. Have you any idea of its value?"

Lanyard lifted a whimsical eyebrow. "Some," he admitted drily.

"And what do you ask for it, sir?"

"Nothing."

The gaze of the Englishman bored into his eyes; but he met their challenge with an unshaken countenance, smiling.

"My dear sir," Stanistreet demanded--"who are you?"

"The name under which I sailed for New York on board the **Assyrian**," Lanyard announced quietly, "was Andre Duchemin."

Disturbed by a startled exclamation, together with a sound of shuffling and a slight thump, he looked round in mild curiosity to see Blensop staggered and astare, standing over a litter of documents which had slipped from his grasp to the floor. Mastering his emotion quickly enough, the secretary knelt with a mumbled apology and began to pick up the papers.

With no more notice of the incident Lanyard returned undivided attention to Colonel Stanistreet.

"I had another name," he confessed, "and a reputation none too savoury, as, I daresay, you know. Through the courtesy of the British Intelligence Office I was permitted to disguise these; but on the **Assyrian** I was recognized--in short, ran afoul of German Secret Service agents who knew me, but whom I did not know. On the sixth night out circumstances conspired to make me seem a serious obstacle to their schemes. Consequently I was waylaid, robbed, and thrown overboard. Within the next few minutes a torpedo struck the ship and the submarine which fired it came up under me as I struggled to keep afloat. By passing myself off as a Boche spy, I succeeded in inducing the commander to take me below, and so reached the Martha's Vineyard base. There chance played into my hands: I contrived to sink the U-boat and escape, as reported in my telegram."

During a brief silence he found opportunity to observe that Mr. Blensop was working with hands that trembled singularly.

"Incredible!" Stanistreet commented.

"Yet here is proof," Lanyard asserted, indicating the papers beneath Stanistreet's hand.

"My dear sir, I didn't mean--"

"Pardon!" Lanyard smiled, with a lifted hand. "I never thought you did, Colonel Stanistreet. But it is your duty to make sure you are not imposed upon by plausible adventurers. Therefore--since my papers have been stolen--I am glad to be able to prove my identity with Andre Duchemin by referring to survivors of the *Assyrian* disaster, among others Mr. Sherry, the second officer, Mr. Crane of the United States Secret Service, and a countrywoman of yours, a Miss Cecelia Brooke, whose acquaintance I was fortunate enough to make."

Stanistreet nodded heavily, and consulted his watch. "Miss Brooke," he said, "should be here shortly. Blensop made an appointment with her last night, which I confirmed by telephone this morning."

"Then, with permission, I shall remain and ask her to vouch for me," Lanyard suggested in resignation, since it appeared he was not to be permitted to escape this girl, that destiny was not yet finished with their entanglement.

"I shall be glad if you will, sir.... Monsieur Duchemin," Stanistreet began, but hesitated--"or do you prefer another style?"

"I am content with Duchemin."

"That is a matter for your own discretion, but I should warn you it may already have acquired an evil odour on this side. To my knowledge it has been used within the last twenty-four hours, and the pretensions of its wearer supported by your stolen credentials."

"I am not surprised," Lanyard stated reflectively. "A chap with a beard, perhaps?"

"Why, yes...."

"Anderson," the adventurer nodded: "that, at least, was his alias when he jockeyed himself into the second steward's berth aboard the ***Assyrian***."

He glanced idly across the room, discovered Blensop once more at pause in a stare, and grinned amiably.

"He came here last night," Stanistreet volunteered deliberately-- "representing himself as Andre Duchemin--to sell me a certain paper, the same which subsequently, I am convinced, he returned to steal."

"And did," Lanyard added.

"And did," the Briton conceded. "Now you have told me who he is, I promise you every effort shall be made to apprehend him and prevent further misuse of the name you have assumed."

"It has," Lanyard said tersely.

"I beg your pardon?"

"I say every effort has been made--and successfully--to accomplish the ends you mention."

"What's that you say?" Blensop demanded shrilly, crossing to the desk.

"My secretary," Stanistreet explained, "was present at the interview, and is naturally interested."

"And very good of him, I'm sure," Lanyard agreed. "I was about to explain, Mr. Blensop, that Ekstrom, alias Anderson, was killed in the course of a raid on the Prussian spy headquarters in Seventy-ninth Street this morning."

"Amazing!" Blensop gasped. "I am glad to hear it," he added, and went slowly back to his task.

"I may as well tell you, sir," Lanyard pursued, "I have every reason to believe the document sold you last night was one of those stolen from me."

Stanistreet wagged a contentious head.

"I cannot conceive how it could have come into your possession, sir."

"Simply enough. Miss Brooke requested me to take care of it for her."

The eyes of the Englishman grew stony. "Miss Brooke!" he repeated testily. "I don't understand."

"It was a document--I do not seek to know its nature from you, sir--of vital importance in this present crisis, with the United States newly entered into the war."

Stanistreet affirmed with an inclination of his head.

"I may tell you this much, Monsieur Duchemin: if it had not reached this country safely.... What am I saying? If it be not recovered without delay, the chances of America's early and efficient participation in the war will suffer a tremendous setback ... Blensop, be good enough to call up the American Secret Service at once and ask whether the document in question was found on the body of this--ah--Ekstrom."

"Pardon," Lanyard interposed as Blensop hesitantly approached the telephone. "It would be a waste of time. I happen to know, because I was there, that no such document was found on Ekstrom's body."

"The devil!" Stanistreet grumbled. "What can have become of it? This business grows only the blacker the deeper one seeks to fathom it. I must own myself completely at a loss. How it came into the hands of Miss Brooke--"

"I can explain that, I think. The document was in the care of two gentlemen, Mr. Bartholomew and Lieutenant Thackeray. The former was murdered by the Huns in search of it, Lieutenant Thackeray murderously assaulted. But for Miss Brooke's intervention the assassins must have succeeded. As it was, the young woman herself found it and, one presumes, took charge of it because her fiance was incapacitated, and possibly with the notion that she might thereby prevent further mischief of the same nature."

"Her fiance?" Stanistreet echoed blankly.

"Lieutenant Thackeray--"

"Her brother, sir!" the Briton laughed. "Thackeray was his nom de service."

It was Lanyard's turn to stare. "Ah!" he murmured. "A light begins to dawn...."

"Upon me as well," Stanistreet confessed. "Miss Brooke and her brother are orphans and, before the war, were inseparable companions. I do not doubt that, learning he had been commissioned with an uncommonly perilous errand, she booked passage by the *Assyrian* without his consent, in order to be near him in event of danger."

"This explains much," Lanyard conceded--"much that perplexed more than one can say."

"But in no way advances us on the trail of the purloined document."

"I am afraid, sir," Lanyard lied deliberately, "you may as well abandon all hope of ever seeing it again. Ekstrom made away with it: no question about that. There was time enough and to spare between his exploit here and his death for him to deliver it to safe hands. It is doubtless decoded by this time, a copy of it already well on the way to the Wilhelmstrasse."

"I am afraid," Stanistreet echoed--"I am very much afraid you are right."

His thick, spatulate fingers of an executive drummed heavily upon the desk.

Stone's figure darkened the windows.

"Colonel Stanistreet?" he called diffidently.

"Yes, Mr. Stone?"

"There's something here I'd like to consult you about, sir, if you can spare a minute."

"Certainly." The Englishman rose. "If you will excuse me, Monsieur Duchemin...." Half way to the windows he hesitated. "By the bye, Blensop, I wish you'd call up Apthorp and ask after Howson's condition."

"Very good, sir," Blensop intoned cheerfully.

"And do it without delay, please. I don't like to think of the poor fellow suffering."

"Immediately, sir."

As his employer passed out into the garden with Stone, the secretary discontinued his checking and came over to the desk, drawing up a chair and sitting down to telephone. At the same time Lanyard got up and began to pace thoughtfully to and fro.

"Howson is the wounded night watchman, I take it, Mr. Blensop?"

"Yes--an excellent fellow.... Schuyler nine, three hundred," Blensop cooed into the transmitter.

Conceivably that ostensible discomfiture whose symptoms Lanyard had remarked had been a transitory humour. Mr. Blensop was now in what seemed the most equable and blithe of tempers. His very posture at the telephone eloquently betokened as much: he had thrown himself into the chair with picturesque nonchalance, sitting with body half turned from the desk, his right hand holding the receiver to his ear, his left thrust carelessly into his trouser pocket, thus dragging back the lapel of that impeccable morning-coat and exposing the bright cap of his gold-mounted fountain pen.

Something in that implement seemed to possess for Lanyard overpowering fascination. His gaze yearned for it, returned again and again to it.

He changed his course to stroll up and down behind Blensop, between him and the safe.

"I understood Colonel Stanistreet to say the watchman was not seriously injured, I believe," he observed, with interest.

"Shot through the shoulder, that is all.... Schuyler nine, three hundred? Dr. Apthorp, please. This is Mr. Blensop speaking, secretary to Colonel Stanistreet.... Are you there, Dr. Apthorp?"

With professional dexterity Lanyard en passant dropped a hand over the young man's shoulder and lightly lifted the pen from its place in the pocket of Blensop's waistcoat; the even tempo of his step unbroken, he tossed it toward the safe, where it fell without sound upon a heavy Persian rug.

"Yes--about Howson," the musical accents continued, "Colonel Stanistreet is most solicitous...."

Swiftly Lanyard moved toward the safe, glanced through the French windows to assure himself that Stanistreet and Stone were safely preoccupied, whipped out the envelope he had prepared, and thrust it into a file of papers which did not crowd its pigeonhole; accomplishing the complete manoeuvre with such adroitness that, like the business of the pen, it passed utterly without the knowledge of the secretary.

"Thank you so much. *Good* morning, Dr. Apthorp."

Lanyard was passing the desk when Blensop rose, and the footman was entering with his salver.

"A lady to see Colonel Stanistreet, sir--by appointment, she says."

Blensop glanced at the card. At the same time Stanistreet came in from the garden, leaving Stone to potter about visibly in the distance.

"Miss Brooke is here, sir," the secretary announced.

"Ask her to come in, please."

The footman retired.

"Howson is resting easily, Dr. Apthorp reports," Blensop added, going back to the safe. "Has Stone turned up anything of interest, sir?"

"Footprints," Stanistreet replied with a snort of moderate impatience. "He's quite upset since I've informed him the man who made them is--"

"***Good God***!"

The interruption was Blensop's in a voice strangely out of tune. Stanistreet wheeled sharply upon him.

"What the deuce--!" he snapped.

By every indication the secretary had suffered the most severe shock of his experience. His face was ghastly, his eyes vacant; his knees shook beneath him; one hand pressed convulsively the bosom of his waistcoat. His endeavours to reply evoked only a husky, rattling sound.

"What the devil has come over you?" Stanistreet insisted.

The rattle became articulate: "I've lost it! It's gone!"

"What have you lost?"

"N-nothing, sir. That is--I mean to say--my fountain pen."

"The way you take it, I should say you'd lost your head," Stanistreet commented. "You must have dropped the thing somewhere. Look about, see if you can't find it."

Thus admonished, the secretary began to search the floor with frantic glances, and as the footman ushered in Cecelia Brooke, Lanyard saw the young man dart forward and retrieve the pen with a start of relief wellnigh as unmanning as the shock of loss had seemed.

With that Lanyard's interest in the fellow waned; he was too poor a thing to consider seriously; while here was one who compelled anew, as ever when they met, the homage of sincere and marvelling admiration.

Yet another of those miracles of feminine adaptability and makeshift had brought the girl to this meeting in the guise of one who had never known a broken night or an hour's care, with a look of such fresh tranquility that it seemed hardly possible she could be one and the same with that wilted little woman whom Lanyard had left in the gray dawn at the entrance to the Hotel Knickerbocker. A tailored suit, necessarily borrowed plumage, became her so completely that it was difficult to believe it not her own. Her eyes were calm and sweet with candour; her colour was a clear and artless glow; the hand she offered the Briton was tremorless.

"Colonel Stanistreet?"

"I am he, Miss Brooke. It is kind of you to call so early to relieve my mind about your brother. I have known Lionel so long...."

"He is resting easily," said the girl. "His complete recovery is merely a matter of time and nursing."

"That is good news," said Stanistreet. "Monsieur Duchemin I believe you know."

"I have been fortunate in that at least."

Gravely Lanyard saluted the hand extended to him in turn. "Mademoiselle is most gracious," he said humbly.

"Then--I understand--Monsieur Duchemin must have told you--?" The girl addressed Stanistreet.

"Permit me to leave you--" Lanyard interposed.

"No," she begged--"please not! I've nothing to say that you may not hear. You have been too much involved--"

"If mademoiselle insists," Lanyard demurred. "I feel it is not right I should stay. And yet--if you will indulge me--I should like very much to demonstrate the truth of an old saw...."

Two confused looks were his response.

"I fear I, for one, do not follow," Stanistreet admitted.

"I will explain quite briefly," Lanyard promised. "The adage I have in mind is as old as human wit: Set a thief to catch a thief. And the last time it was quoted in my hearing, it was not to my advantage. I recall, indeed, resenting it enormously."

He paused with purpose, looking down at the desk. A pad of blank paper caught his eye. He took it up and examined it with an abstracted manner.

"Well, monsieur: the application of your adage?"

"Colonel Stanistreet, what would you think if I were to tell you the combination of your safe?"

"I should be inclined to suspect that you were the devil," Stanistreet chuckled.

"By all accounts a gentleman of intelligence: one is flattered.... Very well: I proceed to demonstrate black art with the aid of this white paper pad. The combination, monsieur, is as follows: nine, twenty-seven, eighteen, thirty-six."

A low cry of bewilderment greeted this announcement. Blensop had drawn near and was eyeing Lanyard as if under the influence of hypnotism.

"How--how do you know that?" he asked in a broken voice.

"Clairvoyance, Mr. Blensop. I seem to see, as I hold this pad, somebody writing upon it the combination for the information of another who had no right to have it--somebody using a pencil with a hard lead, Mr. Blensop; which was very foolish of him, since it made a distinct impression on the under sheet. So you see my magic is rather colourless, after all.... Now, a wiser man, Mr. Blensop, would have used a pen, a fountain pen by preference, with a soft gold nib, well broken. That would leave no impression. If you will lend me the beautiful pen I observe in your pocket, I will give a further demonstration."

The eyes of the secretary shifted wildly. He hesitated, moistening dry lips with the tip of a nervous tongue.

"And don't try to get out of it, Mr. Blensop, because I am armed and don't mean to let you escape. Besides, that good Mr. Stone patrols the garden." Lanyard's tone changed to one of command. "That pen, monsieur!"

Blensop's hand faltered to his waistcoat pocket, hesitated, withdrew, and feebly extended the pen.

"I think you *are* the devil," he stammered in an under-tone--"the devil himself!"

Deftly unscrewing the pen-point, Lanyard inverted the barrel above the desk.

The cylinder of paper dropped out.

"And now, Colonel Stanistreet, if you will call Mr. Stone and have this traitor removed...."

XXIII
AMNESTY

When Stanistreet had gone out in company with Stone, and the broken, weeping Blensop, ending a scene indescribably painful, a lull almost as uncomfortable to Lanyard ensued.

Then--"How did you guess?" Cecelia Brooke asked in wonder. Discountenanced by the admiration glowing in her eyes, Lanyard stood fumbling with the disjointed members of Blensop's pen.

"Do not give me too much credit," he depreciated: "anybody acquainted with that roll of paper could have guessed that an empty fountain pen would furnish an ideal place of concealment for it. Moreover, just before you came in, that traitor missed his pen, and his consternation betrayed him beyond more doubt to one whose distrust was already astir. As for the other, it was true: Blensop did write down the combination on this pad, using a pencil with a hard lead; the marks are very plain."

"But for whose use?"

"Ekstrom--Anderson--was here last night, and saw Blensop alone. Colonel Stanistreet was not at home. Knowing what we know now, that Blensop was a creature of the German system here, bought body, soul, and conscience through its studied pandering to his vices, we know he could not well have refused to surrender the combination on demand."

"Still I fail to understand...."

"Ekstrom, being Ekstrom, could not resist the opportunity to play double. Here was a property he could sell to England at a stiff price. Why not despoil the enemy, put the money in pocket, then return, steal the paper anew for the use of Germany, and collect the stipulated reward from that source? But he reckoned without

Blensop's avarice, there; he showed Blensop too plainly the way to profit through betraying both parties to a bargain; Blensop saw no reason why he should not play the game that Ekstrom played. So he stole it for himself, to sell to Germany, but being a poor, witless fool, lacking Ekstrom's dash and audacity, was foredoomed to failure and exposure."

The girl continued to eye him steadfastly, and he as steadfastly to evade her direct gaze.

"Nothing that you tell me detracts from the wonder of your guessing so accurately," she insisted. "Now I know what Mr. Crane said of you was true, that you are one of the most extraordinary of men."

"He was too kind when he said that," Lanyard protested wretchedly. "It is not true. If you must know...."

"Well, Monsieur Lanyard?"

Her tone was that of a light-hearted girl, arch with provocation. Of a sudden Lanyard understood that he might no longer stop here alone with her.

"If you will be a little indulgent with me," he suggested, "I will try to explain what I mean."

"And how indulgent, monsieur?"

"I have a whim to take the air in this garden. Will you accompany me?"

"Why not?"

As she led the way through the French windows, he noted with deeper misgivings how her action matched the temper of her voice, how she seemed to-day more deliciously alive and happier than any common mortal.

So light her heart! And all since she had found him here!

At his wits' ends, he conceded now what he had so long denied. With all her wit and wisdom, with all her charm of beauty, winsomeness, and breeding, with all her ingrained love of truth and honesty, she was no more than Nature had meant her to be, a woman with woman's weakness for the man she must admire. She liked him, divined in him latent qualities somehow excellent. Something in him worked upon her imagination, something, no doubt, in the overcoloured, romantic yarns current about the Lone Wolf, and so had touched her heart. She liked him too well already, and she was willing to like him better.

But that must never be. He must rend ruthlessly apart this illusion of romance with which she chose to transfigure the prowling parasite of night, the sneaking thief....

The garden was sweet with the bright promise of Spring. A few weeks more, and its formal walks would wend a riot of flowers. Now its sunlight made amends for what it lacked in beauty of growing things; and its air was warm and fragrant and still in the shelter of the red-brick walls.

Midway down that walk, by the side of which a thief had skulked nine hours ago, near that door whose lock had yielded to his cunning keys, the girl paused and confronted Lanyard spiritedly as he came up with heavy step and hang-dog head.

"Well, monsieur?" she demanded. "Do you mean to tantalize me longer with your reticence?"

But something in the haggard eyes he showed her made the girl catch her breath.

"What is it?" she cried anxiously. "Monsieur Duchemin, what is your trouble?"

"Only this truth that I must tell you," he said bitterly: "I merely played a part back there, just now. There was neither wit nor guess-work in that business; once I had seen Blensop's panic over the fancied loss of his pen, the rest was knowledge. I saw him and Ekstrom together last night--skulking in those windows, I watched them; and though in my denseness I didn't understand, I saw him write upon that pad, tear off and give the sheet to Ekstrom. And I knew Ekstrom had not succeeded in stealing back what he had sold to Colonel Stanistreet, knew he was guiltless in fact if not in deed."

"But--how could you know that?"

"Because I was there, in the room, when he entered it after it had been shut up for the night."

Conscious of her hands that fluttered like wounded things to her bosom, he looked away in misery.

"What were you doing there?" she whispered in the end.

"Trying to find that paper, which I had seen Ekstrom sell to Colonel Stanistreet, so that I might make good my promise and relieve your distress by returning it to you. I had opened the safe before he entered, and searched it thoroughly, and knew the paper was not there--though at that time it never entered my thick head to suspect Blensop of treachery. It was neither Blensop nor Ekstrom, Miss Brooke ... it was I who stole that necklace."

She made no sound and did not stir; and though he dared not look he knew her stricken gaze was steadfast to his face.

"I will say this much in my defence: I did not come with intent to steal, but only to take back what had been stolen from me, and return it to you, who had trusted it to my care. I wanted to do that, because I did not then understand the ins and outs of this intrigue, and had no means of knowing how deeply your honour might be involved."

"But you did *not* take that necklace!"

"I am sorry.... I saw it, and could not resist it."

"But Mr. Crane assured me you had given up all that sort of thing years ago!"

"Notwithstanding that, it seems I may not be trusted...."

After another trying silence she declared vehemently: "I do not believe you! You say this thing for some secret purpose of your own. For some reason I can't understand you wish to abase yourself in my sight, to make me think you capable of such infamy. Why--ah, monsieur!--why must you do this?"

"Because it isn't fair to represent myself as what I am not, mademoiselle. Once a thief, always--"

"No! It isn't true!"

"Again I am sorry, but I know. You have been most generous to believe in me. If anything could save me from myself, it would be your confidence. That, I presume, is why I felt called upon to undo my thieving, and make good the loss. The money Colonel Stanistreet paid Ekstrom is now in the safe, back there in the library. The necklace is ... here."

Blindly he thrust the tissue packet into her hands.

"If you will consent to return it to its owner, when I have gone, I shall be most grateful."

Her hands shook so that, when she would open the packet, it escaped her grasp and dropped into a little pool of rain-water which had collected in a hollow of the walk. Lanyard picked it up, stripped off the soiled and sodden paper, dried the necklace with his handkerchief, replaced it in her hand.

He heard the deep intake of her breath as she recognized its beauty, then her quavering voice: "You give this back because of me...!"

"Because I cannot be an ingrate. I know no other way to prove how I have prized your faith in me.... And now, with your leave, I will go away quietly by this garden gate--"

"No--please, no!"

"But--"

"I have more to say to you. It isn't fair of you to go like this, when I--"

She interrupted herself, and when next she spoke he was dashed by a change in her voice from a tone of passionate expostulation to one of amused animation.

"Colonel Stanistreet!" she called clearly. "Do come here at once, please!"

Startled, Lanyard saw that Stanistreet had appeared in the French windows in company with Crane. In response to Cecelia's hail both came out into the garden, Stanistreet briskly leading, Crane lounging at his heels, champing his cigar, his weathered features knitted against the brightness of the sun.

"Good morning, Miss Brooke. Howdy, Lanyard--or are you Duchemin again?" he said; but his salutations were lost in the wonder excited by the girl's next move.

"See, Colonel Stanistreet, what we have found!" she cried, and showed him the necklace. "I mean, what Monsieur Duchemin found. It was he who saw it, lying beneath that rose-bush over there. Your burglar must have dropped it in making his escape; you can see the paper he wrapped it in, all rain-wet and muddied."

Stanistreet's eyes protruded alarmingly, and his face grew very red before he found breath enough to ejaculate: "God bless my soul!" Breathing hard, he accepted the necklace from Cecelia's hands. "I must--excuse me--I must tell my sister-in-law about this immediately!"

He turned and trotted hastily back into the house.

Crane lingered but a moment longer. His cheek, as ever, was bulging round his everlasting cigar. Was his tongue therein as well? Lanyard never knew; the man's eyes remained inscrutable for all the kindly shrewdness that glimmered amid their netted wrinkles.

"Excuse *me*!" he said suddenly. "I got to tell the colonel something."

He got lankily into motion and presently passed in through the windows....

Irresistibly her gaze drew Lanyard's. He lifted careworn eyes and realized her with a great wistfulness upon him.

She awaited in silence his verdict, her chin proudly high, her face adorably flushed, her shining eyes level and brave to his, her generous hands outstretched.

"Must you go now?" she said tenderly, as he stood hesitant and shamed. "Must you go now, my dear?"

The Codes Of Hammurabi And Moses
W. W. Davies

QTY

The discovery of the Hammurabi Code is one of the greatest achievements of archaeology, and is of paramount interest, not only to the student of the Bible, but also to all those interested in ancient history...

Religion   **ISBN:** *1-59462-338-4*

Pages:132
MSRP $12.95

The Theory of Moral Sentiments
Adam Smith

QTY

This work from 1749. contains original theories of conscience amd moral judgment and it is the foundation for systemof morals.

Philosophy   ISBN: *1-59462-777-0*

Pages:536
MSRP $19.95

Jessica's First Prayer
Hesba Stretton

QTY

In a screened and secluded corner of one of the many railway-bridges which span the streets of London there could be seen a few years ago, from five o'clock every morning until half past eight, a tidily set-out coffee-stall, consisting of a trestle and board, upon which stood two large tin cans, with a small fire of charcoal burning under each so as to keep the coffee boiling during the early hours of the morning when the work-people were thronging into the city on their way to their daily toil...

Childrens   ISBN: *1-59462-373-2*

Pages:84
MSRP $9.95

My Life and Work
Henry Ford

QTY

Henry Ford revolutionized the world with his implementation of mass production for the Model T automobile. Gain valuable business insight into his life and work with his own auto-biography... "We have only started on our development of our country we have not as yet, with all our talk of wonderful progress, done more than scratch the surface. The progress has been wonderful enough but..."

Biographies/   ISBN: *1-59462-198-5*

Pages:300
MSRP $21.95

The Art of Cross-Examination
Francis Wellman

QTY

I presume it is the experience of every author, after his first book is published upon an important subject, to be almost overwhelmed with a wealth of ideas and illustrations which could readily have been included in his book, and which to his own mind, at least, seem to make a second edition inevitable. Such certainly was the case with me; and when the first edition had reached its sixth impression in five months, I rejoiced to learn that it seemed to my publishers that the book had met with a sufficiently favorable reception to justify a second and considerably enlarged edition. ..

Pages:412

Reference   ISBN: *1-59462-647-2*   *MSRP $19.95*

On the Duty of Civil Disobedience
Henry David Thoreau

QTY

Thoreau wrote his famous essay, On the Duty of Civil Disobedience, as a protest against an unjust but popular war and the immoral but popular institution of slave-owning. He did more than write—he declined to pay his taxes, and was hauled off to gaol in consequence. Who can say how much this refusal of his hastened the end of the war and of slavery ?

Pages:48

Law   ISBN: *1-59462-747-9*   *MSRP $7.45*

Dream Psychology Psychoanalysis for Beginners
Sigmund Freud

QTY

Sigmund Freud, born Sigismund Schlomo Freud (May 6, 1856 - September 23, 1939), was a Jewish-Austrian neurologist and psychiatrist who co-founded the psychoanalytic school of psychology. Freud is best known for his theories of the unconscious mind, especially involving the mechanism of repression; his redefinition of sexual desire as mobile and directed towards a wide variety of objects; and his therapeutic techniques, especially his understanding of transference in the therapeutic relationship and the presumed value of dreams as sources of insight into unconscious desires.

Pages:196

Psychology   ISBN: *1-59462-905-6*   *MSRP $15.45*

The Miracle of Right Thought
Orison Swett Marden

QTY

Believe with all of your heart that you will do what you were made to do. When the mind has once formed the habit of holding cheerful, happy, prosperous pictures, it will not be easy to form the opposite habit. It does not matter how improbable or how far away this realization may see, or how dark the prospects may be, if we visualize them as best we can, as vividly as possible, hold tenaciously to them and vigorously struggle to attain them, they will gradually become actualized, realized in the life. But a desire, a longing without endeavor, a yearning abandoned or held indifferently will vanish without realization.

Pages:360

Self Help   ISBN: *1-59462-644-8*   *MSRP $25.45*

☐ **The Rosicrucian Cosmo-Conception Mystic Christianity** *by Max Heindel*   ISBN: 1-59462-188-8   **$38.95**
The Rosicrucian Cosmo-conception is not dogmatic, neither does it appeal to any other authority than the reason of the student. It is: not controversial, but is: sent forth in the, hope that it may help to clear...   New Age/Religion Pages 646

☐ **Abandonment To Divine Providence** *by Jean-Pierre de Caussade*   ISBN: 1-59462-228-0   **$25.95**
"The Rev. Jean Pierre de Caussade was one of the most remarkable spiritual writers of the Society of Jesus in France in the 18th Century. His death took place at Toulouse in 1751. His works have gone through many editions and have been republished...   Inspirational/Religion Pages 400

☐ **Mental Chemistry** *by Charles Haanel*   ISBN: 1-59462-192-6   **$23.95**
Mental Chemistry allows the change of material conditions by combining and appropriately utilizing the power of the mind. Much like applied chemistry creates something new and unique out of careful combinations of chemicals the mastery of mental chemistry...   New Age Pages 354

☐ **The Letters of Robert Browning and Elizabeth Barret Barrett 1845-1846 vol II**   ISBN: 1-59462-193-4   **$35.95**
by Robert Browning and Elizabeth Barrett   Biographies Pages 596

☐ **Gleanings In Genesis (volume I)** *by Arthur W. Pink*   ISBN: 1-59462-130-6   **$27.45**
Appropriately has Genesis been termed "the seed plot of the Bible" for in it we have, in germ form, almost all of the great doctrines which are afterwards fully developed in the books of Scripture which follow...   Religion/Inspirational Pages 420

☐ **The Master Key** *by L. W. de Laurence*   ISBN: 1-59462-001-6   **$30.95**
In no branch of human knowledge has there been a more lively increase of the spirit of research during the past few years than in the study of Psychology, Concentration and Mental Discipline. The requests for authentic lessons in Thought Control, Mental Discipline and...   New Age/Business Pages 422

☐ **The Lesser Key Of Solomon Goetia** *by L. W. de Laurence*   ISBN: 1-59462-092-X   **$9.95**
This translation of the first book of the "Lemegton" which is now for the first time made accessible to students of Talismanic Magic was done, after careful collation and edition, from numerous Ancient Manuscripts in Hebrew, Latin, and French...   New Age/Occult Pages 92

☐ **Rubaiyat Of Omar Khayyam** *by Edward Fitzgerald*   ISBN:1-59462-332-5   **$13.95**
Edward Fitzgerald, whom the world has already learned, in spite of his own efforts to remain within the shadow of anonymity, to look upon as one of the rarest poets of the century, was born at Bredfield, in Suffolk, on the 31st of March, 1809. He was the third son of John Purcell...   Music Pages 172

☐ **Ancient Law** *by Henry Maine*   ISBN: 1-59462-128-4   **$29.95**
The chief object of the following pages is to indicate some of the earliest ideas of mankind, as they are reflected in Ancient Law, and to point out the relation of those ideas to modern thought.   Religiom/History Pages 452

☐ **Far-Away Stories** *by William J. Locke*   ISBN: 1-59462-129-2   **$19.45**
"Good wine needs no bush, but a collection of mixed vintages does. And this book is just such a collection. Some of the stories I do not want to remain buried for ever in the museum files of dead magazine-numbers an author's not unpardonable vanity..."   Fiction Pages 272

☐ **Life of David Crockett** *by David Crockett*   ISBN: 1-59462-250-7   **$27.45**
"Colonel David Crockett was one of the most remarkable men of the times in which he lived. Born in humble life, but gifted with a strong will, an indomitable courage, and unremitting perseverance...   Biographies/New Age Pages 424

☐ **Lip-Reading** *by Edward Nitchie*   ISBN: 1-59462-206-X   **$25.95**
Edward B. Nitchie, founder of the New Yorkk School for the Hard of Hearing, now the Nitchie School of Lip-Reading, Inc, wrote "LIP-READING Principles and Practice". The development and perfecting of this meritorious work on lip-reading was an undertaking...   How-to Pages 400

☐ **A Handbook of Suggestive Therapeutics, Applied Hypnotism, Psychic Science**   ISBN: 1-59462-214-0   **$24.95**
by Henry Munro   Health/New Age/Health/Self-help Pages 376

☐ **A Doll's House: and Two Other Plays** *by Henrik Ibsen*   ISBN: 1-59462-112-8   **$19.95**
Henrik Ibsen created this classic when in revolutionary 1848 Rome. Introducing some striking concepts in playwriting for the realist genre, this play has been studied the world over.   Fiction/Classics/Plays 308

☐ **The Light of Asia** *by sir Edwin Arnold*   ISBN: 1-59462-204-3   **$13.95**
In this poetic masterpiece, Edwin Arnold describes the life and teachings of Buddha. The man who was to become known as Buddha to the world was born as Prince Gautama of India but he rejected the worldly riches and abandoned the reigns of power when...   Religion/History/Biographies Pages 170

☐ **The Complete Works of Guy de Maupassant** *by Guy de Maupassant*   ISBN: 1-59462-157-8   **$16.95**
"For days and days, nights and nights, I had dreamed of that first kiss which was to consecrate our engagement, and I knew not on what spot I should put my lips..."   Fiction/Classics Pages 240

☐ **The Art of Cross-Examination** *by Francis L. Wellman*   ISBN: 1-59462-309-0   **$26.95**
Written by a renowned trial lawyer, Wellman imparts his experience and uses case studies to explain how to use psychology to extract desired information through questioning.   How-to/Science/Reference Pages 408

☐ **Answered or Unanswered?** *by Louisa Vaughan*   ISBN: 1-59462-248-5   **$10.95**
Miracles of Faith in China   Religion Pages 112

☐ **The Edinburgh Lectures on Mental Science (1909)** *by Thomas*   ISBN: 1-59462-008-3   **$11.95**
This book contains the substance of a course of lectures recently given by the writer in the Queen Street Hail, Edinburgh. Its purpose is to indicate the Natural Principles governing the relation between Mental Action and Material Conditions...   New Age/Psychology Pages 148

☐ **Ayesha** *by H. Rider Haggard*   ISBN: 1-59462-301-5   **$24.95**
Verily and indeed it is the unexpected that happens! Probably if there was one person upon the earth from whom the Editor of this, and of a certain previous history, did not expect to hear again...   Classics Pages 380

☐ **Ayala's Angel** *by Anthony Trollope*   ISBN: 1-59462-352-X   **$29.95**
The two girls were both pretty, but Lucy who was twenty-one who supposed to be simple and comparatively unattractive, whereas Ayala was credited, as her Bombwhat romantic name might show, with poetic charm and a taste for romance. Ayala when her father died was nineteen...   Fiction Pages 484

☐ **The American Commonwealth** *by James Bryce*   ISBN: 1-59462-286-8   **$34.45**
An interpretation of American democratic political theory. It examines political mechanics and society from the perspective of Scotsman James Bryce   Politics Pages 572

☐ **Stories of the Pilgrims** *by Margaret P. Pumphrey*   ISBN: 1-59462-116-0   **$17.95**
This book explores pilgrims religious oppression in England as well as their escape to Holland and eventual crossing to America on the Mayflower, and their early days in New England...   History Pages 268

QTY

The Fasting Cure *by Sinclair Upton*   ISBN: *1-59462-222-1*   **$13.95**
In the Cosmopolitan Magazine for May, 1910, and in the Contemporary Review (London) for April, 1910, I published an article dealing with my experiences in fasting. I have written a great many magazine articles, but never one which attracted so much attention... New Age/Self Help/Health Pages 164

Hebrew Astrology *by Sepharial*   ISBN: *1-59462-308-2*   **$13.45**
In these days of advanced thinking it is a matter of common observation that we have left many of the old landmarks behind and that we are now pressing forward to greater heights and to a wider horizon than that which represented the mind-content of our progenitors... Astrology Pages 144

Thought Vibration or The Law of Attraction in the Thought World   ISBN: *1-59462-127-6*   **$12.95**
by William Walker Atkinson   Psychology/Religion Pages 144

Optimism *by Helen Keller*   ISBN: *1-59462-108-X*   **$15.95**
Helen Keller was blind, deaf, and mute since 19 months old, yet famously learned how to overcome these handicaps, communicate with the world, and spread her lectures promoting optimism. An inspiring read for everyone... Biographies/Inspirational Pages 84

Sara Crewe *by Frances Burnett*   ISBN: *1-59462-360-0*   **$9.45**
In the first place, Miss Minchin lived in London. Her home was a large, dull, tall one, in a large, dull square, where all the houses were alike, and all the sparrows were alike, and where all the door-knockers made the same heavy sound... Childrens/Classic Pages 88

The Autobiography of Benjamin Franklin *by Benjamin Franklin*   ISBN: *1-59462-135-7*   **$24.95**
The Autobiography of Benjamin Franklin has probably been more extensively read than any other American historical work, and no other book of its kind has had such ups and downs of fortune. Franklin lived for many years in England, where he was agent... Biographies/History Pages 332

Name	
Email	
Telephone	
Address	
City, State ZIP	

☐ **Credit Card**   ☐ **Check / Money Order**

Credit Card Number	
Expiration Date	
Signature	

Please Mail to: Book Jungle
PO Box 2226
Champaign, IL 61825
or Fax to: 630-214-0564

ORDERING INFORMATION

web: *www.bookjungle.com*
email: *sales@bookjungle.com*
fax: *630-214-0564*
mail: *Book Jungle PO Box 2226 Champaign, IL 61825*
or PayPal *to sales@bookjungle.com*

Please contact us for bulk discounts

DIRECT-ORDER TERMS

**20% Discount if You Order
Two or More Books**
Free Domestic Shipping!
Accepted: Master Card, Visa,
Discover, American Express

www.ingramcontent.com/pod-product-compliance
Lightning Source LLC
Chambersburg PA
CBHW080957020726

47505CB00009B/2234